# FRAMED!

The evil joy went out of Smiley's face. His eyes went past Bob Lake toward the window and fastened there with a sort of horrible fascination. Before Lake could turn, the bark of a gun crowded the room with echoes, and Hugh Smiley slumped forward on the table. At the same time there was a heavy impact on the floor.

Bob Lake reached for his gun on the wall. The holster was empty! There on the floor lay the heavy object that had been thrown through the window. It was a revolver, and, as Bob Lake caught it up, he knew at once that it was his.

"Rankin," said a voice behind him.

He whirled to find Smiley propping himself with sagging arms back from the table. His eyes were already glazing. From the outer part of the building Lake heard footsteps coming. There he stood with the gun in his hand from which a bullet had struck the dying man.

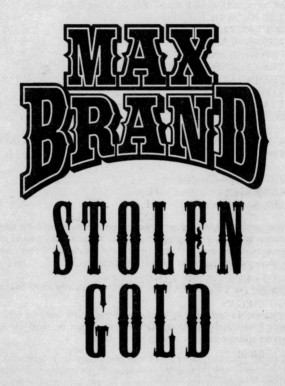

# MAX BRAND

# STOLEN GOLD

LEISURE BOOKS  NEW YORK CITY

A LEISURE BOOK®

September 2001

Published by special arrangement with Golden West Literary Agency

Dorchester Publishing Co., Inc.
276 Fifth Avenue
New York, NY 10001

ISBN 0-8439-4913-9

Printed in the United States of America.

Visit us on the web at www.dorchesterpub.com.

# TABLE OF CONTENTS

# Acknowledgments

with his hands and peered half viciously and half curi-
ly up through the darkness, as if he wished with all his
rt to attack the man who had insulted him, but must first
ke sure that such an attack would be an expedient pro-
ding.

That which he saw was apparently extremely discour-
ging, for he settled back against the tree and changed his
pen defiance to a sullen scowl.

"But," went on Jack Montagne, smiling in spite of himself
at this change of front, "I'm going to do you a good turn, instead of kicking you away from that fire and out into the mud.
I'm going to tell you that there is a house down the road about
a mile. You don't have to stay here. You can go down there
and sleep in the barn, anyway."

"Can I?" asked the tramp. "All right, you go and try it.
That's all I got to say . . . you go and try it!" He wrapped his
arms about him, shivering, as the wind grew fresher out of the
north, and he grinned in mockery at the rider.

"Did you try it?" asked the rider, with a sudden sternness
that was not, however, directed at the tramp. "Did you try it
and get turned out into a night like this?"

"Maybe," replied the tramp.

The rider set his teeth in one of those convulsions of anger
which seemed to be characteristic; and the tramp, peering at
him by the dim firelight, shrank from what he saw.

"But are there no other houses around here?" asked
Montagne.

"Find out for yourself," said the tramp. He had been em-
boldened by the generous indignation of the night rider, as if
this were proof that the larger man would not take advantage
of his superior size, or the revolver that was faintly outlined
under the skirt of his slicker. "Find out for yourself . . . that's
what I had to do."

# Sheriff Larrabee's Prisoner

When this short novel first appeared in Street & Smith's *Western Story Magazine* in the issue for December 3, 1921, the editor assigned Frederick Faust a new pseudonym for the story, Martin Dexter, but this would be the only time that this name would be used as a Faust byline. Currently, Faust's serial, "Ronicky Doone, Champion of Lost Causes" under the byline David Manning, was being serialized in the magazine. In the very next issue there would be a short novel by Faust under the byline George Owen Baxter and a new serial beginning under the name Max Brand. These multiple identities were intended to make readers think that each one was a different and distinct author. In this short novel Sheriff Henry Larrabee must pursue and capture the logical suspect in the murder of an old miser. However much Larrabee's ability to understand human nature astounds members of the posse that include his sons, it is his daughter who proves to be most like him once she becomes convinced that the suspect, Jack Montagne, is innocent.

I

## "NO HANG-OUT"

The rain had been falling steadily, with a northwester to drive it aslant. Now the wind leaped suddenly at Jack Montagne, and, as if its former pace had been maintained only to lure him into a false security, it now drove the rain in level volleys that crashed against his slicker and stung his face. Even his weather-hardened hands resented the fury of the storm. The blast stopped the trot of his pony that remained for the moment leaning into the storm. Presently it again gathered headway, urged on by the tickling spur of the rider. When the anger of the wind and rain had spent itself, Montagne screened his eyes and peered anxiously up the valley.

It was then he made out the two lights — one a mere yellow ray which, passing through the mist of rain, was split into a thousand shivering portions as Montagne squinted at it, and the other merely a dim red blur. They were welcome sights to the rider on this black night, and yet he hesitated before going straight toward them.

Eventually he decided that the news about him could not have preceded him to this desolate valley, and he touched the pony with the spurs again. This time the weary beast broke into a lope, cupping the muddy water on the trail in the hollows of his forehoofs, and sending it up in spurts and showers to drench the rider. But against such physical discomforts Jack Montagne was proof. When the possessions of a man have shrunk to his bridle and saddle and horse and the old gun, sagging at his hip, when, moreover, fear and dread ride at his side, the elements are negligible factors. In truth, the storm fitted in with the mood of Montagne, and his temper rose in fierce bursts of revolt against the world, just as the wind occasionally struck at him with redoubled force, and like the night his mind was filled with a steady, black gloom.

The red light on his right now grew rapidly. The rain streaked down against it, and above the light he made out the outlines of a tree. Someone was sitting by a campfire to the lee of a tree, and that was his only shelter against this furious storm. There was no other conclusion to come to, and Montagne shook his head in wonder. Perhaps the fellow had

not seen that light down the road, that light came from a house. It was partly with a kindly to tell the camper that there was a better shelte partly with the hope of learning a little about which he found himself, that Montagne turned and came squarely upon the fire.

It was a miserable and uncertain blaze, fizzing an constantly, as drops of water filtered down from the of the tree above. And yet the broad trunk made a rath shelter, for the steady wind kept driving the rain at an and the man, whose back was against the tree, was danger of getting wet by the direct fall of water. Only drops, that trickled through the foliage above, came splash about him. He had been stirring weakly at the fire, and it wa not until the pony came within a yard of the blaze, snorting in disgust as the smoke filled its nostrils, that the camper lifted to the view of Montagne a white, rat-like face, out of which little bright black eyes glittered.

"Get your own fire, bo," said the camper, without waiting to learn definitely the purpose of the new arrival. "I ain't got any more'n enough room for myself, and I ain't going to let you in. Get on your way and hustle your own fire!"

He enforced this suggestion with an ugly lifting of his upper lip, very much after the manner of a terrier guarding a bone. But Jack Montagne did not immediately answer. He waited until his observations had taken in all the details of the battered hat, the coat of nameless age and patches, the shoes through the ends of which the toes were thrusting, and the whole atmosphere of unclean suspicion that dwelt about the tramp like a garment.

"You dirty rat," said Jack Montagne, when he broke si lence. "I ought to twist your neck into two pieces!"

"What?" demanded the tramp, starting, as he shad

Jack Montagne considered that lean, pointed face with a thoughtful contempt.

"No," he decided at length, "I won't look any farther. I'll go to that house yonder, and I'll get supper and a bed there, whether they want to give it to me or not. If they'd turn even a dog out into this sort of weather, they don't deserve no consideration, and I ain't going to give it to 'em. If you want to come along with me, I'll see that they put you up, too."

But the tramp merely laughed. "I ain't a fool," he declared. "I ain't going to walk that far for nothing. Besides, I'm doing fine right here."

"S'long, then," said Montagne.

The tramp returned no answer, but he followed the stranger with a bright glance of his little eyes, as Montagne swerved out into the storm again.

Through the crashing of the rain Jack kept steadily for the house. Presently he saw the light in the window grow brighter, and he made out the shadowy form of a big ranch house, one of those long and ragged roof lines that attest many additions built onto the original and central structure. Turn a stranger away from such a place, where there must be room to put up twenty extra men? His anger grew with every stride of his pony; when at length he drew rein, his jaw was set.

It was the rear of the house he had approached, and the light came from a projecting wing that was evidently the kitchen. As Montagne swung out of the saddle, he stepped from the blast of the storm into the quiet shelter of the building. Pausing at the door, he heard two voices, both raised — one the harsh voice of a woman, and one a man's voice.

"If he don't get the money out of that chest," said the man, "where does he get it? Anyway, I'm going to find out if. . . ."

11

"Shut up!" exclaimed the woman. "Let me tell you. . . ." Here she lowered her voice until it became unintelligible to Montagne, and he rapped heavily on the door.

The voices ceased, then there was a shuffling of feet, the turning of the doorknob, as someone called out to him: "Who's there?"

It was the same growling voice of the man whom he had heard speaking inside the kitchen.

"A stranger, partner," said Montagne pleasantly, "held up in this rain, and I'd like to get a place to sleep and a bite to eat."

"This ain't no hang-out for bums," answered the other fiercely. "Get out and stay out!"

And the door was slammed in the face of Montagne. But in that moment he flung himself forward, leaning low, his shoulder and its cushion of hardened muscle presented for the shock, after the fashion of a football player. The door had been slammed, but the latch had not yet clicked home, and the lunging body of Montagne knocked the door wide. The burly fellow was sent spinning across the floor of the kitchen and crashed into the wall, and Montagne, crouched low and staggering, entered.

When he straightened himself, he saw the man of the house scrambling to his feet, uttering a profusion of terrific curses. Then the big-shouldered, loose-jointed fellow sprang to the wall and caught a shotgun off the nails where it was supported. He did not, however, level the gun at Montagne. Something in the face of the stranger arrested the motion. His close-set, bulging eyes dwelt in a sort of daze on the newcomer, and Montagne thought he had never seen features so animal-like, save in the woman. She also had reached for the nearest weapon, sweeping up a great butcher knife in her work-reddened hand, but, like her son — the relationship was

12

proclaimed in their faces — her motion to strike was arrested.

For they saw in the newcomer a man well over middle height, so strong and sinewy that even the loose-flapping folds of the slicker could not entirely disguise his power. More than this, he was in a tremendous passion which his silence made more terrible than a profusion of curses. In relaxation he must have been a handsome man, but now his features expressed nothing but consuming rage. His brows were black above his glaring eyes, his nostrils quivered, his mouth was a straight, white-edged line, and the tendons of his neck stood forth. Moreover, point was given to his anger by the fact that his right hand was under his slicker. Beyond a doubt it was grasping the butt of a revolver.

## II

### "THE HOSTS OF THE HOUSE"

The son had no cunning with which to adapt himself to this terrible stranger; the woman possessed more adroitness. She cast at her son one flaming glance and shook her head; clearly she admonished him to give over the thought of violent resistance to violence. Then she slipped the knife back onto the table and turned to Montagne, with complaints instead of fury.

"What sort of a business is this?" she demanded. "Busting down doors and breaking in on honest folk? Is that a way to act, I say? Is that a way?" She put a whine into her voice, to be sure, but her eyes were still sparkling with rage, although she told her son, with a curse at his stupidity, to put down the shotgun. "I ain't going to have no murder on your head," she declared, "not even if the law wouldn't lay no hand on you for defending your own house and home! Now, you, what d'you want?"

The anger had been gradually departing from Jack Montagne. Like most men liable to fits of murderous temper, his rage passed away almost as swiftly as it had come over him, but his face was still ominous as he replied to the woman's demands.

"I've heard about you folks," he said, "turning people out into this sort of a storm, but I didn't believe it. Now I'm going to talk straight . . . I ain't got a cent, but I'm going to get a dry place to sleep, and I'm going to get a place for my hoss and feed for it in the barn . . . I'm going to get supper for myself. You lay to that. I say I ain't got a cent on me now, but, when I come back, I'll pay you every cent it's worth, and then double. You can trust that. I never been known to break a promise . . . but, whether you trust me or not, I'm going to get what I said I'd get. Now, listen, I'm going to take my hoss out to the barn, yonder, and find feed for him. Then I'm coming back here, and I expect to find supper started for me. Understand? I've fed a hundred gents in my day and never took nothing for it. Now I'm going to get a little part of it back."

So saying, he stepped backward into the night and slammed the door behind him. No sooner had it closed than the son slipped to it and laid the great bolt softly in place. Then he turned with a grin of triumph to his mother. "We'll lock him out, confound him," he said.

"Think you can hold out one like him?" asked the woman. "Not if you were ten times the man you are, Gus. It would have taken your father, aye, or a better one than your father, to handle this one."

"I dunno," replied Gus. "I can do my share, if I got a chance and ain't took by surprise."

14

"I know. If you got a chance to sneak up on somebody, and get a gun trained on 'em, you're brave enough. But don't try to sneak up on the gent that just come in here. Know why?"

"Why?" asked her son, blinking.

She slipped a little closer to him and glanced aside at the door through which Montagne had just disappeared, as if fearful that he might return at that instant and overhear.

"Because he's a killer," she whispered. "I know that kind. You see the way he rocked a little from side to side, he was so mad? You seen the way he went white, and the veins sprang out purple on his forehead? You seen the way his eyes went jumping everywhere? That's because he was a killer. He had his hand on his gun, and he wouldn't have thought nothing of blowing off both our heads. Oh, I know the likes of him, and I know 'em well! He's a bad one, Gus, and you can lay to that! Don't try no fancy work on him."

The pale, brutish eyes of Gus opened wide, as he drank in this information. Then the woman went to the door, removed the bolt again, and shook her fist in a consuming burst of rage. "Why should he have come on this night of all nights?" she snarlingly demanded.

"We'll just have to put it off," said the son.

"You fool!" replied his amiable mother. "Why was I cursed by having a coward and an idiot for a son? But you're like your father before you . . . no sense . . . like a swine . . . just made for eating and drinking and sleeping and grunting in your sleep. Bah!"

The son replied to this outburst of affection with a wicked glint of his eyes and a twitching of his loose upper lip, but, apparently, he had had too much experience of the virago's tongue to invite a fresh outburst.

"How can we put it off? Ain't we got to have the money by

tomorrow?" she went on as savagely as before. "You think you can put off Cusick? No, not that leech! He'd foreclose in a minute. His mouth is watering at the idea of getting the ranch, anyway. And now this killer comes and. . . ."

"Shut up," muttered the son, as an idea flashed across his brutish face. "Maybe this ain't the worst that could have happened . . . this having the stranger with us tonight. Maybe we could make him. . . ."

His mother checked him with a raised hand, and the next moment the door opened, and Jack Montagne entered the room again. This time he came rather carelessly, even whistling, as if he were now an old acquaintance. He settled himself in a chair, leaned back against the wall, and twitched the holster at his right hip so that the butt of the gun fell into a convenient position. He regarded the pair with quiet interest. They gave him a glance in return and then busied themselves in laying out a supper of cold ham and cold fried potatoes and lukewarm coffee, left over from their own evening meal.

Without a word they served him; without a word he drew up his chair and began to eat. As has been said before, he was a good-looking fellow, except when his face was contorted by rage. He had an ominously sudden way of glancing from side to side, and the muscles of the jaw were strongly developed, as in one who habitually kept his teeth set. In actual years Montagne could not have been more than twenty-seven or eight, but hard experience, of one kind or another, had touched his hair with a streak of gray over the temples. He was a man of many expressions. Looking down, he often seemed middle-aged and weary; looking up, he seemed years younger; when he smiled, he was suddenly a boy, filled with geniality.

"And now," he said, as he approached the conclusion of that cheerless meal, "where do I sleep?"

16

"In the barn," said the woman savagely. "I guess hay is good enough for you!"

"Sure," agreed Jack Montagne. "Only you were so kind of generous about making me accept things ever since I landed here, that I thought maybe you'd want me to sleep in a nice comfortable bed in the house."

He grinned, as he spoke, but Gus said: "And so we do. There's a spare bed in the room right next to mine, and. . . ."

"D'you think I'll have him in the house?" asked the woman.

But her son winked at her, and, regarding her steadily, he said: "Shut up and let me talk. Ain't I the man about this house? I say he's going to sleep inside!"

He had raised his voice to a shout, and his mother submitted to him with suspicious suddenness. At the same moment a slow, feeble step was heard descending the stairs, a step that hesitated like the movement of extreme old age.

"You've got the old devil up with your yelling," said the woman. "Now he'll make us all dance for it."

The next moment a bent old man came into the doorway. If the woman and her boy were of bearish temper and bearish conformation, the old fellow who now came before the view of Jack Montagne was certainly of the wolf breed. His eagle nose, his grimly compressed lips, his forward-jutting chin, and, above all, the cold, keen eyes, under the bushy, white brows, told of a predatory soul. Years had bowed him, but there was something so significant about him that the hawk-like figure seemed to tower above them all. It was rather as if he had stooped to come through the doorway than as if the weight of time had stooped him. He carried a long cane, gathered up toward his breast, in a hand that was a blue claw, entirely unfleshed.

He stamped this cane upon the floor. Age had stiffened his

17

neck, but his eyes, for that reason, roved the more keenly. "I told you before," he said, "that I ain't going to have noise in the evening . . . evening is my time for reading . . . evening is my time for quiet. I ain't going to have noise. I heard a racket once before tonight, and now you're shouting. It's got to stop. D'you hear? It's got to stop!" He whipped up his cane suddenly and shook it in malevolent rage at Gus. "You lout! You fool!" he exclaimed. "It's you that makes life a torture around here. Now, mind you, no more noise!"

To the surprise of Montagne this fierce reproof was received in a mild silence. Both the woman and her son lowered their eyes to the floor, and then Gus looked up in apology.

"I'm sure sorry," he said. "I got to arguing and. . . ."

"That's the trouble with fools," said the terrible old man. "They always talk too much. Who's this?" He picked out Jack Montagne with a gesture of his cane.

"A stranger," said the woman, "that we never seen before. But we can't turn folks away on nights like this. We got to show some sort of kindness, even if we ain't rich folks, and even if we don't get paid."

She said this with a sort of cringing humility, glancing sadly toward the ceiling, as if bewailing the ingratitude of a hard world.

But the old man merely grunted, and then grinned at her. "You'll get a reward in heaven for all your kindness," he told her. "You sure will get a reward there. Who are you?" This last was directed at Montagne.

"I'm Jack," said Montagne.

"Jack, eh?" said the old fellow. "Jack the Baker, Jack the Butcher, Jack the Ropemaker, Jack the Killer . . . which one are you?" And, as he concluded the list of fanciful appellations, his narrow chin thrust out, and his keen eyes probed and stabbed at the eyes of Jack Montagne.

In spite of himself Montagne felt a chill running through his veins. The old man knew too much about human nature, and all his knowledge seemed to be of evil.

"I don't like him," went on the old man. "Send him away. I'd have nightmares all night, if I knew that man was sleeping here, under the same roof with me. I don't like him . . . he's too hungry. Them that have nothing want everything. And him . . . you ain't got a cent in your pocket!"

As he said this, he advanced a long step, a light and stealthy step, and thrust his cane almost in the face of Jack. The latter half rose from his chair, alarmed and filled with an almost superstitious fear. The old man began to laugh mirthlessly, his eyes snapping. Then he stamped his cane on the floor, as he stepped back.

"I know you," he went on, nodding to himself, "I know you all . . . starvelings, buzzards. Bah! You'll find no meat on my bones to fatten you . . . not you. Out with you, Jack the Beggar, Jack the Knave, Jack the Killer. Out with you and sleep in the barn! I'll not have you under the same roof with me, I say. I prophesy you won't come to no good end!"

Jack Montagne slowly recovered his poise in the face of this malignant attack. He settled back again in his chair and smiled in the wicked face of the old man. "I'll stay here," he said, "old bones . . . I'll stay here and be comfortable. It ain't none too warm outside."

"You won't leave, won't you?" demanded the hostile old ogre. "You can't throw him out, can you?" he asked of Gus. Then he answered his own question: "Nope, it'd take ten like you to handle one like him. But, if I was forty years younger, I'd . . . well, no matter. Forty years are forty years and can't be changed."

"Mister Benton," broke in the woman, "I'm terribly sorry, I sure am. I do what I can to make you comfortable, but,

19

when gents come and force their way in on me. . . ."

"I thought you took him in out of kindness?" The irritable old man fairly snapped his question. "Don't talk, Missus Zellar . . . don't talk. I see through you, and I don't see no good!" He turned on Gus. "By the way, seen young Walters lately?"

"Seen him this mornin', Mister Benton."

"You did, eh? And what's he say?"

"He's doing fine. Says he'll have his interest money ready for you next week. He could pay it now."

The old fellow nodded his head slowly back and forth, half closing his eyes. "I knowed Walters would be made by the money I loaned him . . . I knowed that. I always know."

"And right here, Mister Benton," said the woman, "I could have used that money fine. Me and Gus could have improved the ranch no end and give you a better rate of interest than Walters does."

"Don't talk," declared the octogenarian. "Don't talk. I see through you . . . like you had a window over where your heart is."

He turned and stalked toward the door. His back was visibly pinched and withered under his coat. From that rear view he seemed suddenly weak, but, when he turned on them again at the door, all thought of his feebleness left Jack Montagne. The withered lips of Mr. Benton continued to writhe, but he uttered no sound. Presently his halting step went up the stairs again and disappeared through a doorway beyond.

When he was gone, there was a sigh emitted by all three. For a moment, exchanging glances, they seemed to be of one mind. Truly they were all, in differing ways, grim people, but compared with this terrible old man they were weaklings.

"That bed I told you about," said Gus suddenly, "I'll

show you where the room is, if you like."

Jack Montagne nodded, rose, and followed his guide up the stairs, noting the empty bareness of the house. Dissolute spending, which had impoverished the ranch, had gutted the house, it seemed. The very hall seemed to beg for new voices and cheerier footfalls — certainly less stealthy ones.

When they came to the room, Gus deposited the lamp on the table beside the bed and left without a word. Jack Montagne sat down and buried his face in his hands. He had come to another halting place in his downward progress through life. Had the old man been right? Was he, indeed, bound for damnation?

He shrugged away that fierce prophecy. In the meantime, the fact was that he needed money, needed it terribly, must have it, and the old fellow, beyond doubt, possessed what he wanted. Had he not heard the two in the kitchen speak of money and a chest? All was as clear as day. The old usurer kept a store of coin in his room and loaned it out about the countryside.


## III


## "LARRABEE LISTENS"

The sheriff, Henry Larrabee, jerked up his head and listened.

"That phone call is for me," he said instantly, as the first ring ended. Two long and three short was the sheriff's ring on that country line, and the ring was ground out on a little crank, without summoning the assistance of a central. This first long ring was made in what might have been called a breathless fashion, the crank turning so swiftly in the middle of the motion that it produced only a rattle, not a true ring.

"Not for you! Not on a night like this!" exclaimed his wife, as the good woman lifted her head and listened to the crashing of the rain against the roof.

A second long ring had begun. "It's for me, right enough," said the sheriff, and rose to his feet.

His daughter, Mary, rose, also, staring with excitement. "Oh, Dad, what could be happening?"

"On a night like this . . . anything. There it goes."

The second long ring had ended, and there followed three short rings in swift succession. The sheriff ran to the phone with great strides. "Hello!" he called.

"Sheriff Larrabee," said a woman's voice, "come quick, for there's been a murder here."

"Who are you?"

"Missus Zellar . . . murder . . . ah!"

The last word was a half scream, and there was the sound of the telephone receiver dropping with a jerk.

"You devil!" the sheriff heard a man's voice shouting.

Larrabee smashed up his own receiver. "Jud!" he thundered. "Chris!"

His two sons answered with shouts from the upper part of the house.

"Come down to me, quick! We got riding to do!"

"Henry," breathed his wife, stammering with fear, as she ran to him. "What is it? Where?"

"Nothing," he answered sternly. "Don't hang onto me. I got work . . . that's all. When I'm gone, call the Gloster house and get the Gloster boys to ride toward the Zellar place, as fast as they can saddle and get under way. I'll meet 'em on the road. That's all. Don't ask questions. Just do what I say."

Catching up his hat, he plunged from the house, the front door banging heavily behind him at the same time that the thunder of his sons' feet began on the stairs above. Within five minutes they were in the saddle and racing out onto the muddy road. For they kept their horses in a shed near the house, ready for quick saddling at any hour of the day or night. Going up the first steep hill, they could talk.

"I knew," said Jud, "that they'd be trouble some day in the Zellar house. What's up?"

"I dunno," answered the father. "Just heard a woman talking, and woman talk don't mean much usually. But it sure sounded like trouble was busted loose. Come on, lads!"

They had reached the crest of the hill, and now they lurched down into the valley at a reckless gallop, the horses sliding and slipping over the mud. Turning down the valley road, they presently came in view of a fire beneath a tree, and the sheriff headed straight for it. He swung out of the saddle in front of the tramp whom Jack Montagne had seen earlier in the night. The tramp straightened up — he had been dozing, with his head almost dropped into the flame of the fire — and blinked at the new arrivals. The stern hand of the sheriff helped him to his feet, and he stifled his yawn.

"Who're you?" asked the sheriff.

"Slim," said the tramp. "Some call me Mississippi Slim."

"What else?"

"Disremember being called any other name."

"You come with me, Mississippi Slim. Jud, take him along and follow me to the Zellar place. This is the kind that know things, this Slim. Chris, come on with me. We got to ride hard."

"What can you get out of Slim?" asked Chris, as the two spurred on through the mud.

"Never can tell. But, if you ever step into my boots, boy, and get my job, you want to pick up them that look like Slim. If there's trouble around, they're 'most always down-wind

23

from it, and they know all about what's going on. They smell it before they see it, and they see it before us ordinary folks dream it."

He concluded with a brief admonition. "If Gus Zellar is mixed up in this killing, or whatever it is, that we're moving toward, and we come across him armed, don't waste no time arguing. If he shows fight, shoot . . . and shoot to kill. Handle him the way you'd handle a dog. He ain't no better, much."

He had no chance to say more, for now they came to the house, where lights were burning in half of the windows. The sheriff's son was for a careful approach. The sheriff, however, scoffed at such an idea, and, advancing to the kitchen door, he cast it open and stepped into the presence of Gus Zellar and his mother.

There was no need to fear Gus Zellar. He was a white-faced, trembling wreck of a man, shrinking against the wall. His mother was ten times more formidable. Her eyes were gleaming, her hands clenched, and her whole attitude that of one ready to fight a great battle.

"You sure come slow," she said to Larrabee. "Come upstairs, and you'll find it."

There was something so ominous in that last syllable that even the sheriff, time-hardened by contact with crime and criminals, was a trifle shocked. As she took up the lamp, he swung in behind her, first ordering Gus Zellar to follow close to his mother. The order threw Gus into a sudden panic.

"But what've I got to do with it?" he asked tremulously. "I didn't do it! I swear I didn't do it, Sheriff!"

"I'm not saying you did," said the sheriff, disgusted by such cringing. "But you step along. I want to keep you under my eye."

Gus skulked into line, glancing fearfully behind, as if anticipating a kick. They hurried up the stairs, the woman exclaiming eagerly: "You got to hurry, Sheriff! He left in a rush, and he'll be riding like a fiend all night. Every minute counts, when you're trailing a gent like him!"

"Like who?" asked the sheriff.

"I'll tell you about him after you see what he's done."

They had hurried up to the floor of the second story of the house, and now they went straight behind Mrs. Zellar into the room, directly opposite the head of the stairs. They passed through a broken door. It had been splintered exactly in the center, and both halves were still attached — the one by its hinges and the other by the lock. Mrs. Zellar placed the lamp on the table near the center of the room.

"There!" she exclaimed dramatically, stepping back. "Nothing ain't been touched. There you are!"

They looked past her and saw, within the bright circle cast by the lamp, the figure of old Mr. Benton, lying on his back. Both hands were caught up to his breast, and he lay in a crimson pool that had run from a great wound in his head.

The sheriff's son gasped, turned sick, and caught at the wall for support. But the sheriff himself showed not the slightest emotion. He merely leaned over the body, saying: "Never knowed he was that tall . . . never saw the old codger straightened out before."

"Now you've seen," said Mrs. Zellar shrilly, "and now go get him!"

"How long ago did he leave?"

"Only forty minutes by the clock. I been watching for you to come and watching the clock and thinking you'd never come. But he can't get far through the mud."

"Forty minutes?" asked the sheriff, and he suddenly lost all eagerness. "Well, let's hear about this. Get over here, will you?"

The last words were a savage roar, and they jerked Gus

25

away from the door, toward which he had been sneaking. He stood back against the wall, shuddering, and his eyes twitched nervously from face to face.

"They ain't no call to talk to Gus like that," said Mrs. Zellar. "He didn't do nothing."

"Perhaps not," said the sheriff, and, maintaining his aggravating calm, he produced a cut of chewing tobacco and worked off a comfortable bite between his front teeth.

"Say, Dad," broke in his son, "you ain't going to stand around while he gets away?"

"You talk less and listen more," said his father sagely. "And you cotton onto this . . . before you start following a trail, find out where it leads. Now, Missus Zellar, what happened?"

"He came here and made us . . . ," began the woman.

"Who's he?"

"Wouldn't give no name . . . that kind never do. Just said he was Jack. But Mister Benton knew right off, the minute he laid eyes on him, that Jack was no good, and he said so right to his face. Well, Jack come and knocked open our kitchen door and asked for a meal and a bed. I didn't like the looks of him, but, when I told him there wasn't nothing for him here, he pulled a gun and started ordering us around. Ain't that right, Gus?"

"Every single word," said the truthful Gus, rolling his eyes.

"Leave Gus out and talk to me."

"Afterward, Mister Benton come down, like he mostly always does, to say a word or two to us before he goes to bed, him knowing that we're about the only friends he has in the world."

The sheriff was now walking around the room, carelessly examining every corner of it. Mrs. Zellar followed him a pace or two in every direction he took, raising her voice, when he was far away, lowering it slightly, when he was close.

"He seen Jack, as I was saying, and Jack seen him. And while Benton was talking, Jack found out that the old man kept a pile of money in his chest in his room."

"You knew that, did you?" asked the sheriff, his back turned.

"Does it mean anything . . . my knowing it?" asked Mrs. Zellar.

"Go on."

"Finally, after Mister Benton left, and Jack got through eating . . . he ate like he hadn't had food for a couple of days . . . Jack went up to bed, and he wouldn't be suited with nothing but Gus's own room, right next to Mister Benton's room.

"Gus come downstairs afterward. 'I don't like the looks of him,' says Gus. 'Nor his ways,' says I.

" 'I'm going to sit up a while,' says Gus, 'till Jack turns out his light.'

"So we done it. We turned down the lamp in the kitchen, so it didn't make no light, just a glooming through the room. Then we waited and waited. All at once we heard a scream. Quick as a flash, Gus jumps to his feet.

" 'I been waiting for just that,' he said, and starts running up the stairs, with me after him."

"Are you sure he went first?" asked the sheriff.

"Sure he did. Ain't he the man of the house?"

"Go on," said Larrabee dryly.

"Gus tried the door, and it was locked. He took a run and broke the door open . . . you see . . . and there he found Mister Benton lying, poor soul, with the chest open and the papers and everything all ruffled up, just the way you see. Nothing ain't been touched . . . not a thing is touched,

Sheriff, since we first seen it."

The chest in the corner of the room, indeed, was open, and a confusion of papers tumbled in it and on the floor around it.

"And then the door of Jack's room opens, and out he comes, rubbing his eyes like he'd just waked up, as though he could have slept through all that noise.

" 'What's all the racket about?' he says. Well he knew, the murderer. Look here!"

She led the way to the window. Below it was the roof of the verandah that wound around the side of the house. Opposite was another window.

"That window yonder opens into Jack's room, where he was supposed to sleep . . . the liar. What he done was to slip out of that window of his room and walk right across the roof and open this window and come in. He had first throttled the old man. You see?"

She advanced to the body and, leaning about it, pointed to some discolorations on the throat. There was something hideous in this eagerness, something unnatural for her sex. She was giving the scent of Jack Montagne to the bloodhounds.

"But the old boy died hard," went on Mrs. Zellar, stepping back again. "He wasn't dead, when Jack finished the throttling. He come to life, got his breath, and let out the screech that I heard down below and near stopped my heart beating."

The sheriff, in the meantime, went to the window, leading onto the roof, and tried it. It opened frictionlessly and without sound under the lift of his hand. He turned, nodding, and marked the last of Mrs. Zellar's words with more apparent interest.

"And, when he screeched, Jack, who was getting the money out of the chest, turned around and hit him over the

28

head with a chunk of wood from the fireplace. There it is."

By the open hearth of the fireplace there was a pile of cut wood, each piece well over two feet in length. But one of these pieces lay in the middle of the floor, an ugly stain splotched about its sharp edge.

"You sure he got the money?" asked the sheriff.

"There ain't a cent in the chest!" she exclaimed. "Look for yourself, the way I done."

"I thought you didn't touch anything?" he asked sharply.

"Are you going to lay the stealing on me?"

"What did Jack do then?" asked the sheriff.

"When he seen the body, he tried to act surprised, but me and Gus drew back and looked at him. He tried to talk the thing off, but we just kept on looking. Pretty soon he run out of the room. Next thing we knew, he was jumping downstairs. He didn't hit more'n twice, all the way to the bottom. Out-doors he went, and the next minute he was tearing down the road on his hoss . . . riding west."

"Thanks," said the sheriff. "What did he look like?"

"Good looking, but mean. About five feet eleven . . . dark, straight-looking eyes, dark hair . . . about thirty years old, or less . . . gray around the temples. Rides a gray hoss. Gus went out and seen it in the barn, after Jack went to bed . . . or after he was in his room. That's all I can think about, except that he looked like a killer. Mister Benton said so, right to his face."

"Hmm," said the sheriff, and raised his eyebrows. "Wait a minute," he added. "Here come the boys."

# IV

## "LARRABEE WINS HIS BET"

He went to the door and called down. There was a sound of horses snorting in the rainfall outside, and presently a cluster of five men climbed the stairs in answer to the call. The three Gloster boys came first. They had answered with all speed the summons from the house of the sheriff. Behind them came Mississippi Slim with his guard.

The sheriff greeted the Gloster boys with a word of thanks for their promptness. "We got a bad ride ahead of us," he said. "This is the work the gent we're after done." He pointed to the body of Benton. "And the man that done it has taken the west road. We'll start right away. Chris, you stay here and keep everybody out of this room. Wait a minute."

He turned and eyed Mississippi Slim. The latter was moving stealthily about the room, with his head thrust forward and bent low. He was oddly like a sniffing dog.

"Slim," called the sheriff.

Slim whirled, as if at the sound of a shot. He had been leaning over the chest full of papers.

"You had your fire near the road. See anybody passing tonight?"

Slim raised one finger.

"What was he like?"

"Bad looking . . . on a gray hoss."

"Know anything about him?"

"Nope."

"Did he say anything?"

"Nothing much."

"Talk out, Slim. What did he say?"

"Asked me why I didn't come down here and get a hand-out and a bed. I said it couldn't be done, because the lady didn't waste no time on gents that was wandering on the road looking for work."

Here Mrs. Zellar snorted her contempt.

"But this gent on the gray hoss allowed that he'd get a hand-out and a bunk. Said he'd see if he couldn't get treated right."

"Did he come on to this house, then?"

"I dunno."

"You didn't follow him?"

"Follow him? Let my fire go out?" Slim shook his head in wonder at such a thought.

The sheriff turned on Gus. "That door was locked when you came up?"

"Yep, it sure was, and I busted it in," he said defiantly. "Ask Ma if I didn't."

"Where's the key?"

"I dunno. I didn't look for it."

"Look on the floor," said the sheriff, himself joining the search. "Whether that door was locked from the inside or the outside makes a pile of difference."

The floor of the hall and the floor of the room revealed no key. The sheriff desisted from the search and gave his final directions. "You stay here, Chris, and you hold Slim."

"Why?" asked Slim. "What I got to do with all this killing?"

"You're a material witness. You'll get chuck and a free bunk. Ain't that good enough for you? We got good enough bunks to suit anybody in the jail."

"Jail!" Slim exclaimed. His rat eyes jerked from face to face and then became fixed on the floor, while a violent shiver ran through his meager body, but he said no more.

"And get in touch with the coroner . . . tell him to get his men down here, first thing," went on the sheriff to Chris. "We'll hit the trail, boys!"

"Now that he's clean gone," put in Mrs. Zellar malevolently.

The sheriff turned on her with a mild and curious glance, but the effect of it was to make her wince and change color. Then the men passed on out of the room.

The Gloster boys, Pete and Bob and Jerry, were first in the saddle, with Jud Larrabee and his father following after, but, as the former started down the road to the west, the sheriff called him back.

"Where you going?" he asked.

"Why, follow the trail, I guess."

"You think he went that way?"

"Why not?"

"If he's got any sense at all, he knows that Missus Zellar seen the way he started, and the first thing he'll do'll be to switch off."

"Which way, then?"

"What d'you see?" asked the sheriff. "Look around through the rain. What d'you see?"

The storm had fallen away to a faint misting, but still it blanketed the landscape. Indeed, nothing could have been visible, had it not been for the high-riding moon that was itself unseen, but served to outline the rain clouds in varying shades of deep gray and black.

"Don't see nothing," said the sheriff's son, "except the mountains, yonder. I can just make them out."

"Then," said the sheriff complacently, "that's where he's

gone, and we'll go the same way. Chris!"

His other son came a pace closer.

"Start using that telephone," said his father. "Get Boonetown and tell the central there to spread the description of Jack around. Get old Miller in Boonetown, too, and tell him to get to work, talking. That's the best thing he does, anyway! Good bye, boy!"

Once under way he made up for his seeming inactivity in the house of the Zellars. He was a heavier weight than the younger men, and his horse, an old buckskin campaigner, was inferior in speed to the mounts of the rest, and yet, before they had gone half a mile, the sheriff was in the lead, pushing his horse along with such skill that it seemed he could sense through the dark the obstacles that came in his way. Where the others floundered six times, the wise-footed buckskin slipped once.

The first excitement wore off with the posse, too, but the sheriff seemed to be spurred on by a steady and unflagging interest that kept his head high and his eyes straining on through the dark. The gray of dawn, which found them in the foothills, following trails that began to wind with the contours of the land, discovered the sheriff as agile of eye as ever and cheerfully examining the hills and the trees as they passed along.

The others awakened, also, as the day began. A freshening north wind chopped the sheeted storm clouds into thin drifts that served to shut the sun out, but allowed most of its light to sift through. In this invigorating air the sleepless quintet kept on until presently the sheriff raised his hand.

"Now," he said, "I figure it's about time for us to look about."

His followers had been very prone to beat up every thicket along the way, and they were quite disgusted by the careless

33

methods of their guide and leader. To their minds a thousand men might have hidden along the way and laughed as the posse went by on a wild-goose chase. The sheriff had chosen to stop on the top of a bare hill, with a bare country all around him. Why waste time here?

They conveyed their ideas bluntly and immodestly. The more so since the sheriff scratched the stubble on his chin, a far-away look in his eyes, while they talked and seemed to be almost persuaded at every other word. What he said at length was: "Are you hungry, boys?"

"Sure," was the chorus.

"So's Jack," said the sheriff.

His followers glanced at one another in disgust, and Jud Larrabee flushed with shame. Certainly the old man was growing old and simple. He glared defiantly at the Gloster boys. But it certainly was a very foolish remark — this reference to the appetite of Jack. What had that to do with a man-hunt — the appetite of the hunted?

"He's hungry," said the leader, "and most like he's smelled the bacon going up in smoke, yonder." There were three or four streaks of smoke in view, very dimly perceptible against the gray of the sky. "Nothing like the sight of smoke to make a gent uncommon hungry," went on the sheriff.

"Let's start on," urged his son uncomfortably. "We can talk on the way."

"On the way to what?" asked his father gently. "Let's make that out, first."

"That's what I'd like to know," burst out Jud. "Looks to me like we're all wrong. Who'd ride this way . . . clean out into the open . . . if he was hunting shelter?"

"Maybe he wouldn't," said the sheriff. "It's just my guess. But, if you don't do no guessing, you don't catch no men at the end of the trail. I figure Jack pictures us riding hard along the west trail. He's come up here to the hills. He's got a lot of hours ahead of us, he's thinking. So he comes over the hill, here, with a raging, tearing hunger, and he can't help stopping to eat. Now, first thing is . . . where'd he go to eat?"

"There's the biggest smoke, yonder," said Jud, very miserable, but striving to seem as if he took his father seriously. All the time he was wretchedly conscious of the smiles of the Gloster boys.

"That's the biggest smoke," admitted the sheriff, "and that's the one he wouldn't go to. That little house over the hill would be the place that a gent would run for, unless he was professional and had done murders before."

"Ain't that just what he is?" asked Pete Gloster. "Ain't that what Benton called him at sight?"

"A murderer? Nope, he called Jack a killer. They's a pile of difference. Jack's an amateur."

"What?"

"Sure. He turned his trick before he made sure the other folks was in bed. He took a room in the house, when he could have pretended he had to keep on his way, and so he could have ridden off and come back and done the job with nobody knowing. Nope, Jack's an amateur. Killers don't pick out old men. Jack needed money and needed it bad. He started to get it. He choked the old man, not with no pleasure, but because it had to be done. And then, when the old boy screeched, he picked up a piece of wood and batted him over the head. That was plain clumsy."

"Why?"

"A professional wouldn't have trusted to choking. He'd have used a touch of the knife. Nothing like a knife for neat, silent work, and dead men don't come back to life and start hollering. So I think Jack's an amateur . . . for that and other reasons. And, being an amateur, I'll just lay you boys even that he's in that little old house over the hills yonder . . . or has been there."

"I'll take you for twenty," said Jerry Gloster instantly.

"And me," chimed in Pete and Bob. Then the cavalcade started forward at a gallop toward the house.

They dipped over the hill and came upon a wretched little cottage leaning up the slope. A woman came to the door at their call, wiping her hands on her apron.

" 'Morning!" called the sheriff. "We're trying to catch up with our pal. That gent on the gray hoss that was here a while back. Which way did he go?"

"Right on over the hill, there," she answered, pointing. "Funny he didn't say nothing about the rest of you coming along, though."

"We got a surprise party for him, in a way of speaking," said the sheriff. "How long ago did he start?"

"About half an hour."

"Thanks."

With a glance the sheriff gathered up his posse, and they started on. The silence behind Henry Larrabee was a tremendous thing. It set him smiling, as he rode to the top of that hill to which the woman had pointed. There he drew rein again. Below, lower hills tumbled this way and that, but the landscape was empty of all signs of a rider.

"By the way," said the sheriff, "that bet we made a while back . . . I forgot that I don't bet that way."

"I sure ain't going to be let off that easy," said Pete Gloster generously. "I was getting to think that I knowed more'n you, Sheriff, and I'm getting off cheap at twenty dollars' worth. Besides, why won't you bet?"

"It don't pay, somehow," said the sheriff, "to win money out of the life of another man, even if he's a murderer."

## V

## "LEFT IN THE RAIN"

There was no chance for further argument or comment on the sheriff's ideas. Not half a mile away, climbing out of a hollow and slowly mounting the hillside beyond, they saw a rider passing on a gray horse. Without a word, even of exultation, the posse lurched down the hillside. It was like the sudden breaking of a storm, this coming on the trail of the fugitive, after the meeting with the woman in the house. To his young companions the quiet-mannered sheriff seemed suddenly a prophet, a man of mysterious foreknowledge.

It was unquestionably the man they wanted. No sooner had he sighted the riders on the far slope than he leaned far forward over the saddle and urged his weary horse to fresh efforts, scurrying rapidly up the hill.

Tired his horse must be, but he had come the distance from the Zellar house at a far slower gait than the sheriff, and, accordingly, his mount had greater reserves of energy. He shot out of sight over the crest, and, when the sheriff and his men reached the same point, they saw Jack Montagne halfway up the farther slope. In spite of their frantic spurring he had gained on them, and he was still gaining.

"He'll run us into the ground," said the sheriff. "I'll see if I can't tag him." Then he whipped the long rifle out of its case, tucked the butt into the hollow of his shoulder, and fired. The fugitive and his horse were flattened to the slope beyond, as if a great weight, falling from above, had crushed them. While the sheriff calmly tucked his gun back into the case, his posse

37

rushed forward with a yell. They had their man.

Still, it seemed that Jack Montagne would flee blindly, pitting his speed of foot against the speed of galloping horses. Yet there was nothing to which he could flee. The hills were pitilessly bare, and there was not a tree — only scatterings of rocks, here and there. Yet he raced to the top of the hill and disappeared beyond it. A moment later the object of his flight appeared. He had run for the rocks of the summit in order to use them as a fort, and now he opened fire with the rifle which he had taken from the saddle when his horse fell.

Suddenly the sheriff drew rein with an oath, and the oath caused his companions to pull up their own mounts, for the sheriff was not a profane man. "Look!" said the sheriff, as the echo of the first shot died away. "He's put his hoss out of misery, instead of trying to pot us."

The gray horse had straightened out on the slope and now no longer struggled. While the horsemen stared, the rifle spoke again, three times. Not three yards away from the sheriff's horse the bullets thudded into the mud, and all three landed within the compass of a man's arm.

"He's warning us back," said the sheriff with another oath. "I told you he was an amateur murderer. If he can shoot like that, them three shots might have knocked three of us off our hosses. But he ain't going to shoot to kill unless he has to. That's his way of saying it." Such seemed to be the only explanation. "That's what I call politeness," went on the sheriff, "but the law don't make no allowances for such things. That gent yonder has done a murder, and he's got to hang for it. Jud, skirt around to the right and get behind him. Pete, you go to the left. Bob and Jerry, ride back to the top of the hill and get down behind them rocks. I'm going to try a little politeness of my own."

His directions were swiftly followed. Jud Larrabee and

Pete Gloster, riding left and right, scurried off for the positions that had been assigned them, thereby placing Jack Montagne in the center of a circle of foes. Three or four times, as they rode, the fugitive fired, but each time the bullet struck a few feet in front of the running horse.

The sheriff turned straight to the right, disappeared for ten minutes, and came in view again at the top of a tall, steep-sided hill which overlooked the fortress of Montagne. Here the sheriff dismounted, ensconced himself on the crest, and placed himself flat on his stomach, with his rifle ready, his slicker keeping him out of the mud. From his position, only exposing the top of his head to the fugitive, he could look down on Jack and hold the latter at his mercy. And mercy the sheriff intended to show, if he could.

He saw Jack Montagne in the center of a number of low-lying rocks, among which he stirred about, keeping a strict lookout on all sides. The sheriff drew out his glass and focused it carefully, until he could see the face of the man distinctly. What he saw was of sufficient interest to keep him motionless for some time. But he knew that appearances are not half the story. The man had committed murder, he kept telling himself over and over, and yet, in spite of himself, the sheriff's heart was weakening. The generosity which had induced the fellow to end the suffering of his wounded horse with his first shot, instead of directing that bullet against the charging posse, and the manner in which his rifle had been used merely to warn the sheriff and his men away, these things struck directly to the heart of Henry Larrabee. He had had many a gruesome experience with outlaws and killers, but never before had he trailed a murderer who would not shoot to kill. Moreover, the consummate marksmanship of the man appealed to him. It was hard to believe that such an artist could have been guilty of the foul crime in the Zellar house.

But facts were facts. The sheriff, warned by the stinging impact of a drop of rain that he had not much time in which to work, gathered the butt of his gun closer and prepared to fire. Montagne was surrounded by rocks which would serve admirably to protect him from direct fire on the level, but there was none of sufficient height to protect him the angling fire of the sheriff in his commanding position. Moreover, Jack Montagne was hopelessly surrounded. Pete Gloster to the northeast, Bob and Jerry to the south — they lay in a loose circle around the central position. Sooner or later the fugitive would be starved into submission. There was only one chance for his escape, and that was in a driving rainstorm which might blot him out of sight and give him freedom to slip through. But the sheriff had a way of forestalling the storm that was now blowing again out of the north.

He took careful aim and, with exquisite nicety that would have done justice to Montagne's own skill with a gun, planted a shot on the rock just beyond the fugitive. That warning ought to be sufficient to make the fellow see that his position was commanded, and that he would have to come out and surrender, unless he wished to be shot as he lay there. Larrabee laid aside his rifle and took up the glass minutely to observe the results of the shot.

He saw that Montagne had sprung up and was busying himself in a strange fashion, tugging at another deep-buried rock just before him The sheriff gazed and wondered what this might mean until, with a supreme wrench, he saw the stone torn from its bed. Then he understood. With a shout of vexation he dropped the glass and snatched up the rifle again. But it was too late. Before he could draw the bead the second rock had been placed on the first — a Herculean feat of strength — and now the two stones made a perfectly safe shelter against the bullets of the sheriff, even in his commanding position.

Larrabee ground his teeth. After all, he had been a fool not to kill this man on the first sight. Now he looked anxiously to the north, but what he saw was greatly reassuring. The storm clouds were piling high, but along the horizon a rift had appeared. Rain was falling steadily, and heavier rain was coming, but it was obviously only a clearing-off shower, and the heart of it would pass over in a few moments.

Nearer and nearer came the sheet of rain, blotting out the whole north and consuming hill after hill in obscurity, as it swept along. Now he could no longer see the hill where Jud lay, and suddenly the storm struck his own position. In thirty seconds he could not see ten yards before him or behind, so terrific was the downpour.

Unquestionably Jack would attempt to break through the circle, but, before he traveled a quarter of a mile, the storm would have passed, and he would be in clear view and rifle range, point-blank.

Sweeping his slicker about him and sheltering the rifle under it, the sheriff waited, probing the heart of the downpour, in case the fellow should attempt to slip past, close beside him. But that was not likely. He would run down through one of the hollows between the hills and never risk meeting with the members of the posse.

Still the rain continued, unabating. In the sheriff's anxiety it seemed to him impossible that so much water could ever have been drawn up into the atmosphere. But still it poured down, moment after precious moment, although at last he saw a gradual brightening to the north, and the hill where Jud lay came into view again like a ghost.

It was at this moment that his horse snorted, and the sheriff turned with an appeasing word to see the figure of a man rushing straight on him from behind. There was no time

41

to handle a rifle. As the man drew out of the dense rain, a set, savage face came into view. Larrabee went for his revolver.

It stuck in the holster. The rain had got into the leather, so that it was glued for a moment to the gun, and, when the weapon came into his hand, the other was upon him. The sheriff dodged and fired, but, as his finger curled around the trigger, a long arm darted forth, a fist gleamed before him, and the blow landed flush on the point of his jaw. It did not knock him down, but it paralyzed both brain and body. As he staggered back, the revolver fell from his nerveless hand, and the next instant he was swept to the muddy ground in the embrace of bear-like arms.

What followed was done with lightning speed and precision. In the space of half a dozen breaths the sheriff found himself trussed securely, hand and foot, gagged and lying on his back, with the merciless rain whipping down into his face. The fugitive gave him hardly a glance, but caught up the fallen sombrero, flung it over the face of his victim to shelter him from the torrent, and, with this final and almost insulting act of grace, he was gone.

The splashing of the departing hoofs came back to Larrabee. His destined victim was galloping off on his own horse! That tale would be caught up and told and retold by a hundred tongues. In his anguish Sheriff Larrabee wished that he had died before this day ever came to him. Death was the final meed of every man, but shame should come to cowards only.

The rain diminished now, as if, like a traitor, it only wished to endure until Jack Montagne had used its shelter to escape. A moment later the brightness of the sun was about him. But when would they find him and set him free? How long before they rode again on the trail of that hard-fisted, slippery devil? How long?

# VI

## "ALL ABOARD!"

Two days later the joyless eyes of Jack Montagne looked down from the side of a foothill upon a streak of black, hurrying across the valley, with a trailing cloud of white drawn out above it. Montagne drew a great breath of relief. He looked back instinctively toward the mountains, rolling huge and sullen above him, as if he expected them to put forth an arm and catch him back.

After all the perils, he had escaped and come to easy-striking distance of the railroad, and the railroad meant freedom. In a few days it could carry him away to the ends of the country, where the names of Zellar and Benton were never dreamed of. He visualized himself in a far-off city, reading an obscure notice in an obscure paper about the futile hunt for Jack Montagne, wanted for murder. For by this time they had surely hunted back to the town of his origin, and there they had learned that other and shameful story, and his name with it.

He bowed his head at the thought of it. Then he shrugged back his shoulders and started his pony down the mountainside and toward the rambling collection of houses in the distance.

Two miles from the outskirts he came to a pleasant meadow, where a brook tumbled brightly in the sunshine. Here he dismounted, took off the saddle and bridle, and waved the horse away to freedom. The invitation was accepted with a snort and a flirt of the heels. For a moment,

Montagne watched with a sigh, and then turned back to take up his trail.

He so timed his approach that he reached the vicinity of the town at dusk and then skirted about it to the railroad. Of course, it would not do to linger near the station, but that would not be necessary. Hardly a mile away the tracks started a stiff grade, where a freight train would have to labor slowly — so slowly that a man, agile of foot and sure of hand, could certainly take it with ease.

To this point he went, and, selecting a shelter between two bushes that would shelter him from the too-active eye of some brakie, as the train approached, he sat down to wait. The moon rose during his vigil, before he heard a far-off humming on the tracks, and then made out a train stopping at the town and starting again. That it was a freight train he had not the slightest doubt, as soon as he heard the redoubled labor of the engine as it reached the grade. Montagne rose, stretched himself, and, finding all his muscles playing smoothly in spite of the long period of inactivity, crouched again between the bushes and watched the train roar nearer.

The sound grew louder. The humming of the rails was now a heavy vibration. The rush of the exhaust was like the deafening noise of a great waterfall. With his brain reeling from the uproar, the blow fell that had been so long avoided. There was a sharp command from behind, and he wheeled to look into the muzzles of three revolvers held by grim-faced men.

It is said that remembered dreams are those which occur during the very act of waking. The mind, unencumbered by the slow processes of the senses that burden it during waking moments, plunges through enough events to fill a lifetime, all crammed into a second or two of actual time. So it was with Jack Montagne, as he faced the leveled guns and calculated

44

the chances. There was not a line on a single face that he over-looked. Had there been a single symptom of weakness in a single face he would have taken the suicidal chance rather than submit. But there was no weakness. Every eye told him the same story: a readiness to kill on the slightest provocation on his part. So he pushed his hands above his head. To those who held him up it seemed that the gesture of surrender was made instantly!

"Suffering cows!" exclaimed Jack Montagne to the sheriff, recognizing his antagonist whom he had met during the rain-storm. "Is it possible that you've trailed me here?"

"Trailed?" asked the sheriff gently. "Not a bit. I just did a little guessing that you'd come over the mountains in this di-rection, and, if you did, you'd be sure to head for this town, and, if you headed for this town, you'd be sure to strike for this grade to nab a freight. All simple as daylight. Go through him, Jud."

The last was addressed to his son, who now adroitly went through the pockets of Jack. The revolver, the pocketknife, tobacco and brown papers, and a square of sulphur matches was the total of the effects of Jack Montagne.

"He's cached the money, somewheres," said Jud. "Ain't any sign of it."

"Sure he's cached it," said the sheriff. "Any fool would do that, considering how much there is of it. Where'd you put it, Jack?" He added casually: "Of course, anything you say to us may be used against you."

"I know," said Montagne, "so I won't say anything about the money." And he smiled at the sheriff with what might have been resignation or mockery.

Larrabee considered that smile with the most intimate at-tention. "Bring down your hands," he said, "but bring 'em down behind you, then keep moving slow."

"Afraid I got another gun tucked up my sleeve?" asked Montagne.

"I'm afraid of you every minute," replied the sheriff with astounding frankness. "I might as well tell you, so's you'll know that I'm on the watch for you, every minute. Come to think of it, we'll handcuff your hands in front of you. Here you go."

As Montagne obediently offered his wrists, the manacles were snapped over them. "A nice, new pair," observed Montagne calmly, looking down at them.

His quiet manner shocked the younger men of the posse, but the sheriff seemed more and more interested in his victim.

"What'd you do with my hoss?" he asked. "I suppose you knew we'd sent descriptions of the hoss all over, together with descriptions of you. Did you drill her through the head and let her tumble down a ravine, some place?"

"I let the hoss run loose," said Montagne, "just above town, yonder."

"I take that kind of you," said the sheriff gently. "I take that mighty kind. All right, boys, jump on your hosses, and we'll start. Climb on this one, Jack."

Montagne hesitated. "You going to walk, Sheriff?"

"I can do it better'n you. Ain't handy to walk when you can't swing your hands."

It was strange to hear these politely diplomatic moves between the two. Presently Montagne was seated on the horse, and they started back for the town, with the sheriff walking a little behind the captive. Suddenly he drew up beside his prisoner.

"Jack," he said, in a purely conversational tone, "why did you do it?"

"Do what?" asked Montagne out of a dream.

46

"The old boy . . . old Benton . . . ? Why did you finish him?"

"You're a pretty good guesser," answered Montagne without emotion. "Suppose you try to figure this puzzle out."

So the matter was allowed to rest. They took a midnight train out, and in the dawn they arrived at the sheriff's county seat, where Montagne was escorted to the jail. He preserved his careless demeanor throughout, even when the front door of the jail slammed heavily behind him.

When they reached the door of the cell designated for Jack, the sheriff drew forth his bunch of keys. "Just hold onto your patience for a while," he said to Jack. "Take me a while to find the right key."

"You don't need one," answered Montagne. "Here you are." And, folding his hands small, he slipped them deftly out of the handcuffs. The sheriff watched with intense interest.

"You could have done that any time and made a play to get loose," he observed. "Why didn't you, Jack? I know you got plenty of nerve for a break."

"Because I've made my play and finished it. I'm beat, Sheriff, and that's all there is to it." Then he walked calmly into the barred enclosure.

## VII

## "PUBLIC OPINION"

Boonetown, the county seat, was so small that the uninitiated were apt to call it a village, but it was not too small to be without that mysterious and uncontrollable voice, usually called public opinion. Public opinion on this occasion was wakening from a long, long sleep.

For some years public opinion had expressed itself only at elections and similar unimportant and formal functions. But, when the news arrived that the murderer of old Benton was in town and in jail, the man whom the district attorney had arraigned beforehand with terrible eloquence in the little Boonetown newspaper, public opinion wakened with a start, yawned forth a growl from some four hundred throats, and stretched its thousand arms to find something on which to vent its rage.

For public opinion is a blind beast, even when it wakens. The maladministration of officials, the legal cruelties of business oppression, and business betrayals are very apt never to reach the sleepy ear of the creature. But it may suddenly start up to yell itself hoarse with applause, because a politician gives birth to a neat phrase. Then it falls asleep with a grunt and a smile, when the lucky fellow bows his thanks and dips his fingers in the public purse.

This great, stupid beast, public opinion, having long slumbered in Boonetown, now roused itself with a roar and called for a victim. And on this occasion there was some justification for noise. The district attorney had called attention to the brutality of the crime — to the youth of the murderer — to the white-haired feebleness of the murdered man. Finally, the district attorney had declared his intention of suppressing such crimes, of ending the reign of violence in that violent county, of bringing in a golden age of peace, by hanging this red-handed devil, called Jack, from the highest gallows. A good beginning, he pointed out, was nine-tenths of a good ending; and a good example was the better part of a good beginning. The broken neck of Jack was to furnish the good example that would, thereafter, make crime hang its head and slink away from the precincts favored by the presence of the district attorney.

It may be gathered that he was a very young man to hold such a very old office. Fitzpatrick Lavigne was one of those who love the practice of criminal law; and he loved the prosecuting end of it, because, he said, that end was morally cleaner. In reality his love for the attorney's office was like the love of the barbarian for the sword — Fitzpatrick Lavigne liked to kill. His summing up to a jury was delivered with both violence and relish; he expanded his naturally meager inches; he became huge and dominated a courtroom, while he was whipping a victim toward death. He never recommended mercy to a judge on any occasion.

In appearance he was small, rather plump, with clear, red cheeks, a childishly smooth brow, and eyes of sparkling brightness. He was a favorite among ladies, young and old; among men he was highly prized for his contagious good cheer and his thrilling anecdotes, generally about his own experiences — because, as he was fond of saying, a man generally talks best about himself. He was about twenty-seven years old, but he seemed five full years short of that age, and his youthful appearance was a tremendous advantage to him. When, with fiery indignation, he assailed a criminal in the court, the jury felt that so young a man, with so smooth a brow, must be filled with legal inspiration to use such violent words. He spoke with a sort of indignant virtue that was wholly convincing. He could make twelve honest men sway and stiffen with him. And, when he turned and shook his extended forefinger at the accused, twelve pairs of eyes would generally turn and glare in the same direction. No one would understand, no one could be expected to understand that this Apollo-faced man was consumed with a fanatical zeal to sacrifice a fellow creature on the altar of justice.

Fitzpatrick Lavigne knelt at only one shrine — this was his

percentage of convictions. He worshipped that god, and he prayed to it. He dreamed of a time when his picture would appear in some metropolitan newspaper, setting forth the record of that brilliant young lawyer, Fitzpatrick Lavigne.

But Boonetown did not act, as Lavigne's legal experience in other parts of the country had led him to suppose it would act. No, it rose up and seized guns and rushed to the jail and demanded that the murderer of old men should straightway be handed over to it, to be torn limb from limb.

From a window of the hotel the young district attorney stared thoughtfully down upon this troubled sea before the jail. What oil could he throw upon the waters? Not that he cared for the life of Jack Montagne, but Jack represented a sure conviction. If the mob rent him limb from limb, a scalp, that should hang at Fitzpatrick's belt, would be gone. He went down and waded through the mob to the jail.

Cries accompanied him: "Give the skunk to us, Fitz! We'll teach him manners! Feed him out the window to us, Fitz. We'll teach him!"

Fitzpatrick Lavigne reached the door of the jail. Two pale-faced men, with double-barreled shotguns, guarded the prison, but they were not the force which held the mob at bay. That force the district attorney found in the office, a large quid of tobacco bulging his cheek, his heels cocked up on the desk. The sheriff rolled dull, contented eyes toward his visitor.

"Hello, Lavigne," he said. "Kind of noisy, ain't they?"

Lavigne despised the sheriff, and the sheriff knew it. The sheriff despised Lavigne, and Lavigne knew it. Consequently they were extremely amiable on all occasions.

"But," said Lavigne, consternation in his face, "aren't you going to do anything?"

"About what?"

Fitzpatrick saw visions of the murderer torn from the jail, a conviction hopelessly lost. It was like a conspiracy, and the sheriff would not raise a hand.

"About the mob," declared Fitzpatrick. "Are you going to let them take him?"

"Take nothing," replied the sheriff. "They know me, son. If you don't like the noise, go out and quiet 'em. You started all this with your talk in the paper about 'white-haired innocence' and 'youthful brutality.' "

"Well," said Lavigne, "I only told the truth!"

"Did you? Ever know Benton?"

"Not exactly."

"Well, sir, he was exactly a devil. He didn't have one corner of a good deed tucked away in his make-up. You can lay to that! But there's your mob, Lavigne. What are you going to do with it?"

"You're not afraid they'll get him, then?" asked Lavigne, immensely relieved.

The sheriff laughed softly. "Sooner than see them get him, I'd arm the prisoner, son."

"But what could you two . . . ?"

"Wait till you see him, Lavigne. He's a man. With him at my back . . . well, there ain't any use talking about it, because the crowd ain't going to bust any doors down. They'll just holler out there and have a good time. If I get an earache, I'll just go out and clear the street. Otherwise, it don't amount to nothing."

Lavigne walked to one side, pondering. As the sheriff had said, he had raised the crowd. What should he now do with it? An idea leaped into that young and surprisingly fertile brain. First he seized two officers of the law, such as he usually liked to have with him on similar occasions. They were both broad and correspondingly small of forehead and brain. With them

51

he went to the cell of the prisoner. He waited outside, until his two worthies had secured the arms of the prisoner with handcuffs. Then the district attorney led the way to a back room of the jail, a small room fenced in with almost sound-proof walls. Here Jack Montagne was seated near the wall, with an officer on either side.

"You heard that racket outside?" asked the district attorney, taking his stand with spread feet before the prisoner. "And you know what it means?"

"They want me?" asked the prisoner, and yawned.

The yawn startled Lavigne. "And," he said ferociously, "they'll probably get you, and you know what that means?"

"Tolerable well."

"There's no use in talking," said Lavigne. "We can't afford to have the jail attacked and risk the lives of law-abiding citizens to protect a worthless dog like you. There's only one thing that'll quiet that mob, and that's to know that the law is going to finish you up in its own way and its own time. There's only one way that the law can be absolutely sure of you, and that's through a confession. You understand?"

Montagne nodded.

"Now," said Lavigne, "I don't mind telling you that you haven't a chance, and you're going to hang. Everything is against you. I could hang ten men on what I have against you. It's only a matter of time and legal formalities which have to be gone through. So the best thing for you, all around, is to let me have a full confession. I can make things pretty miserable for you, my friend, if you hold out. But, if you talk out and tell the whole story, I'll see that you live on the fat of the land . . . up to the last day." He smiled generously on his prisoner and went on: "Besides, there's no sense in this fool silence of yours. You won't tell your name, except to call yourself Jack . . . you won't give the name of the town you come from . . . and all this is really evidence against you. A man who is afraid to have the law know his past is a man the law handles without gloves. Will you talk, Jack?"

"I'll talk," said Jack Montagne.

The district attorney sighed with relief. In another minute he had spread out a pad on his knee, for shorthand was included in his accomplishments.

"Start in," he said, "where your story begins to be different from what Slim and the Zellars have sworn to."

On a previous occasion he had listed all the sworn facts to Jack in a vain effort to elicit a confession.


# VIII


## "LAVIGNE LEARNS A LESSON"

"Well," said Jack Montagne, "that makes me begin at the beginning, or pretty close to that. Mind you, I don't expect you to believe me, but I'm going to talk so's you'll stop bothering me."

"Start with when I got to the Zellar house . . . and make it brief. It runs like this . . . I didn't have a cent. I had to get a place to sleep, and I wanted chuck and wanted it bad. Besides, I hated skunks that would have turned a gent out into a storm like that. So I made the Zellars give me chuck. While I was eating, the old man came in and called me a crook, or words to that effect, and right after that young Zellar took me up and showed me into a room.

"I was so sleepy I didn't take off my clothes. I hit that bed and was off in a flash. A scream woke me up. I jumped out of my room and found a light shining under the door of Benton's room. I smashed that door, when I found it was locked, because, inside that room, I heard a scampering of feet. When I ran in, there was nobody there, but old Benton was lying dead. The chest was open, and the papers were ruffled a good deal.

"I went downstairs and called Missus Zellar and her kid. They came up and looked. Then, while I was talking to the kid, Missus Zellar sneaked out. I went after her in a minute, and I heard her telephoning the sheriff, so I knew her plan was to send Larrabee after me.

"I was alone. I knew that both the woman and Gus would swear their lives away to stick me for the murder, because that was their only way of taking suspicion off their own shoulders, where it belongs. What was my word against both of theirs? I didn't wait . . . I grabbed my hoss and started. The sheriff followed. You know the rest."

As he concluded, Fitzpatrick Lavigne smashed the pad to the floor. "That's your confession, is it?"

"Yes."

"By heaven, I've a mind to let that mob in! Listen to 'em."

Outside, the crowd set up a fresh clamor, surging toward the jail. For half an hour the good men of Boonetown had been shouting to keep their anger alive, shouting to find a leader.

"I hear 'em," said the prisoner, "and I'd a pile rather face them than face you and your crowd in the courtroom."

The lip of the district attorney curled. He cast one glance at his henchmen, and they rose instantly to the occasion.

"You skunk," said the red-headed man at Jack's right. "Take this to teach you manners!" And he smashed his fist into Montagne's face. The impact toppled man and chair. He was jerked to his feet, and the district attorney, first making sure that the prisoner was securely pinioned on both sides, stepped close and shook his fist under the nose of Montagne.

54

"There's more of the same stuff coming for you," he said, "unless you stop lying and tell the truth. Are you ready to talk?"

It was only the beginning of the third degree; it was only the beginning of that process which Fitzpatrick Lavigne loved above all else. In the meantime, he watched, fascinated, the progress of a crimson stain rolling down from the mouth of Jack Montagne.

The stain was doubly red, because Montagne had suddenly become deathly white. At sight of that badge of fear, the heart of the district attorney leaped with pleasure.

"I've told you the truth," he said, "and I ain't going to lie even to give you the pleasure of hanging me. But . . . don't have one of these gents hit me again."

In reply Fitzpatrick Lavigne smiled slowly, as a connoisseur smiles when he inhales the bouquet of a favorite vintage. He raised one finger, and this time the black-haired man, at Montagne's left, acted. His burly fist drove home with a sickening impact. Jack went down, his head striking the wall. He rolled forward on the floor and lay quiet.

"Pick him up," said Fitzpatrick Lavigne. "I'll teach the dog to threaten me. You heard him threaten me, Dick?"

Dick grinned and, reaching down, jerked Montagne up with one exertion of his burly arms. But it was like lifting a wildcat. Montagne came to his feet, the handcuffs dangling from one wrist. The sheriff very foolishly had neglected to warn his assistants about the great flexibility of those slender hands of Jack, and now his hands were free.

He swung the manacles into the face of Dick, and the black-haired man dropped without a cry. Then Jack spun on his heel and smashed his right hand into the face of the red-head and sent that worthy crashing back against the wall.

The district attorney leaped for the door, but, between

glancing over his shoulder in terror to see how long it might be before the danger assailed him from the rear and the shaking of his hand, he could not fit the key into the lock of the door.

The redhead was battling with noble vigor and calling wildly on Dick to come to his aid, but his voice was choked and stifled in a rain of blows. He got to his revolver only to have it kicked out of his hand.

It exploded, as it fell on the far side of the room, and the explosion drew a fresh shriek of amazing power from the district attorney. At the same instant the red-headed fellow was backed to the wall, and the whipping fists of Jack Montagne, driven with uncanny speed and terrible power, smashed his face until he cringed down, moaning for quarter.

Then Jack Montagne turned on the district attorney. The latter, with one last, despairing effort, strove to get the key from the lock. The key merely stuttered against the door, and Fitzpatrick Lavigne fled to a corner. Here he crouched, shielding his face with both arms. "No, no!" he exclaimed. "Don't! I'll see that you go free. I'll get you out. You . . . you . . . but don't come near me!"

At that moment a hand turned the knob of the door from without, and the prisoner worked his free hand deftly into the manacle, the palm doubling to half its ordinary compass. The sheriff opened the door to find Jack Montagne leaning carelessly against the wall on the far side of the room, his hands in irons. Dick lay with his face down, unstirring, and the red-headed man was just beginning to straighten up, while the district attorney peered in terror between his arms, as if through the bars of a cage.

"Kill him! Kill the devil!" Fitzpatrick Lavigne yelled. "He's tried to murder me! He's tried to murder us! He got those handcuffs off and. . . ."

"What," demanded the sheriff sternly, "have you been doing with him in here?"

"What my office compels me to do . . . trying to get a confession out of him. And the devil. . . ."

"How," said the sheriff, "did he get his lip cut?"

"He attacked us," began Lavigne.

"He attacked the three of you . . . two of you with guns . . . and him with none? He started this game, did he?"

The sneer of the sheriff suddenly made it impossible for the glib tongue of the district attorney to wind itself around a plausible lie. He could only moan: "I'll make him suffer for this. . . . I'll make him sorry for the day he was born!"

"Look here," said the sheriff, staring mildly at the district attorney, "I guess I didn't see you kneeling over there in the corner and begging Jack not to hit you? I guess I didn't see nothing like that. If I did, I'd try to forget it, but listen to me, Mister Hang-'em-quick Lavigne . . . if you lay a hand on him again, I'll have to do a pile of remembering. What's more, I'll have you and your two thugs laughed out of town for yaller-livered skunks . . . which you are. District attorney? Bah! You ain't worthy of licking the boots of Jack. Maybe he's done a killing, here and there, but he's been a man, according to my lights. That's more'n you and the two of 'em there can say. Now get out, and don't come sneaking back to raise trouble here. I'm running this jail, and I'll keep on running it!"

The two slipped without a word through the door. Dick was jerked to his feet, kicked into semi-consciousness, and pushed after them. Then the sheriff, turning his back on the terrible man-killer, asked him to follow. And Jack did follow very meekly back to his cell, where the manacles were gravely unlocked and removed. There the sheriff spoke to him for the first time.

57

"I'm sure sorry," he said, "that you got your lip all cut up."

He proceeded to the front door of the jail, took from one of the white-faced guards a double-barreled shotgun and, with this terrible weapon under his arm, stepped out in full view of the milling crowd. He waited until the hoarse roar subsided. In that roar they were demanding Jack, the murderer of old men.

"Gents," said the sheriff, "I'm plumb tired out today, and I'm trying to get a nap. You folks bother me a lot. Matter of fact, I got to have sleep, and you're disturbing the peace. So . . . get off this street . . . *pronto!*"

Up went the shotgun, and the sheriff looked about him. It seemed to every man in the mob that Larrabee's keen eyes were glaring at him, as at a ringleader, and then the gaping mouth of the gun pointed down at him. The crowd wavered, split in the center, rolled away on both sides, and vanished. The sheriff spat upon the steps and reëntered the jail.


IX


"UNFORESEEN SUCCOR"

The late October day dawned with a warm, steady breeze out of the south. The air was soft as the air of latter May, and the sun as kindly warm and bright. Mary Larrabee, in honor of the tender, blue sky above her, put on a dress so white that it dazzled, so crisp that it rustled with every step like an autumn wind among the gay leaves. And, while she smiled at her pretty face in the mirror, she knotted at her breast a red ribbon to match the red feather that flowed along the side of her white hat. Then she

58

went forth like some ancient warrior to battle, conscious of invincible armor.

Her own neat little buggy, with her own span of bright-eyed bays dancing before it, waited in front of the house; they whirled her off down the road so fast that the heart of her mother came into her throat. She would have called a warning after her girl, but in her heart was a sublime conviction that no living creature could possibly have the will or the power to injure Mary Larrabee.

As for Mary herself, in those rounded young arms of hers there was ample power to keep the bays in hand, or, if they wished to dash off at too reckless and bounding a trot, she could soothe and control them with her voice. For she had owned them since the day they were foaled, and she had raised them to know and to love her whistle, her voice, and her hand. She could have brought them back to a more sedate gait, but there was no love of sedateness in Mary Larrabee. That clear tan on her face and on her small, strong hands told of many a wild drive and many a wilder gallop through all weathers and over all manner of roads. And across the bridge of her tip-tilted nose there was still a suggestion of the mottling of freckles that had been so prominent during her girlhood.

Sedate? She only waited until she had turned the corner of the hill, and then she let her dainty-footed mares go. And they went like the wind, while she laughed them on to greater efforts. She darted around sharp curves on two wheels, and with a shout she roared across shaking bridges. She flashed through Boonetown, joyously conscious of drawing eyes after her on either side of the one real street. When she stopped before the jail, the bays were dripping and entirely willing to pause, but still, as she tied the hitching strap to the rack, they pricked their ears and tried to reach her hands with their foamy muzzles.

She ran lightly up the steps of the jail and whisked through the dark hall and carried into her father's office a rustle like the wind of the honest outdoors, a brightness like the kind sunshine.

Sheriff Larrabee, as usual, had his heels perched on top of his spur-scarred desk, and he turned his slow-moving eye upon her. Since she had grown up to pretty, young womanhood he had made a point of making no fuss over her, as a sort of antidote to the atmosphere of admiration through which she moved. But today she bore such a radiance about her that a very Diogenes might have dropped his lantern and his cynicism into his tub and stood forth to answer her smile.

So the sheriff asked: "How come? Going to get married?"

She merely laughed at him, as he ran his eye over the whiteness of the frock. He worshipped every turn of her head, every rise and fall of her voice; all the profound kindliness of his heart poured forth around her — in silence. Mary understood.

"I've come to see the insides of this old jail," she declared.

"I'll call Bud," said the sheriff, yawning. "He'll show you around the place. How come? Want to take up my business after I quit?"

"I might," she answered. "I hit nine out of ten with my twenty-two, yesterday. I beat Jud, and he hasn't hardly spoken to me since."

"Hmm," said the sheriff. "I'll call Bud."

"But I don't want you to call Bud."

"All right, go around by yourself."

"You know what I really want. I want to see this terrible man . . . Jack?"

"You do?"

"Of course."

"Want to see what a real, honest-to-goodness murderer

looks like, eh? Well, I guess Jack will be glad to see you and have you stand around and look him over like a wolf in a cage. That'll be a pretty fine party for Jack, right enough."

She sat forward in her chair, regarding his grave face intently. "Isn't he worse than a wolf, a man that's done a murder?" she asked. "Does he deserve to be treated kindly?"

"How d'you know he killed Benton?"

"Why, everybody knows it!"

"Then everybody knows more'n I do! And I'll tell you this . . . he's going to be treated like a white man, right up to the time that twelve men say he's done a murder. After that, while he's waiting to be hung, he's going to be treated like a white man again. If a girl or a boy of mine. . . ." He broke off in his tirade, staring ominously at her.

Mary Larrabee sat back in her chair, nodding. "You like him, don't you?" she asked. "Why?"

"He's a man," said the sheriff. "He had your brothers and me under his gun once, and he didn't shoot to kill, but just to warn off. Keep that idea in your head, Mary."

She grew pale at the thought.

"You still want to see him?"

"I want to see him and thank him," she said eagerly. "Why, Dad, how could such a man be a murderer?" She did not quail before the grim accusation which the world had placed against Montagne. Suddenly she was asking: "Has he a ghost of a chance of proving himself innocent?"

"I dunno," replied the sheriff, "but he don't seem to care. He's stopped hoping, what with the crowd yowling to get at him, and that little sneak, Lavigne, badgering him. Jack don't seem to care whether he lives or dies. When a gent stops being interested in life, he's about through."

She bowed her head. In the Boonetown paper she had read every word of the damning evidence against Montagne.

Now she ran over it, bit by bit. Truly it seemed a perfect case against the stranger, unless her father's prejudice in favor of Jack might be based on good grounds.

"Will you introduce me to him?" she asked gently.

"Sure," said the sheriff. "If you're going to meet him like that, I'll take you in."

He led the way to the rear of the jail, to the cell of Montagne, where the latter was rolling a cigarette with careless skill.

"This is my daughter, Mary," said the sheriff. "I've been telling her how you played white, when we were giving you a run, and she thinks she's got something to thank you about. I'm going back in front, Mary."

As the sheriff sauntered away, he saw Jack Montagne rise and nod to the girl. He heard him say: "No call for thanking me . . . matter of fact, I took the sheriff quite a bit out of his way." And he grinned as he spoke.

"There's nerve," muttered the sheriff. "Enough for ten ordinary men."

But Mary Larrabee was unable to answer that careless speech for a moment. She stared steadily into the lean, brown face of the man, the straight-looking eyes, remembering what her father had said: *He's a man.* That, after all, summed it up. And, when the prisoner merely nodded to her, she suddenly stepped close to the bars and stretched her hand through them.

"I do want to thank you," said Mary Larrabee, "and I want to say how sorry I am that you're in trouble."

His carelessness disappeared. He straightened, flushing to the roots of his hair, and, advancing slowly, took her hand. "Mighty good of you to come in to say that," he said huskily.

She waved that idea away. "First of all," she said, still probing him and finding nothing sneaking or elusive about his return glance, "I want to know what you're doing to protect yourself?"

"Nothing," he answered, "because nothing can be done."

"Because you have no money?"

"That's partly it."

"Dad would help you, I know," said the girl, "but, as the sheriff, he can't very well do that. However, I can, and I have money. I know the lawyers in town, too . . . and I can get one to work for you."

He shook his head. "I've always been dead set against taking charity," he replied.

"Will you tell me only one thing?" she pleaded. "Will you simply tell me that you didn't do this horrible, impossible thing?"

He watched her for a moment, with a singular hunger, but at length he shook his head with decision. "It's no use," he said, "because there's nothing that can help me, and I've made up my mind not to speak again."

"That's a final decision?"

"Absolutely."

"Then," she answered, "I'll tell you that I'm perfectly convinced that you didn't do it. I know you didn't do it, and . . . and I'm going to prove to the world that you didn't."

The flush grew darker and darker on his face, as his eyes expanded. "It's plumb easy to see," said Jack Montagne, "that you're your father's daughter. He's the squarest shooter I ever met, and you sure take after him. Why, if you were a man. . . ."

He paused, but she urged him on with: "Well?"

"You'd be the sort I'd tie to, the sort I'd want to have around in a pinch. But the way it stands . . . well, there's just one good thing you can do, and that's to forget all about me."

He was so calm about it that the tears rushed to her eyes.

To hide them she turned abruptly away, waved her hand to him, and ran out to find her father. The latter was walking up and down outside the jail, scuffing up the sand and studying it absent-mindedly.

"I've made up my mind to fight for him," said the girl, on fire with enthusiasm. "There must be some way."

"Most like," said her father carelessly. "Most like there is. Never can tell when something will turn up."

Up and down they walked, past the side of the long, low building. She knocked her shoe against a bright bit of metal and stooped and picked up an old house key. She pocketed it automatically, as some people do in such cases.

"How," asked the girl, summing up the case with energy, "can twelve men with good sense look at Jack and think he could commit a crime?"

"Hmm," replied her father. "It's pretty rare to get twelve men together and get good sense out of 'em . . . and it ain't hard for that little snake, Lavigne, to hypnotize an average jury. No, Mary, you sure got no hope . . . not against Lavigne. He's a man-killer, but he uses the law to do his killing."

She stamped in her anger. "How many other men is he going to hang?" she asked furiously. "How many other men are in the jail there, waiting until that little rat has time to come out and worry the lives out of them?"

Her father smiled a little at this vigorous denunciation. "We're having dull times," he said. "Only one other gent in the jail, and that's the hobo, Mississippi Slim."

At this the girl stopped short. "Where's Mississippi?"

"In the jail."

"I know . . . I know, but what cell?"

"Got an idea?"

"I don't know, but, for heaven's sake, tell me. What's his cell?"

"Right yonder." He pointed to a grating a few paces away. "He may be hearing us now."

"Oh," exclaimed Mary Larrabee, "it's turning my brain upside down. Is there a chance?"

"Of what?"

"Nothing," said Mary, and she bolted for her buggy in front of the jail, running with the speed and the grace of a boy.


X


"THE KEY TO THE DOOR"


She whisked out of Boonetown, as she had whisked into it, the bays sweeping the light rig along at a terrific clip. Presently she turned onto a dim country road, made by the wear of travel, but never graded. Straight out of it she drove until she came to a sight of the house of the Zellars. She drew back her horses to a slower gait and finally pulled up behind the house. Instantly her eye met a reminder of the crime — two parts of a door, split cleanly down the center, were leaning against the wall near the kitchen window. This was the door that both young Zellar and Jack Montagne claimed to have broken through, in an effort to get at the room of the dead man.

She tied off her horses and, turning away, found Mrs. Zellar, in the act of wiping a milk tin, standing at the door of the house.

The big, ugly face of the woman stirred a reluctant smile of welcome. "Mary Larrabee!" she exclaimed. "How long since you come this way? Pretty nigh onto three years, I guess."

"I've heard so much about this murder," said Mary, as she

shook hands, "that I wanted to see the place. May I, Missus Zellar?"

"A terrible thing," replied Mrs. Zellar. "The shock it give me . . . I ain't over yet. Gus was hit pretty hard, too. You want to see the room?"

"If you please."

"Come right up," she started to lead the way. "A terrible thing," she repeated. "And me and Gus sure was fond of old Mister Benton. I know some folks didn't like him much. He had his ways, but all old folks do. We were used to him and knew how to make allowances. Yes, we were fond of old Benton. They's an empty feeling around the house, now he's gone."

Mary Larrabee shivered with disgust. One glimpse of Benton's face would be sure warrant that no human being could ever find a spark of affection to waste on the old fellow. They stood at the door of the room.

"There's the place," said the woman. "There's where he laid, with his head turned a little to one side. Do you see the mark? Soap and hot water . . . nothing does any good to take that stain out. I've worked till my arms ached, and still it won't come out. Poor Mister Benton. I hope they hang that Jack as high as the moon!"

"You really think he did it?"

"Think? Child alive, don't I know? Didn't I hear him talk? Didn't I see the way he looked, when he heard that the poor old man had money in his room? Right then I says to Gus . . . 'There's no good in this man, Gus, there's no good in him.' And it sure turned out that there wasn't any."

"Well," replied Mary Larrabee solemnly, "may the guilty man hang."

She turned away, sick from what she had seen, and went slowly down the stairs. Down those stairs Jack had fled, according to his story. Up those stairs old Benton had dragged himself for the last time, on that terrible night. Every detail of that night of storm and horror came back to her.

In the open air she drew a great breath of relief, and, approaching the broken door, she drew out the key, that she had picked up beside the jail, and tried it hastily. The lock turned smoothly under the pressure and turned back again. Mary Larrabee drew it forth and dropped the key back into her pocket, her heart racing with excitement.

"How come?" asked Mrs. Zellar, following with aggressive curiosity.

"I forgot to say," said the girl glibly enough, "that my father asked me to bring back the lock of the door to Benton's room. Will you let me saw it out?"

Mrs. Zellar fixed her big, startling eyes upon the face of Mary Larrabee, frowning. Evidently she was not at all pleased.

"It don't sound like your father, sending you around on jobs like this," she declared. "It don't sound the least bit like him."

"He knew I was coming out here, anyway," explained Mary.

"Hmm," said Mrs. Zellar gloomily. "You want the lock, but why d'you want it?"

"I never could make any sense out of these legal matters," said Mary, managing to smile in the face of that dark suspicion, "but that's what Dad asked me to bring. Of course, if you don't want to part with it, I'll simply go back and have him. . . ."

"It ain't that," protested Mrs. Zellar, "but it'd be more regular, if the sheriff was to send out a written order for it, or a request for it, being that he wants it for evidence."

"I suppose it would," said the girl, "but I've already done

what he told me to, by asking you for it."

She made as if to turn away, but Mrs. Zellar, in a quandary, called her back. "I don't want to hinder the law none," she said. "If this'll help to hang Jack, why, take it and welcome to it. I'm sure I ain't got any purpose in keeping things back. I ain't got anything to hide from your father . . . or any other sheriff."

"Of course not," said Mary. "Then I'll take the lock back, if you'll let me have a saw."

Mrs. Zellar was gone a long time in the house, apparently hunting for the saw, but Mary heard the voice of mother and son in heated argument. At length, Mrs. Zellar came out with the saw and, gloomier than ever, proceeded to cut out the lock and hand it to Mary. "I hope it brings bad luck to Jack Whatever's-his-name. I hope this lock is the thing that hangs him," she said savagely.

Mary untethered the horse and climbed back into her buggy. "Why do you hate Jack so much?" she asked, when she had turned the buggy around.

"Why? Because he's a crook," said Mrs. Zellar fiercely. "And because he done a murder under my roof and robbed me!"

"Robbed you?" asked Mary Larrabee.

"Sure he did. Wouldn't Mister Benton, if he'd died natural, have left me something in his will? Of course, he would have. Who robbed me of it, then? Why, this Jack, this devil did! Ain't that clear as day?"

Mary shook her head. "I don't know," she said, "but, if Jack is a murderer, I don't know where we can find men we can trust."

"Wait a minute," said Mrs. Zellar suddenly, starting for the heads of the horses. "Wait a minute! Hold on, Mary Larrabee! I've changed my mind about. . . ."

But a sharp cut of the buggy whip sent the bays sprinting away. "I can't wait," called Mary in explanation. "I have to hurry back!"

Then she dashed past the big woman and out onto the road. Mrs. Zellar followed a step or two, then paused with her arms akimbo, and stared after the flying little equipage. At length, she turned sullenly back toward the house.

"There's a devil in these young girls," she confided to her son a little later. "And I'd give a lot to know what she's up to, the little vixen."

The first thing that Mary did could have been seen from the house. She halted her team beside the tree, where the tramp was known to have kept his fire on that night of nights. The site of the fire she examined carefully and then swung the team back onto the road. The bays were in a foam, when she brought them back into Boonetown and drew up before the carpenter shop. She found the proprietor in the very act of starting for the country.

"Old Missus Purvis just phoned in," he said. "If your dad has some business for me, Mary, I guess it'll have to wait. Missus Purvis is plumb rushed. That's the way it goes with old folks. They want everything done so fast you'd think they was afraid death would come along before it was done."

"But Mister Hands," said the girl, "this is a matter of life and death."

"Hmm," said the carpenter, and pulled his glasses down on his nose, so that he could peer at her over them. "Life and death?"

She placed the lock on the workbench. "Is that a common lock, Mister Hands?"

He examined it, took up a bundle of keys, and tried some, one by one. Presently the lock was turned under his manipulation. "Common enough lock, all right," he said. "I got twenty old keys, right here, that could turn it."

Mary Larrabee uttered an exclamation of despair. "But," she protested, "I want to prove that this key belongs to that lock. And now you've spoiled everything for me!"

She drew forth the key and handed it to him. "Lemme see," muttered the carpenter, who was locksmith as well. "Lemme see, now. Maybe it does belong, but what difference does that make? I can fix you up with other keys for it."

"Other keys? No, no! Mister Hands, you must prove that this key belongs to this lock."

"Well, maybe I could. You see where the bit of this key is worn off a little? That comes from being used in a lock that has a rough place in it. I can find out in a minute."

He set to work with a screw driver, taking the lock apart, examined it carefully, and then straightened with a grunt of satisfaction. "Look for yourself," he said. "Don't need no microscope for this. See this place, sticking out in the lock? That's what's worn away the key. Must have took a tolerable lot of use to do it, but there ain't any doubt. See how it fits into the worn place?"

"Mister Hands," asked the girl, "how can I thank you for showing me? You've saved him!"

"Saved who?"

But lock and key were snatched from the carpenter's hand, and she was gone, whirling through the door.

## "THE WHOLE STORY"

At the jail she swept her father into the storm of her enthusiasm. Key and lock were placed in his great brown hands.

"You see," she explained, "that key has to belong to the lock!"

"Well, Mary," he admitted, "it sure looks like it. And what d'you make of it?"

"It must have been brought from the Zellar house?"

"That's nacheral . . . no doubt about that."

"And who could have brought it?"

"Jack, I suppose."

"Oh, Dad, don't you see that his cell is on the other side of the jail? How could he have thrown it there?"

"Eh?"

"It's the tramp, Dad. He's the one who threw it out the window to get rid of the only clue that connected him with the murder. Isn't that clear?"

Her father shook his head, frowning. "Don't sound like a strong argument, girl."

"But how could that key have come there?"

"I don't know."

"Did you search Slim when you picked him up?"

"Why should I search him? He wasn't near the house."

"Then he might have had the key on him, when he was brought to the jail?"

"I suppose so."

"How long would it take to walk from the tree where he

had his fire to the house? Not more than ten minutes, do you think?"

"Not more'n that, I guess, if a gent stepped out lively."

"Dad, he's the murderer!"

"But, if he got rid of the key by throwing it out the window, he didn't get rid of the money that was taken from Benton's chest."

She pondered a moment. "Will you take a drive with me out to Slim's fire?"

He nodded, and a moment later they were spinning down the road toward the Zellar place, once more.

"He might have cached the money any place around this tree," said the girl enthusiastically, as she dismounted from the buggy at the site of the fire.

"That's true," said the sheriff, and he began an ardent search. But there was nothing to be found. In half a dozen places, where boughs joined the trunk, at a steep angle, he looked, but there was no sign of the money.

"Or he might have dug a hole," suggested the girl at length.

They examined the ground around the tree, within a radius of a hundred feet, but there was no sign of earth having been broken.

"Still," said the girl, "it must be here. He wouldn't wait to hide it any other place, because he'd be in such a hurry to get back to his fire. Isn't that logical? Before the murder he was seen drowsing by the fire . . . after the murder he was back at his fire again. That is his alibi."

"You got all the terms down pat," said her father. "And it sounds reasonable, too. But what next?"

"What about the fire itself?"

"Buried paper money in a fire?" Larrabee was chuckling.

"See where he scraped that fire to one side. He first had

the fire going on the left, then he moved it to the right, where it is now . . . scraping the whole bed of coals. Well, is it reasonable that a man would move his fire, once it's going? Isn't the hot bed of coals the most important part of a campfire, Dad?"

"That's gospel, Mary."

"Then, perhaps, he moved that fire to cover something."

The sheriff said not a word, but simply kicked away the ashes and the charred remains of the fire. He thrust his hand down into the half-baked earth below it, tearing it away in clods, until at last he uttered a cry, worked a moment longer, and then stood up, holding a handful of dirty greenbacks!

But Mary Larrabee, staring, saw two visions pass before her eyes — and money had no part to play in either. She saw Mississippi Slim, hanging with a rope knotted around his neck, and she saw Jack walking out of the jail, a free man. There in the hand of her father was the evidence that would accomplish both purposes.

"The money and the key," the sheriff was saying. "Well, it sounds pretty good, but we can't be sure. The thing to do, Mary, is to get a confession out of Slim, if we can. That's the way to clear Jack. Otherwise, even if he gets off, his name won't be plumb cleared. Once a gent is accused of a bad crime, his name is black the rest of his life. I'll have to call in the snake, Lavigne, to help. My, won't he grind his teeth when he finds out what I've learned?"

On the way back to Boonetown he detailed briefly the scene between Jack and the district attorney, which he had interrupted, and the mad fervor of the attorney's desire to hang the prisoner. She had the pleasure, an hour later, of seeing the district attorney swallow the bitter pill and admit that he had been wrong. But in five minutes he had regained some of his happiness. One trail was lost, but another had been opened.

No matter what man died, a death was a death. Indeed, with marvelous elasticity of spirits, he was rubbing his hands and walking up and down his office in a fine heat of inspiration, rehearsing the evidence bit by bit. At length he said: "It's clear as day! He did it, but a good lawyer could get him off, probably. Somebody else might have buried that money under the tree . . . somebody else might have tossed the key into the sand. The confession is what we need, and the confession is what I'm going to get. Come along!"

Never in her life could the girl forget the scene that followed. She and her father accompanied the district attorney back to the jail and into the cell of Mississippi Slim, where the latter was walking busily up and down, "getting my exercise for the road," he told them.

The attorney took out his pad at once. "Now, Slim," he said, "I want to go over one part of your evidence."

"Many times as you want, chief," said Mississippi glibly.

"It was about what time when you first saw Jack?"

"I dunno. Ten or after, maybe."

"He disappeared down the road toward the house?"

"Yes."

"Good! Now, when you asked for food at the Zellar place earlier in the evening, what did you do when you were turned from the door?"

"Went up the road."

"You didn't stay about for a while?"

"No."

"Didn't try to get into the house, maybe, and walk off with something to get even with them for turning you out?"

The district attorney chuckled, and Slim laughed loudly.

"I wish I had," he said.

"Did you ever see this?" asked Lavigne, with a sudden and

harsh change of voice, and he produced the key in the flat of his hand.

There was an even more startling change in the rat-sharp face of Slim, as he settled back on his bunk and sneered at them. "Playing tricks, eh?" he asked. "I'll do no more talking . . . not until I got a lawyer here."

"All right," said the district attorney, "but I suppose you're willing to hear a little story?"

"Talk your head off," said Slim fiercely, "but don't ask me no questions."

"It begins," said Lavigne, "with the moment Jack rode on toward the house. You looked after him . . . you began to wonder if he might not have better luck than you did. Particularly, you wondered what would happen when that big fellow tried to force the Zellars to give him a hand out. Eh?

"Well, you got so curious that after a time you decided it was worth getting a soaking to see the party. So you got up and followed . . . you came to the kitchen door and saw him go inside . . . you listened for a while outside the window until you were sure that he was being fed.

"And, the moment you knew that, you were wild with anger! You wanted to do something to injure those people. So you sneaked around the house, looking for a place to get in, eh?"

The face of Slim was grave with boredom. There was no other expression in it.

"Finally," went on the district attorney, "you found you could shinny up one of the verandah posts and get onto the roof. By the time you got up there, the old man, Benton, was just coming back into the room, and he settled down in a chair near the window. Only for a moment, though. After a time he went over to his chest and opened it. You saw him take out some money and make sure of it . . . you saw him lock

75

the chest and saw the pocket into which he dropped the key. Is that right?"

Slim merely yawned.

"Then," said Lavigne, "the old man came back to his chair and sat down to read. A minute later you began to work . . . you tried the window behind his chair. It came up without making a sound. Inch by inch you lifted it, pressing very softly for fear of a squeak. And all the time the old man kept right on reading, eh?"

"This is sure a fool story," declared Slim. "Maybe you think anybody would believe it?"

"You got the window up, at last," insisted Lavigne, "and then you slipped your hands in and settled them around the throat of Benton. He hardly made a struggle. At least, whatever struggle he made was not loud enough to be heard above the roar of the rain on the roof. So you slipped in, when Benton stopped wiggling, and you gave him a look.

"His face was purple . . . he wasn't breathing. His eyes were popping out of his head, and he looked dead as a doornail. You locked the door. Then you fished out the key from his pocket and took out that money.

"But, while you were stuffing it into a pocket, you heard a shriek behind you . . . the old fellow was only partly stifled. You saw him getting up out of the chair and staggering toward you to fight for his money. You had to act quick. You had to get rid of him and get back to your fire. You caught up a piece of firewood, hit him over the head, and, without waiting to see how it ended, you jumped through the window, ran over the verandah roof, jumped off, and made it back to your fire, and. . . ."

There was a sound of gasping breath. Slim had risen from his bunk with staring eyes. "Where were you hid in that room?" he asked. "Say, how did you see it?"

The Boonetown paper gave much credit to the district attorney for the cleverness with which he had fastened the meshes upon the real criminal and freed an innocent man. It gave a long write-up to Fitzpatrick Lavigne, while the part which Mary Larrabee had played disappeared in a single paragraph. Lavigne, as usual, took all the credit to himself.

But Mary Larrabee cared not a whit about reporters and papers. She was too preoccupied that evening in hearing from Jack his name and the history of his past. She was interested to the point of tears, while he told of his life before that wild night of storm and murder; how he had lived with his sister and brother-in-law, how, to raise much-needed money, his brother-in-law had made a practice of changing brands on the cattle that he caught off the range; how exposure had threatened; and how he, the man without a family, had taken the blame on his own wide shoulders and slipped away out of the country, penniless and despairing, but determined to give his sister's family a fighting chance to live in honor.

For the first time and the last she heard all this with misty eyes, and it was never again referred to. Nor were any of the events of the Benton murder ever mentioned in the house. But, when she was Mrs. Jack Montagne, Mary kept in a secret place, to be looked at on holy days, the little worn key that had saved the life of one man and sent another to his death.

# A Shower of Silver

This short novel, titled "A Shower of Silver" by Frederick Faust, was first published as "When the Wandering Whip Rode West" under the byline John Frederick in Street and Smith's *Western Story Magazine* (6/18/21). Bob Lake, like many of Faust's impulsive knights of the range, ends up on the wrong side of the law — as had long been predicted by those who knew him — once he finds himself doing the wrong thing for the right reason in an act of chivalry toward Anne Rankin.

I

### "A WHISPER AND A WOMAN"

The last three months had been a dull time for Bob Lake. He had in the beginning coiled his rope, bidden a profane farewell to his favorite broncho, oiled up his best .45 Colt, planted a gray Stetson on his head, packed a grip, and started to see New York. And he saw it — at a considerable expense. Eventually he parted with everything except the gun and the Stetson, which were holy things to Bob, and, with his last five-dollar bill in his pocket, he sat in at a game of poker with a fat roll and an urgent desire to leave for the land of open skies and little rain. Two hours later he was bound West.

Impulse ruled Bob Lake. Give a man some hundred and ninety pounds of iron-hard muscle, a willingness to fight plus a desire to smile, no master except necessity, and no necessity except the wish for action, and the result is a character as stable as a hair trigger. He had one of those big-featured, but ugly, faces that have all manner of good nature about the mouth, and all manner of danger behind the eyes. He had both enemies and friends in legion, but they all united in the opinion that sooner or later Bob Lake was due to fall foul of the law.

At present Bob Lake was melancholy. This morning he had chuckled with joy to see the mountains of the land of his desire rolling blue against the western sky. It was now noon, and, although the train was rocking along among those same mountains, the joy had departed from the face of Bob Lake. The reason sat in the seat ahead of him.

A newly married couple had boarded the train at ten o'clock that morning at a town in the foothills. The party that accompanied them to the station had swirled about them, laughing, shouting, throwing rice, and out of the confusion had come the girl on the arm of her husband. He was a man as big and Western as Bob Lake, but the pallor of his face bespoke an indoor life. A very handsome fellow, although there were qualities of sternness in him. Bob would not soon forget the grim smile with which he shook the rice from the brim of his hat and looked back on the shouting crowd.

Then Bob Lake saw the girl. His first impulse was to pray that the seat of the pair would be in his car. His second impulse was to pray that the seat might be elsewhere. For he had a profound conviction that, if he had a chance to look into the eyes of this girl at short range, there would be trouble brewing in no time.

After they had climbed the steps he held his breath, and then straight down the aisle they came. A battery of smiles and chuckles on either side of them marked their progress, and the shouting of the crowd volleyed from outside. The girl was very conscious of it. She came timidly, and her little side

80

glances seemed to beg them to look in another direction, and every step she made down that aisle was straight into the heart of Bob Lake.

Perhaps they would go on through to another car. No, they paused near him, and the crowd with flowers and candy and gay-colored parcels poured around Bob's seat. He saw a gray-haired woman with tears streaming down her cheeks; he saw a gray-haired man with twitching lips that attempted to smile. When the warning — "All aboard!" — had sounded, and the crowd had swept out again, Bob Lake found that the pair were in the seat directly ahead of him.

When he made this discovery, he felt that it was fate. He was as certain of it as if he had seen a shadowy figure in retrospect bidding him rise from that poker table in New York and rush on board the train.

Ordinarily Bob Lake was the very soul of honor; he would rather have blinded his eyes than let them look twice at the wife of another man. But in this case he felt a shrewd difference. Something was taking him up and carrying him on against his own volition as a tide sweeps a man out to the open sea. The irony of it made him wince. Women had never been anything to him. A few had laughed their way into his life for an evening at a dance, but they had all yawned their way out again, and Bob Lake remained essentially heart free. At last it was the wife of another man.

*It's fate,* he kept repeating to himself. If the thing had not been preordained, why that sudden mad rush from New York? Of course, Bob did not at the moment recall that everything he had ever done had been on spur of the instant. Why, he went on to ask himself, did her glance take hold on him like a hand, if there were not some weird power to blame?

He was glad of one thing — that she was not facing him. He could only see her hair. When he turned to shut out this

81

sight by staring out of the window, the sound of her voice pursued him, tugged at him, made him turn to look at her again and listen with held breath to make out the words. He felt like an eavesdropper, but, nevertheless, he could not help damning the roar of the train. Something, he kept assuring himself, was going to happen. And when a hundred and ninety pounds of manhood feels that way, something usually does happen.

He made out snatches of the conversation. The marriage ceremony had taken place an hour before they boarded the train. The man's name was Rankin, and the girl's name was Anne. *The most wonderful name in the world,* Bob instantly decided. They were going into the mountains to Al Rankin's country, which the girl did not know, and to his home there that she had never seen.

But what could happen? A train wreck, perhaps. There was a good deal of the boy in Bob Lake. An instant picture was launched in his mind of himself striding through smoke among smashed timbers, carrying the body of the girl. He brushed the dream away and concentrated on reality. For at any moment the train might stop among the mountains — the girl and the man might leave his life forever. The thought turned Lake cold.

Once he got up and walked down the length of the train in order to return a little later and approach the girl so as to see her face. But when he came back, he saw nothing. He was afraid to look. He, Bob Lake, afraid to look a girl in the face. But, although he saw nothing, there was an impression. It was as if a light had shone on him in the night. When he slipped back into his place, his pulses were hammering. And then it happened.

It was the end of a division, and, when the train stopped, a chunky man with a great spread of hat, with baggy-kneed trousers, and riding boots came to the head of the car and squinted down its length. At the same time a newspaper was raised before the face of Al Rankin and shaken out. The result was that Bob Lake did not see what immediately appeared until a pudgy, brown hand appeared over the edge of the paper, pulled it unceremoniously down, and the chunky little man stood looking down at Rankin. He leaned and murmured something.

In fact, his voice was most carefully guarded, but Bob Lake had been training his ear to catch whispers through the roar of the moving train. Now he made out one word: "Arrest."

And he heard what Al Rankin answered: "What charge?"

The whisper which replied to this missed his ear, but Al Rankin immediately rose. His wife was on her feet at the same moment.

"Infernal nuisance," Rankin told her calmly enough. "Meet Bill White . . . an old friend of mine. Bill has a message that takes me off the train here."

"I'm ready, Al," Anne stated.

"Ready for what?"

"To go with you, of course."

"Nonsense! Break up the trip for this? Certainly not. You stay aboard. When you get to the station, old Charley will be waiting. You can tell him by his beard . . . just like a goat's. He'll take you out to the house and make you comfortable. I'll be up tomorrow."

He turned and nodded to Bill White, who was watching the girl steadily. He had bowed in a jerky fashion to acknowledge the introduction, and now he was looking at the young wife with a sort of hard sympathy.

"Al, there's nothing wrong?"

Just a moment of pause. Something gathered in the face of

83

Al Rankin. "Haven't I told you there's nothing wrong?" he said sullenly. "You stay aboard and don't worry. They don't make enough trouble in these parts to bother me."

He had changed his tone toward the end of this speech and qualified the scowl with the beginning of a smile. But the blow had fallen. Bob Lake saw the girl wince and whiten a little about the mouth, but she made no further protest. Al Rankin turned with a careless wave of farewell and strolled down the aisle, followed by the little gray-headed man. It seemed to Bob Lake that the girl started impulsively to follow. Perhaps it was the memory of the gruff rebuke that stopped her short and made her sink slowly into her seat again.

From the window he saw Al Rankin sauntering away with his companion. Whatever their business might be, they seemed in no hurry to accomplish it. Then he saw the girl was not looking after them through the window. She sat close to the side of the car with her head turned straight before her.

*Al,* Bob Lake thought, *you sure made a bum play with the rough talk . . . a rotten bad play.*

He felt the preliminary lurch of the starting train, and it pressed him back against the seat — just as Al Rankin, he recalled, had lurched back when the chunky little man had whispered into his ear the charge on which he was being arrested. Bob Lake became solemnly thoughtful. There was only one charge which could have disturbed the fine calm of Al Rankin, he felt, and to himself Bob whispered the word: *Murder!* When the thought entered his mind, he glanced guiltily around the car, half expecting to see pitying eyes directed at the young wife. But, instead, everyone was settling back to sleep through that stretch of dreary mountains.

*Murder!* He was as certain of it now as though he had heard the whisper. And this was the thing for which he had waited to happen. A sudden self-loathing took possession of Bob Lake. He hated himself for the gleam of joy that he had felt as the first surmise came to him. What of the girl? Would she not go through life even as she sat now, looking straight ahead of her, fearing to meet the eyes of men and women in her shame? All the beauty of her smile would be straightened from her lips, he knew, and the thought made him grind his teeth.

The wheels were beginning to groan as the train slowly started.

And then Bob Lake acted. It was one of those sudden, mad, unreasoning impulses. Two sweeps of his arm planted his hat on his head and gathered up his suitcase. He fairly ran down the aisle and at the door turned for a last look.

She was, indeed, pale, unsmiling, as if she knew the doom that hovered over her. Her glance cleared a little, and, under the fierce probing of Bob Lake's stare, her eyes widened, became aware of him with quiet wonder. The train was gathering headway, and still he lingered to throw all the meaning that was in his heart into his eyes. Everything that he felt was in his glance. Too much, perhaps, and too legible. For now she flushed, and she leaned forward, gazing at him in a sort of horror. It was almost as if she were going to cry out and call him back.

Then he tore himself away, pushed open the door, and poised on the lowest step. The ground was already shooting past with terrifying speed. Yet he gauged his distance, leaned back, and dropped free of the train. The blow crumpled his legs. He went down in a confused mass of whirling arms and legs and suitcase, yet he laughingly scrambled to his feet in time to see a white face pressed against the window as the car shot past. He waved his hand to that face. *How much would she understand?* That thought held him gaping, until the length of the train had rushed past, and the rear end was whipping off into the distance with a mist of dust drawing after it. Then he turned back to take up the adventure. Al Rankin must be saved from the law.

## II

## "RANKIN'S RECORD"

He had no time to balance reasons nicely or appreciate the folly that had started him on this blind trail. Al Rankin and the stranger had stepped into an automobile where two other men already sat. He saw that Al was put into the back seat between the other men. Then the car shot down the south road.

There were two questions to be asked. One was where that south road led, and a youngster near the platform told him that it went directly to Everett, twenty miles away. The second question was where he could get an automobile for his own use. It was almost as easily answered, and five minutes after he dropped from the train he was in a machine, speeding down the south road for Everett.

The owner of the car drove him, and he looked a cross between a mechanic and a farmer. Old buckboard customs now made him press the feed with his right foot while his left dangled over the side of the car, and he kept his right shoulder habitually turned to his passenger. Bob Lake had made the necessary explanations about a short business trip, and the first five miles shot past — wild driving over wild roads — without another word exchanged.

They climbed a steep grade and pitched forward at fifty miles on a downward stretch. "You know Bill White?" asked Bob Lake in a different voice.

"Sure, I know the sheriff."

That was all Bob wished to know. He settled back against the seat until they rushed with open exhaust into the town of Everett. It was rather a village than a town. There was the inevitable single street, deep with dust, and the only up-to-date thing that Bob Lake saw was the automobile in which he sat. His driver came in as the cowpunchers in the good old days used to "come to town." He came wide open in a dense cloud of dust and came to a stop with jammed brakes, skidding the last few yards into place before the hotel.

"Here you are," he announced, and one corner of his eye glinted in expectation of applause.

Bob Lake paid him while the dust cloud they had torn up slowly overtook them and enveloped them in white. Then he went into the hotel. When he had secured a room on the second floor and thrown his suitcase on the bed, he slumped into the rickety chair and buried his face in his hands to think. He had great need of thought. Indeed, the last hour had been so dream-like that he would not have been surprised at all if, when he looked up, he had seen the head of Al Rankin leaning against the back of the seat before him and the mountains rushing past the windows of the train. The dust with which he was covered brought him to a realization of the facts. He dragged in a breath through his set teeth and cursed. Once more he had played the impulsive fool.

Perhaps the sheriff had not made an arrest. Perhaps he had only taken Rankin from the train because he needed him badly on a manhunt. Rankin had impressed him as a fighting type. Of course, it was strange that a man's honeymoon should be interrupted for such a purpose, but, Bob Lake knew, stranger things than this had happened in the mountain-desert country.

He made brief preparations to hunt for information. The

shoes came off his feet. The riding boots that he had been unable to leave behind when he started in New York, and which he had never been able to trust to the chance delivery of a trunk — those priceless shop-made boots — were drawn upon his feet. He took a step in them, and the clinking of the spurs was music to his ears. He stepped to the mirror and grinned at the face he saw — the red necktie, the high stiff collar, the coat. Ten seconds tore away that mask. The collar and tie were gone, tossed to a corner of the room, and a voluminous silk bandanna knotted in place around his neck skillfully. Out of the suitcase came the old cartridge belt, and the gun, that had been worn so long in concealment, came into the open and was dropped with a thud into the holster. Last he tossed off his coat and unbuttoned his vest. He was ready again to take his place in the world as a man. But first he walked up and down the room to ease his feet into the familiar boots with their paper-thin soles. Then he tried his gun half a dozen times for the sheer joy of feeling it come out in his fingertips as freely as the wind and the hug of the butt against the palm of his hand.

Then he started out to find information. It came to him at once and not through a coincidence. The whole town was buzzing with it, and most of the buzzing concentrated on the verandah of the hotel. With a little patience he could have gathered the whole tale piecemeal from exclamations and bits of irrelevant news. But he preferred to get his facts in a lump. He found a man young enough to tell the truth and old enough to yearn for an audience. Bob Lake cornered him, and appealed as a stranger for the story.

The fellow was delighted. First a leisurely examination assured him that Bob "belonged" and was "right." Then he launched into the narrative.

"Them boys think they know a lot," he said. "But what

they're short on is the facts. I know, because I'm the only one that seen the sheriff since he brought Rankin to town."

"Is Rankin an outlaw?"

"Worse."

"Eh?"

"I mean he's the kind that does things and never gets picked up for 'em. Most boys that goes wrong are plumb fools, or else the booze gets 'em, or they get mad about a little thing and do a big thing that's worse. Al Rankin ain't none of them. He's crooked because it pays him. Oh, everybody has known it for a long time. A lot of things happened around these parts. There was that gang that stole Chet Bernard's cows three years back. There was the killing of young Murphy, and there was the shooting of Lanning and Halsey. Self-defense, you see?" He winked at Bob Lake without mirth. "I leave it to you, stranger. When a gent practices two hours a day with the cards and never loses when he's playing for big stakes, would you call him a gambler or a card sharp?"

"Hmm," murmured Bob Lake.

"And when a gent goes out and practices with his gun, shooting from all kinds of positions, fanning 'er and wasting a hundred shots a day, would you say that gent was a straight gunfighter who knew he would have trouble and was getting all set to meet it?"

"Hmm," repeated Bob Lake.

"And when a gent kills another man in self-defense . . . well, that's all right. But, when he shoots two more, that self-defense looks kind of thin, eh? And when you add all the facts up, you begin to figure that you've got a gambler and a robber and a man-killer. But with a smart one like Al Rankin, it ain't easy to nail anything on him. They even say he's got a home in another part of the mountains, and that he's pretty well thought of up there. He goes other places and raises his trouble and gets his income.

"Well, Bill White has had his eye on Al for a long time, but he couldn't get nothing to use on him. There was always a lot of bad talk, but bad talk ain't any good with twelve men in a jury box that want facts to hang a man with. So Bill kept waiting for facts, and pretty soon the facts come.

"You see, there was a killing about a year back that nobody thought much of. Sam Coy was a bad one . . . bad all the way through. When he was found dead at the door of his shack, nobody did much except shrug their shoulders. Good riddance, everybody said.

"Well, sir, I'll come back to the Coy killing pretty soon. In the meantime, Al Rankin was pretty sweet on Hugh Smiley's daughter, Sylvia. He kept taking her around to all the parties, and folks begun to say maybe Al would marry and settle down. Worse ones than him has turned out straight. And Sylvia is a pretty fine girl by all accounts. But after a while Al Rankin drops her. That's his way.

"This time he had her expecting to marry him sure, and it about broke her heart, they say. Well, the next thing you know, there comes talk that Al Rankin is down to Polkville trying to marry another girl, and Hugh Smiley gets all heated up about it. Polkville is over behind the mountains, you know.

"Then Hugh Smiley comes into town and says to the sheriff . . . Bill White told me this himself not more'n half an hour ago . . . Hugh says to Bill . . . 'I got something that'll hang Al Rankin.'

" 'Give it to me,' says Bill.

" 'Not while Al is ranging around loose,' says Hugh. 'I ain't ready to die.'

" 'How come, then?' says Bill.

" 'Put him behind bars, and then I'll give you the

testimony that'll hang him.'

" 'Are you sure?' says the sheriff.

" 'Sure as I live,' says Hugh Smiley.

" 'But you got to get it to me, quick,' says the sheriff. 'If I lock up Al, I got to have the testimony in my hands within the day. I can't hold him on a trumped-up charge longer'n that. Besides, I'd have him gunning for me after he got turned loose.'

" 'Partner,' says Hugh, 'they ain't any doubt about it. I got something that'll hang him. Just show me that I'm safe first, and I'll bring it. But not till you got Al behind bars.'

" 'What'll it convict him of?'

" 'The murder of Coy.'

"Well, it didn't take Bill White long to start up some action. *Pronto* he wires to Polkville and hears that Al is all married and on his way to his home. The sheriff cuts across the country and grabs Al off'n the train with a trumped-up warrant that don't amount to nothing. Then he sent out word by a machine that was driving past Hugh Smiley's place to get Hugh to come in with the evidence. Hugh'll be coming in on the west road 'most any time now on his old, one-eared roan. I sold him that hoss, and Hugh still rides him . . . ten years, I guess."

There was more talk of it, but Bob Lake closed his ears to the tiresome chatter. He needed some thought.

# III

## "PHILANTHROPIC INTERFERENCE"

There was no doubt in his mind that Al Rankin was guilty of all the crimes that the old man had charged against him, and even more. But a cold syllogism looked Bob Lake in the face. He had vowed himself to secure the happiness of Anne Rankin. Anne Rankin loved Al Rankin. To secure her happiness he must make the criminal safe. A more foresighted man might have pondered long before he reached the same conclusion; certainly he must have weighed much evidence pro and con. But Bob Lake was not foresighted, nor was he fitted to ponder nice questions. He had a hundred and ninety pounds of muscle suitable for action, and by action he was accustomed to cut the Gordian knot.

Moreover, spurring him on into the service of Al Rankin was the fact that he had coveted the wife of another man the moment he laid eyes on her. To the spotless honor of Bob Lake that was an indelible stain. Indeed, the honor of Bob Lake was almost a proverbial thing on his own ranges. And now he was determined to wipe away the blot, if he could, by assiduously serving the man whom he had in thought shamefully wronged. A very nice distinction, some would have said — to Bob Lake it was as clear as day.

The important thing was, if possible, to keep the evidence of Hugh Smiley from reaching the hands of the sheriff. To that end Bob secured a horse as soon as possible, saddled, and rode at full speed for the west road out of Everett. When he was clear of the town, he sent home the spurs and proceeded at a wild gallop.

It was a matter of four or five miles before he saw a small dust cloud ahead of him, and, as soon as he had made sure from the slowness of its approach that it was a horseman and not a wind drift of dust, he checked his own pace to a lope. The dust cloud eventually cleared, and he was aware of a middle-aged fellow on a roan, one of whose ears was close-cropped. Bob Lake made straight for him and reined in beside the other.

"You're Hugh Smiley?"

"Maybe," said the other without enthusiasm, and he studied Bob with intense interest not untinged with alarm.

"If you are, speak up. I'm from Sheriff Bill White. New man of his. Name's Bob Lake."

"What are you doing out here?" asked the rider of the roan uneasily.

"The word's out," said Bob Lake cheerfully, "that you're bringing in the evidence that'll hang that skunk, Al Rankin. The sheriff doesn't want to take any chances."

"Any chances of what?"

"Chances that some friend of Al Rankin's might cut in on you and keep you from landing the evidence in Bill White's safe."

"Who ever heard of Al having any friends around these parts?"

"You never can tell. The sheriff ain't taking any chances."

"Maybe not."

Hugh Smiley remained entirely uncommunicative. He was a rat-faced fellow with one of those noses that dip out to a point, forehead and chin receding at exactly the same angle, and yellowish teeth of prodigious length, and his little eyes roved over and over the big body of Bob Lake.

"Anyway," said Bob, "they ain't any harm in me riding in

93

beside you, and if anything should happen . . . why, then I'll come in handy."

"But nothing'll happen," protested Smiley in growing uneasiness, and he shifted his glance to search the hills through which they were riding. "Nothing'll happen. Everybody knows that Al never played no partners. He was always a lone hand."

"Sure. The point is, Bill ain't taking any chances of any kind. Ain't hard to see why. If he hangs Rankin, it'll be a feather in his cap. He can have his job for life . . . pretty near."

"Yep, pretty near."

"I ain't an old hand around these parts, but I been here long enough to find out that Rankin is a skunk."

Under this stimulating talk, Hugh Smiley grew more communicative. "Yep, I guess I'm doing a pretty good thing all around for the boys."

"And a thing that takes a lot of nerve," Bob Lake said frankly. "I been raised in a pretty hard country, and I've had my knocks, but I'd hate to come up ag'in' a gunfighter like Al Rankin, even if he was behind bars."

"Would you?" Smiley shuddered at the prospect. "What's him to me?" he declared bravely. "Ain't he flesh and blood just like me?" He was trying to bring back his courage, but his color changed.

"Just flesh and blood," admitted Bob Lake, "but a pretty dangerous sort. I tell you there's going to be a pile of the boys around town that'll want to shake hands with you, when Rankin is strung up, Smiley! I've heard talk already. They was some even said they didn't think it was in you."

Smiley warmed again half-heartedly. "All that glitters ain't gold by a long sight," he declared. "You can lay to that. I ain't around blustering and bluffing like the younger gents, but I stand for my rights and most generally git 'em."

"Sure you do," returned Bob Lake. "I could see you was that kind at a glance."

Hugh Smiley now expanded like a flower in the sun of this admiration. "And I'm the man that's going to hang Rankin," he declared.

"A good thing, too."

"Is it? I'll tell a man it is, son!"

"What I can't figure is how a smooth one like him would ever leave the evidence lying around?"

"Sounds queer, don't it? I'll tell you how it was. He got into a little trouble with Coy, I figure. Maybe he didn't go there to kill him on purpose. But Al has a devil of a temper, and it must have flared up on him while he was talking to Coy. Must have begun first with a lot of wrestling around. The ground was all stamped up in front of the door. Then they went for their guns. Al maybe dropped his, but he got Coy's away from him and shot him plumb through the heart.

"I was coming by, and I heard the noise. I let out a yell and started on the gallop. Most like Al heard me yell and didn't think of nothing except to get on his hoss and get away. Which he done, but he left his gun behind him. I come up, find Coy dead, and Al's gun on the ground. I put the gun up and let the sheriff know how I found things, but I left out all about the gun.

"Because why? Because Al was paying a lot of attention to Sylvia, my girl, along about then. That was why. But then he turned around and treated her like a dog, and I started to lay for him. Today I got my chance. I'm waitin' and hungerin' for the minute when I shove this gun under Al's nose and say . . . 'You skunk, here's what hangs you!' "

He had grown so excited in his recital that now he suited the action to the word and, whipping out a pearl-handled revolver, he brandished it in the air close to Bob Lake.

"But there's a lot of pearl-handled guns," said Bob. "How'll that tie the murder of Coy on Rankin?"

"There's not a lot with Al's initials on 'em," triumphantly replied the rat-faced man. "Besides, everybody knows this gun. Al's mighty fond of it. A thousand has heard him say that he wouldn't trade it for a ten-thousand-dollar check, because it saved his life too often. And now it'll hang him." He broke into horrible laughter. "What he'll have to explain away is how come he parted with that gun. And I'll be there to swear where I found it, and how I found it."

"Suppose he says that he gave it to you?"

"He never gives anything away. They's them that can tell how Sandy McGregor offered him a cold thousand for that gun and got refused . . . got laughed at. No, sir, they ain't any way for him to wriggle out. Not with twelve men out of this here county trying him."

"Then," said Bob Lake, "it looks pretty clear that the whole case hangs on the gun. Without the gun your testimony wouldn't be worth a plugged nickel."

"Not a nickel, son."

"Sorry, Smiley," murmured Bob Lake, "but I'll have to take the gun."

"Eh?" asked Smiley, frowning.

He found a gun held close beneath his chin, and behind it there was a determined, savage face.

"Hand over the gun, you rat!"

"You!" exclaimed Smiley. "You're playing with Rankin?"

"Maybe. Come out with the gun. Slow . . . slow . . . take it by the barrel . . . that's it."

He received the handsome weapon, set with jewels, flashing in the sunlight.

"They'll lynch you," said Smiley. "You fool!"

"You won't come into town to tell 'em about it till

Rankin's out of jail, Smiley. You're going to turn around and ride down this here road till I see you out of sight. If I catch you in town, I'm going to trim that ugly face of yours with bullets. Now, get out!"

There was a parting leer of terror and rage, and then Smiley whirled his horse without a word and galloped down the road looking back over his shoulder. Unquestionably, had Bob Lake turned his back for a moment, the little man would have wheeled and tried a pot shot from the distance, but Bob did not turn, and eventually he had the pleasure of seeing Smiley disappear around the turn.

Then he spurred toward Everett, not far away, for they had covered most of the distance during their talk.

How he should dispose of the weapon was the next trouble, for, if it were found on him, and Smiley explained how the weapon had come into his possession, the gun would still hang Al Rankin.

The sound of running water suggested the solution of that problem. A narrow stream cut across the trail, hardly fetlock deep, but to the right it dropped into a deep pool. Into that pool he dropped the pearl-handled revolver after a last admiring examination of the jewels with which it was set. Then he continued the journey.

Al Rankin was freed by his act. By the same act Anne's husband was returned to her. A gambler and murderer returned to her! For the first time the full force of that combination came upon Bob Lake, and he sighed. Forethought was not his strong point, but in afterthought he was something of a philosopher. However, the act was irretrievable. By it he had determined the destiny of Anne; by it he had automatically excluded himself from her life. There was a hope, perhaps, that Al Rankin might change his ways. But, as he remembered that pale, handsome, calm face, the hope dwindled and grew thin in the heart of Bob Lake.

He reached Everett in a black melancholy, and, when he had returned the horse and gone back to the hotel, he learned that there was not even an escape from the town. If he went back to the railroad, a timetable told him that he could not get another train until the next morning about noon.

He lounged gloomily through the rest of the afternoon, forced himself to eat dinner, and then returned to his room for the night. He was unhappy, more desperately unhappy than he had ever been in his life. Truly the way of the philanthropist was a wretched way.

He had hung up his cartridge belt at this point in his reflections, when the door was flung open without the warning of any preliminary knock. He glanced over his shoulder and saw the hall blocked with armed men.

## IV

### "ALL FOR ANNE"

At their head was the chunky little man with the gray hair — Bill White.

"You're Bob Lake," he said bluntly, pointing a stubby forefinger at Lake. "You're Bob Lake, alias what?"

"Alias nothing," returned Bob with equal bluntness. "What in thunder are you doing in my room?" As he spoke, he removed the cartridge belt from the hook on the wall and shook the gun out of the holster.

"None of that," returned the sheriff.

But Bob Lake had forgotten reasonable caution. That mad mood was on him which had made his best friends prophesy that sooner or later he would fall afoul of the law. "Step high, partner," he said to the sheriff warningly. "Step light. It looks to me like I got the drop on you gents, and I'm going to keep it. Hands away from guns, if you please."

They had entered so full of the courage of numbers — there were half a dozen of them — that they had not taken the precaution of drawing a weapon against him. And now he stood close to the wall, swaying a little from side to side with a murderous light in his eyes.

"Son," said White, who seemed less daunted than the others, "you're talking fool talk. I'm the sheriff."

"You don't say so. Am I going to take your word for that?"

Bill White exposed the badge of his office and then grinned triumphantly. "Now, Bob Lake," he said, "will you listen to reason?"

"Maybe, maybe not. I feel sort of irritable, Sheriff, and you got to talk sharp. What you want?"

"To search you and your room. Start in, boys."

"You stay put, gents, you hear?" said Lake. "Let's see your search warrant, eh? Trot it out, Sheriff!"

The sheriff growled: "Search warrant be blowed, Lake!"

"Maybe. But you don't touch a pocket till you show me one."

"What'll keep me from it?"

"This!"

"Lake, I'd ought to arrest you on the spot."

"Arrest me without a charge, Sheriff, and you'll wish you'd arrested the devil sooner before you're through. You hear me talk?"

"Fool talk," said the sheriff. His calm was breaking into anger.

"Listen," said Lake, growing calmer as he saw the temper rise in the sheriff. "If you lay a hand on me, partner, you'll be the first that ever did it. My record's clean. In my part of the country I've got friends, and I'll use 'em to make your trail hot. Now, get out of this room!"

"Just a minute. Hugh!"

Smiley appeared from the rear of the crowd. "Is this the gent?"

"It's him right enough." Smiley looked evilly at Bob Lake.

"Lake, you took Al Rankin's gun off Smiley. Talk up and confess. You'll come to no harm that way."

"I never saw your rat-faced friend before."

"How does he know you, then?"

"I've been in town since morning, and my name's on the register downstairs. That's easy enough."

"Why, if this ain't the grandpa of all liars!" exclaimed Smiley. "D'you mean to say . . . ?"

"Wait," said the sheriff, raising his hand. "Loud talk don't lead nowheres. Now, Lake, talk sense. You're in the hole."

"I don't see how."

"And you can't fight your way out. Lake, you horned in to help Rankin. We know it."

"Never met Rankin in my life."

"Will you stand to that?"

"Sure. What's your story?"

"That Smiley was bringing in evidence against Rankin in the shape of his gun, picked up at the scene of the Coy murder, and that you took it from him."

"Smiley lies. Probably he was talking loud with nothing behind it. You ask him to show, and call his bluff. All he can do is shift the blame on what he ain't got. He picks a stranger, and I'm the man. Ain't that simple?"

"Suppose we search the room?"

"Go ahead. If it means anything serious, I'm sure ready to oblige you, gents."

His calm and the readiness with which he now submitted to the search staggered the sheriff. Under his directions, while he kept an eye upon the actions of Lake, the others went over every inch of the space. Closet, suitcase, the clothes of Bob Lake, the bed — there was not the space of a pin that was not seen to or probed, and, as the search progressed and black looks began to be cast at Smiley, the excitement of the little man grew intense.

"He's thrown it away, Bill," he declared. "That's what he's done. He knew we'd search, and he threw it away."

"You're a fool, Hugh. That gun, jewels and all, is worth a thousand, if it's worth a cent."

Hugh Smiley groaned in despair. And the search, coming to an end, resulted in a dark-faced semicircle gathering around the rat-faced man.

"Sheriff," said Bob Lake suddenly, "has this little rat got any grudge ag'in' this Rankin you talk about? Any grudge that'd make him try to get Rankin in trouble?"

"Grudge? Sure." The sheriff turned with a new and ugly glance upon Smiley.

"Take this gent and put him in front of Rankin . . . sudden . . . and see what Rankin does," suggested Smiley.

It was not an altogether brilliant idea, but the sheriff, seeing his greatest of prizes about to slip through his fingers, was quite willing to grasp at straws. Bob Lake readily assented, and they journeyed across to the jail. By this time Hugh Smiley had lost all aggressiveness and was lingering in the back of the group. But the others dragged him along. He had never been a popular member of the community. Behind him was an unsavory youth full of a cunning smoother and infinitely meaner then the crimes attributed to Al Rankin. Now he was carried along in the rear of the little crowd, and his courage was subjected to their sarcastic comments.

When they reached the jail, a little, low-lying building, the sheriff marshaled them into an outer room and cautioned them to silence with a raised finger.

"Now, follow me," he whispered to Bob Lake. Leaving the others behind, he threw open an inner door.

"I got a friend of yours, Al," he called as he entered with Bob Lake behind him. Then he stepped aside to watch the expressions of the two men.

Al Rankin sat behind a heavy set of bars on his cot, and the door opened into a narrow passage between the bars and the wall of the building. In this passage stood the sheriff and Bob Lake, and upon the latter the prisoner now bent a calm glance.

"Friend?" he asked. "Ain't had the pleasure of meeting him yet, Sheriff."

"You forget," said the sheriff. "Think it over. You remember now?"

"Bill, you ought to know that I never forget faces. I never saw this gent before. Wait a minute . . . no, I never saw him before."

The sheriff was dumbfounded. There was no doubting the sincerity of Al Rankin unless he were, indeed, a consummate actor.

"It's a queer case," said the sheriff gloomily. "I told you what I expected from that rat, Smiley?"

"Sure."

"Well, Rankin, it looks like you're coming clean through all this. Smiley swears that Bob Lake, here, met him on the road into town and swiped the gun from him. We searched Lake and his room and found never a trace of it."

Al Rankin turned his handsome face toward Bob Lake, and a faint smile touched the corners of his mouth. What it might mean the sheriff could never guess, but Bob Lake knew that the smile meant a perfect understanding. There was something even a trifle alarming in that quick apprehension.

"Al," went on the sheriff, "you're free. I'm sorry that I had to bust in on you the way I did, but. . . ."

"Business is business," answered Al Rankin cheerily. "And this ain't the first time that you've showed me attentions. No hard feelings, Sheriff, but you might have picked a better time for jailing me."

"The wife and all that . . . ," returned the sheriff. "That was pretty hard, Al, and I'm the first to admit it. Are we quits?"

"Quits?" asked Al Rankin in an indescribable voice. "Quits?" He smiled, and the sheriff shuddered. He took no care to conceal his emotion.

"All right," he said, "we'll have it out then, sooner or later."

"Sooner or later," said Rankin, "we sure will."

"But there's one thing more, Al. This fellow Smiley is scared to death. Will you shake hands with him before me, and tell him that you don't bear any malice?"

"Why," said Al Rankin, "from what I've heard, it looks as if he'd ought to be more afraid of this gent" — he indicated Bob Lake — "than he is of me."

"Maybe. But will you shake hands with him, Al?"

"If that'll make you any happier, sure I will."

"I'm glad of that. I don't want him on my conscience. I told him it would be safe, you see?"

"Very thoughtful of you, but go ahead."

"I'll get the keys."

He left the room, and Al Rankin made a long, light step to the bars; his debonair calm was gone.

"Who are you?" he asked curtly.

"Easy," murmured Lake. "Maybe they're listening."

103

"Can't hear a thing through these walls. Come out with it."

"My name is Lake. The sheriff told you the rest. I got the gun from Smiley and threw it away."

"What gun?"

Lake smiled. "Still bluffing?" he queried.

"But why?" asked Al Rankin.

"I was on the train in the seat behind you," replied Lake.

"Ah, I thought I remembered something about your face."

"When White came and took you. . . ." He paused, finding it difficult to go on. "As a matter of fact, Rankin, it seemed a shame that a girl like your wife should lose her husband . . . I. . . ."

"You did this for Anne . . . all this?" asked Al Rankin slowly.

"Rankin, you'll be thinking me a fool, but I'm talking straight to you. I'll never see the girl again, and I'll never see you again. She turned my head, Rankin. I envied you. And for a minute I was almost glad that the sheriff had grabbed you. Then I changed my mind. You know the rest. Now . . . good bye and good luck to you. But one thing before I go, Rankin. If I ever hear that you haven't straightened out after marrying a girl like that, I'll come from the end of the world, if I have to, and skin you alive!"

"You'd do all that?" asked Rankin with a sneer. Then he straightened his face. "Shake on it, Lake."

Their hands closed, and Bob Lake felt a grip that he had never dreamed possible in a man.

"This ain't the last time I see you," said Rankin. "A gent like you is the kind I want for a friend. You're coming up to Greytown with me, and you're going to visit at the house. The wife will want to know you."

But Bob Lake shook his head, and he laughed bitterly.

104

"Never in a thousand years, partner. I don't trust myself that much. I'd be a fool."

They had no opportunity to say more. At this moment Bill White returned.

## V

## "THROUGH THE WINDOW"

The sheriff shook his little bunch of keys and unlocked the barred door and stepped aside to allow Al Rankin to come out. He was perfectly frank in his attitude. "You know how I stand, Al," he said. "Sooner or later I'm going to get the goods on you. Long as you stood alone, it was a hard fight. But now you've started to play partners." He indicated Bob Lake with a jerk of his thumb. "The minute a gent starts doing things like that, he's done for. I've seen too many of 'em come and go."

But the temper of Al Rankin refused to be disturbed. "You're all wrong, Bill," he assured the sheriff. "I'm married, and I'm going to lead a life nobody can point a finger at."

The sheriff met this speech with a cold smile of deep wisdom. "I know you'll try to get me sooner or later," he said. "But I'll try to be ready. Now come along and shake hands with Hugh Smiley. The little chap is half dead with being scared. And I don't blame him."

He led the way out of the cell room and into his office. The rest of the little building was already deserted. The crowd had learned that the last hope of the sheriff had failed, when he could establish no proof of past relationship between Al Rankin and Lake. In the office stood only Hugh Smiley. It was plain that he was in the throes of a panic. He would far

105

rather have been outside, flying for his life, but he felt it was hopeless to flee from Al Rankin. Other men had tried it and failed. The only thing for him to do was to stay and face the music and try to effect a reconciliation.

But it was only by dint of clutching the edge of the table that he was able to remain there, facing the door. As it opened and he saw the handsome face of Rankin, the little man shivered violently. He stood like one waiting for the death sentence from the judge.

"Here you are," said the sheriff. "Al, maybe you think you've got reason to be sore at Smiley. But, as far as I can make out, Hugh has reason to be sore at you. Suppose you shake hands, here, and call everything quits."

The face of Al Rankin, it seemed to Lake, was a study in controlled emotion. The quivering of his eyelids showed the tremor of fierce anger that was passing through him, yet he maintained the calmest of smiles.

"Most generally," he said, "I aim to square things up with a gent that double-crosses me. However, I let a promise drop to the sheriff, and I like to live up to my promises. Besides, you have a grudge against me, Hugh. D'you think it's all cleared up, now?"

"All cleared," said Hugh Smiley. His little rat eyes went restlessly to and fro. "I was wrong, Al. I don't mind tellin' you now that I was wrong and . . . and I want to ask your pardon for it."

"Why," said Rankin, "if you feel that way, we will call it quits. Go back home and sleep easy and forget about me, Hugh. I guess that'll do, Sheriff, eh?"

"I suppose so." The sheriff was not entirely satisfied.

"If anything goes wrong," said Hugh Smiley, pointing a trembling finger at White, "remember that it was you that got me into this."

"I know it," returned the sheriff, and he made a wry face.

"Wait," cut in Bob Lake. "I think they ought to shake hands first, eh, Sheriff?"

"Good idea. That's what they met for in the first place. Go ahead, Al."

A glance from the corner of Rankin's eyes fell upon Lake, a glance gleaming with such venom that the big fellow winced. The handshaking was duly performed. And the sheriff sighed.

"All right, boys," he said, "I've got to run along. Sit around and talk things over. Here's your gun, Al. Here's yours, Lake."

He hung the cartridge belt and the revolver on the wall, while he put Rankin's gun before him on the table. Then he left the room.

"All I got to say," said the rat-faced man, "is that I'm glad you showed some sense, Al."

Al Rankin looked up from his gun that he was balancing lightly in his long fingers. "By the way," he said, "I've got to say something to the sheriff before he leaves."

Tossing his weapon back on the table, he left the room hurriedly. They heard a door close outside, and the keen eyes of Smiley turned for the first time upon Bob Lake.

"Why you done it," he said gloomily, "I dunno. But it was sure a fool play. D'you think Al is grateful? He don't know what gratitude means, stranger, and you'll live long enough to find out. Grateful? Right this minute he's plannin' something ag'in' you. For why? Because he knows that you know where that gun was put, and the minute the gun's found, they's a noose around his neck. Does that sound reasonable?" He leaned across the table and grinned maliciously into the face of Lake.

"Reasonable enough," replied the other carelessly, a great deal more carelessly than he felt about the matter.

107

"And how does he know that you won't use what you know to squeeze money out of him? He's got lots of coin, Al has. He got a lot from his father. He's got a house that's a regular palace, Al has, and the only reason he's been around raisin' trouble is because he likes action. That's all. He'll be kind of wishing you was out of the way, maybe, and the minute he does that, you'll sure cuss the day when you held me up for that hanging evidence. Wait, son, till. . . ."

The evil joy went out of that face. The eyes went past Bob Lake toward the window and fastened there with a sort of horrible fascination. Before Lake could turn, the bark of a gun crowded the room with echoes, and Hugh Smiley slumped forward on the table. At the same time there was a heavy impact on the floor.

Bob Lake reached first for his gun on the wall. The holster was empty! There on the floor lay the heavy object that had been thrown through the window. It was a revolver, and, as Bob Lake caught it up, he knew at once that it was his.

"Rankin," said a voice behind him.

He whirled to find Smiley propping himself with sagging arms back from the table. His eyes were already glazing. From the outer part of the building Lake heard footsteps coming. There he stood with the gun in his hand from which a bullet had struck the dying man.

The whole devilish scheme dawned on his mind. Al Rankin had left his own weapon, lying on the table. On his way out of the room he had slipped Lake's gun out of its holster, and then, circling the building on the outside, he had fired through the open window. What could be neater?

It was known that Lake and Smiley were at odds, and there were plenty of grounds for a quarrel between them, whether Lake had actually held up the little man as Smiley had sworn, or whether Smiley had evened the score between them. And the blame of that bullet was thrown upon Bob Lake, removing him from Rankin's path, just as Smiley had prophesied the gambler and gunfighter would wish to do.

He leaned over Smiley.

"Witnesses!" was all the little man could say. He seemed to be saving his strength for a later moment.

Then the door was burst open by the sheriff. "You murdering idiot!" he shouted and wrenched the gun from Lake's hand.

But the latter pointed mutely to the dying man.

By this time High Smiley had slumped back in the chair with his arms dangling in odd positions at his side. He was plainly far gone, and only his eyes showed a sign of life as his chin sagged down against his chest.

The sheriff dropped to his knees beside the little man, still covering Bob Lake with his own gun.

"Not him," whispered Smiley. "Al Rankin . . . through the window . . . I seen his face." He sank limp against the shoulder of the sheriff.

Bob Lake raised the dead body and laid it on the table. Others were coming through the building, shouting to one another. Gunshots in Everett generally had aftermaths.

"Is it clear?" asked Lake.

"Not at all," said the sheriff. "A minute ago I left you here all chummy as so many partners. Now here I am with the gun that killed Smiley, and that gun is yours, and Smiley gives me a dying declaration that Al Rankin is the man, and there's Rankin's gun, lying on the table cold." He wiped his forehead.

"Rankin went out, Sheriff, and took my gun with him. He fired through the window and then threw my gun inside. His plan was to come running back after the hubbub started and show surprise. But. . . ."

"Then where is he now?" asked the bewildered sheriff.

"He heard Smiley yell his name a minute ago and saw that his whole plan had been spoiled because Smiley had seen his face, when he fired through the window, Where is he now? He's riding out of Everett on the first horse he found saddled, most like."

The sheriff's amazement cleared itself in one tremendous curse, then he bolted from the room. But Bob Lake went back to the dead man and looked down into his face. No doubt Hugh Smiley was a bad one and not worth his salt, but he would have served to apprehend a murderer had Lake not interfered. Now the rôles were reversed, and, as surely as the sun shone, Bob Lake was responsible for the tragedy.

He went out from the jail and back to the hotel a free man, but a very thoughtful one.

## VI

### "MOSTLY ABOUT ANNE"

The result of his reflections was one clear perception: he had made a terrible mess of things from the start. A worthless gambler and murderer without honor or faith or gratitude had been taken out of the proper hands of the law; a man, innocent of crime in this affair at least, now lay dead. And finally the man to whom he had been a benefactor had come within an ace of saddling the guilt of a murder upon his own shoulders.

It was sufficient, one would say, to make Bob Lake swear himself in as a deputy and join the posse in the pursuit of the renegade, Al Rankin. But there was another residue of Bob Lake's thought, and that residue was the face of Anne Rankin as he had last looked back to her from the head of the car. His memory of her was astonishingly clear. The few attitudes and expressions that he had seen remained before his mind like so many pictures, and in his leisure he could take them out and examine them in detail, one by one. Long before reaching this point, another man would have taken a train back for Manhattan or some other more distant point. But, when all was said and done, Lake only knew that he must see that girl again — at once.

The next morning he was on the train for Greytown, and early in the afternoon he dismounted at the little station in the heart of the mountains. It was bitterly cold in spite of the spring. An unseasonable snow had fallen several days before, and now it was frozen and packed hard by a stiff northerly wind. Over this the clear sunshine fell, blinding to the eye where the snow fields lay level. The nearer mountains were crystal outlines against the sky. The farther peaks were a bluish white, but here and there, where the snow had slid away, there was a raw, bare, black cliff.

The train pulled away and left another man standing on the platform, a middle-aged man whose eyes were extremely old and whose smile was extremely young. He had dropped his suitcase and was bundling himself into an overcoat, when Bob Lake approached.

"D'you know this layout?" asked Lake.

"Not a thing. I'm a stranger here, and I'm looking for Albert Rankin's house."

"Albert Rankin? Oh, Al Rankin, eh? Well, I'm trying to spot the same place."

He found himself regarded with a new and vital interest. "Friend of Rankin's?"

The voice was even, but there was no doubt of the hardness that crept into the tone. Plainly this man was not apt to

111

take kindly to the friends of Al Rankin. He might, perhaps, be an officer of the law sent to watch the newly made outlaw's headquarters.

"Nope. Only talked to him once."

"Where was that, may I ask?"

"In Everett."

The other started. "When?"

"Last night."

"The deuce you say," exclaimed the older man. "You were in Everett last night?"

"I'll say I was."

"Then you know about the whole fracas."

"All there is to be known."

His companion bundled him off to a corner of the platform for the station agent had come out to watch them.

"I have an unfortunate interest in this matter," he said. "Let me introduce myself. I am Paul Sumpter. I see that name means nothing to you, but I am the father of Al Rankin's wife."

"I'm Bob Lake. Glad to know you."

"And you, sir. Sheriff White advised me of everything that had happened last night by wire. Of course, it was told in brief. I have come up here to see to my girl, but, above all things, I'd like to find out exactly what happened in Everett last night."

Bob Lake drew back. He was ordinarily talkative enough, but he was filled with aversion to this man who had allowed his daughter to marry such a fellow as Al Rankin.

"I can tell you what happened in a nutshell . . . murder, Mister Sumpter."

The other drew his knuckles across his puckered forehead. "Murder," he repeated softly. "There were extenuating circumstances?"

112

"Sure, there was a chance for him to shift the blame on another gent. That was why he took a pot shot at Smiley."

"And who was the other?"

"Me."

It was Sumpter's turn to fall back. "You are the man who . . . ?"

"Oh, I'm him, all right," returned Lake. "I'm the fool who stepped in and got messed up."

They stood regarding one another curiously. "I see," said the older man quietly. "You're up here, hunting for Rankin? Well, sir, I hope to heaven that you find him."

"Don't start jumping to conclusions. Right now I got an idea that I'm the best friend Rankin has in the world."

His companion gaped in amazement. "After he has tried to saddle a murder on you? But possibly the sheriff is wrong, and I'm wrong. There are qualities in Al Rankin that can make a man stick to him through thick and thin, even as you seem to be doing."

"There are."

"I'm glad of it," said Mr. Sumpter. "I've been making up my mind that my daughter shall never see the fellow again. But he may be an extraordinary sort of man. The reports against him may be exaggerated. Tell me, Mister Lake, the good things you have noted in him."

"I can do that short, Mister Sumpter . . . his wife."

"His wife?" Then, as he understood, Sumpter frowned. "It's on account of my girl, Anne, that you're prepared to stay by Rankin? Is that it? I've never heard her mention your name among her friends."

"She doesn't know me. But let that go."

"Mister Lake, let me tell you, once and for all, that the best thing you can do for Anne is to let the law take its course. You have already done too much, I believe. You are the man who removed from Smiley the evidence which would have hung Rankin. Far better if he had swung on the gallows. There would have been an end to him and another beginning for Anne. The best thing you can do is to turn around and go back."

"Your daughter will be the best judge of that."

He was favored with a long and searching scrutiny, and then, at the approach of the station agent, he turned to the man and asked for directions. They were easily given. One had only to take the road and keep on around the side of the next hill. It was easy walking because the snow was firm. No one could mistake the Rankin house. There was no other in sight.

Sumpter and Lake started out side by side. They talked little at first, but Sumpter seemed to have taken a determined liking to the younger man, and finally he began on the story of the marriage.

It was by no means a novel tale. The life of his daughter had fallen into two distinct divisions, it seemed. First, she had been a romping girl typical of the West. She did anything that boys could do and sometimes did it a good deal better. The tomboy period ended when she was sent East to a girl's school. On her return she was a new personality, it seemed. But one undercurrent of her nature remained the same — she continued to love the outdoors and the life of the mountains. The time she had spent away from her homeland had served to idealize it. The East to her had always remained the country of the efféte. Constantly harking back to the wild days of her girlhood, she came back expecting in a measure to take up the old times as she had left them, and she had been shocked to find she could not. The thing she admired she could no longer do, and she was physically incapable of the thirty miles a day in the saddle that had once been nothing to her. So she transferred her interests; she began to idolize the

Western men. She loved their freedom. She professed a liking even for their dialect. At this crucial moment in stepped Al Rankin.

He was everything that she admired. He could almost literally ride anything that walked on four feet. His courage was known. Although he was a comparative stranger in their town, tales followed out of the mountains, and it was said that he had killed "his man."

This was enough to startle Sumpter and put him on his guard. He went so far as to forbid the girl having anything to do with the stranger until he had been able to learn more about his past. But the prohibition, as usual in such cases, merely confirmed the girl in her liking. She refused to see other men. She concentrated stubbornly on Albert Rankin and wasted on him all of her inborn aptitude for idealization. When her father attempted to argue, he was met with stubborn silence.

He decided, more indulgently than wisely, to let her have her own way, trusting to her woman's intuition, and fearing to drive her to rashness by a prolonged opposition. For stubbornness was a Sumpter characteristic, and, under all of her gentleness of exterior manner, Anne Sumpter at heart could be firm as a rock. And the father, recognizing the family trait, gave way.

No sooner was the ban lifted than Al Rankin was constantly in the house. Their engagement followed, and at once he pressed for an early marriage. The girl consented. She declared it was the way of the West. Her father and even her mother protested only half-heartedly. They had been won over by the pleasant manner and easy social address of handsome Albert Rankin. Financially they easily learned that he was sound enough. The marriage followed.

Even before the ceremony Mr. Sumpter received the first

serious warnings in the shape of several anonymous letters, and one was signed by Hugh Smiley. They made various unsavory charges against young Rankin, but Sumpter gave them slight attention. In the first place because he despised anonymous blackmail, and in the second place because in the case of Smiley he felt a bitter personal spite.

"But, when I took her to the train," concluded Sumpter, "I had a premonition that she was embarking toward a disaster. It came over me all at once, when we stepped into the coach. But then it was too late to do anything.

"It was not long. Last night the telegram came from Sheriff White of Everett, informing me in outline of everything that had happened. He also told me that Rankin is now outside the law. So that nothing can prevent me from taking my girl back to her home and teaching her to forget this horrible affair. It might be that I shall need help. In that case, may I call on you?"

"When you get her consent, call on me," said Lake.

"You don't think she'll come?"

"I've stopped thinking," said Bob Lake bitterly. "The things I figure on all come out wrong."

## VII

## " 'FOR BETTER OR WORSE' "

Rounding the hill, they paused by mutual consent and stared at one another. Stretching to the right before them, the hillside flattened into a spacious plateau heavily forested, and above the trees in three tall gables rose the roof of the house. To Bob Lake it seemed to have the dimensions of a palace, and his heart fell.

To him a house in the mountains meant a three-room shack. How would he be able to face the mistress of this mansion and talk to her of the things that he began to feel vaguely forming in his mind?

"I remember hearing something about it," Sumpter was saying. "But can you imagine the owner of a property like this becoming a common gunfighter and gamester?"

Bob Lake returned no answer. They struggled over the slippery snow up the hillside, and on the level of the plateau every step among the trees revealed the more and more imposing proportions of the house. Built of the heaviest timbers, it was settled to the natural slope of the ground like a piece of landscape. At night and unlighted it must have seemed merely the peaked crest of the mountain.

"But why a house like that . . . up here?" asked Bob Lake.

"Rankin's father had a great deal of money. He was an Easterner, but he built this hunting lodge and raised Albert in the wilds. Wanted to get him back to nature, as I understand it, and he succeeded."

They came out onto a semicircular opening in the woods before the lodge, and presently they rang the doorbell. A Chinese boy admitted them and took their names. When he had gone, Bob Lake pointed to the big logs that were smoldering in the fireplace of the hall. "No real use," he said, "but just for folks to look at when they come saunterin' in."

Then they admired the paneling in the great style of redwood. The stonework about the fireplace alone, Bob Lake decided, would have cost his entire fortune to reproduce. Wherever his eye fell, it reported back to his mind a detail which made him more gloomy.

There was light, rapid fall of feet, and then down the generous curve of the great staircase came Anne. She was huddling a wrap of blue, shimmering stuff around her shoulders

117

as she ran; Bob Lake did not miss even this detail. The light from a window that opened on the stairway showed her brightly for a moment, and then she descended into the shadow of the hall and was in the arms of her father.

A dozen half laughing and half excited questions tumbled out all at once, and then, as her father stepped back gravely, she saw Bob Lake. If he had any fear that she might have forgotten him, that fear was banished instantly. There was a flash and paling of color as she looked at him and, it seemed to Lake, no little alarm in her manner.

"You know Mister Lake?" her father was saying.

She bowed to him, recovering her self-possession. "I've seen Mister Lake before. But, Dad, what brought you here? Have you missed me already? And have you seen the house? And isn't it wonderful? And the servants . . . and everything you could imagine."

"I have missed you," said Sumpter. "But that isn't exactly what's brought me here. If Mister Lake will excuse us for a moment, I wish to talk with you alone."

They made their brief excuses to Bob Lake, and then she drew her father into the library, lined with more books than Sumpter had ever seen in one room before.

"It's serious?" she murmured to him.

"Very serious. The first thing for you to do is to pack up your things and come back home with me. I can explain things on the way in detail."

He could have been more diplomatic, but he was not in a tender mood. He felt that she had so thoroughly messed matters in her marriage that there was not a little of "I told you so" in his attitude. And the result was that he hurt her cruelly with his very first speech.

"It's Al!" she exclaimed. "Something has happened to Al. I knew it, when I saw you come!"

"Something has happened to Al," repeated her father grimly. "Besides, what's more to the point, Al has done a good deal to others."

"But what?"

"Anne, I want you to take your father's word. I don't want to go into details just now. The main thing is that you've married a hound, and you've got to get away from this house as fast as you can. Will you trust me for that?"

He might as well have trusted a mother to send her child to the gallows. "Are you trying to drive me mad?" she asked. "What's happened to Al? Is . . . is he hurt?"

"Never better in his life."

"Then . . . ?"

"Which is more than can be said for at least one of his acquaintances."

"There's been a fight?"

"Not a fight."

"Tell me everything . . . everything. I knew there was something serious about it from the manner of that man who took him off the train."

"Do you know why he was taken off the train?"

"No."

"It was an arrest."

"Ah! On what charge?"

"Murder!" He drove the word at her brutally. He was determined that, before he ended this interview, he would have her so thoroughly subdued to his will that she would never question it again. But, instead of crumbling before his attack, she rallied to meet it.

There was an unexpected basis of strength in her nature that always came to the top in an emergency. All his life her father had been astonished when he was confronted by it.

"It's not true," she said quite calmly.

119

"Do you think I'd lie to you, Anne?"

"Someone else has lied to you . . . or else they trapped Al with a false charge. At this very moment I know as surely as I know that I'm standing here, that Al is a free man!" She said it proudly.

"You're right. He's free."

It staggered Anne in spite of her surety of the moment before. "Then . . . ?"

"Do you know who to thank for his freedom? The romantic fool downstairs . . . Lake. Who is he?"

"Lake? Thank him? What do you mean by that?" She came close to him with eagerness that he could not understand in her face. "What did Mister Lake do? What did he do?"

"Saved the neck of Al Rankin, that's all."

"I knew it . . . almost."

"You knew what?"

"Nothing. Tell me what Mister Lake did."

"The sheriff arrested Al Rankin without evidence. He was waiting for evidence that a man didn't dare to bring in, for fear of having his throat cut. That's the sort of a man your husband is. This Lake . . . the idiot . . . intercepted Smiley on his way and took the evidence from him. That evidence was the revolver with which Rankin had killed a man named Coy . . . deliberate murder, Anne!"

"I don't. . . ."

"Don't say you don't believe it. Don't act like a stubborn child, my dear."

"But why did Mister Lake do it? Did he know Al?"

"Never saw him before that day. He was riding behind you on the train. Can you figure out why he did it?"

Her flush was a marvelous thing to see. "I don't know," she said softly. "No, I can't understand. I've never spoken to him before today."

"Everybody seems to have gone mad," said her father. "But I have told you enough to convince you that you've got to go back with me?"

"Do you think I shall leave Al for a charge that even the law can't hold against him?"

"But there's a new charge, Anne."

"And this time?" she queried.

"Murder again."

"Ah!" She winced from that blow and then made herself meet his eyes.

"You've made a fool of yourself, and that's the short of it, my dear. You've let a crazy, romantic idea run away with you. Now, come back home and face the music and forget this devil of a Rankin. I never liked him. I warned you against him from the first."

"They'll never convict Al! They can't."

"Not with eyewitnesses?"

"Who?"

"The man who was killed lived long enough to name his murderer. That man was Smiley."

"He lied out of malice."

"Did he? There was another man. It was a man who had just saved Rankin from the gallows at the risk of his own neck. It was a man who had done these things out of the bigness of his heart. To repay him for what he had done Al Rankin tried to shift the blame for the murder on his shoulders. That's the sort of a cur Rankin is. And the name of the living witness against Rankin is the man downstairs . . . Bob Lake! Will you call *him* a liar?"

She was struck mute. Feeling her way, she found a chair and sank slowly into it. Still she watched her father with haunted eyes.

"And now, Anne," he went on, growing suddenly gentle,

121

"the thing for you to do is to come back to people who love you and people you can trust. I'll keep you from this murdering devil, this ungrateful, hard, scheming sneak."

"Oh, Dad," she whispered, "how can I go back? How can I go back and face them and live down their whispers and their smiles?"

"Why, curse 'em," said her father. "I'll knock off the head of the first man that raises his voice against you or insults you with a grin. And as for the gossip of the women . . . why, honey, you can silence the whole pack of 'em with a single smile."

A very wan smile rewarded him for his flattery. Still she shook her head. "What right have I to desert him? 'For better or worse.' I've no right to leave him . . . and he'll still be proven innocent."

"You can't meet my eye, when you say that."

"Dad, I can't go. I can't!"

"Anne, why not?"

"Shame . . . pride . . . everything keeps me here."

"It's ruin, Anne."

"I've brought it on my own head . . . besides . . . I won't admit that he's wrong. I'm going to stay."

"Then, by heaven, I'm going to stay here with a gun. If your husband comes inside the door, he's a dead man."

## VIII

### " 'A STRANGE COMBINATION' "

She left him raging up and down the room and pausing with a stamp of the foot from time to time, when he recalled her stubbornness. He felt very much like one who has brought a chance of escape to a prisoner and finds the obstinate fool unwilling to accept freedom.

But Anne slipped out and came on Bob Lake, sitting in the hall where she had left him. He sat with his chin propped upon one great brown fist while he studied empty space. On his puckered forehead there was the wistfulness of a man who submits to inevitable defeat. She paused on the stairs to study him. He was by no means a handsome fellow, she decided, and yet she liked his very ugliness. There was a certain dauntless honesty about that face that others had felt before her. She saw, too, as any woman with the feel of the West in her blood will do, the breadth of his shoulders, his fighting jaw, and the size of hands capable of holding and retaining what they seized — or else crushing it under the fingers. Anne Sumpter liked these things, and, having finished her catalogue of details, she went on to surprise him.

A man who is surprised, she knew, is always half disarmed and left open to the eye of a woman. Smiling faintly, she reached the hall before he sensed her coming.

"My father has told me about you," she said, taking pity on his confusion, but she had not by any means intended to. "He has told me," she went on, "that you have done a good deal for Mister Rankin."

Then she waited, she hardly knew for what. He was not quite so clumsy as she had expected. She discovered that he had a way of looking at one so that it was difficult to bear his eye. His seriousness was contagious.

"Lady," he said gravely, "I dunno what your father has said. But if you want facts, I'll give 'em to you."

"By all means," said the girl, and paused for the recital. There would be much boasting in it, she had no doubt.

"The facts are these," said Bob Lake, reflecting on them as

123

though to make sure that he was correct. "It come in my way to do a little favor for Al Rankin, and I done it."

Was that the way he phrased a service that had kept her husband from the gallows?

"Then it came in Al Rankin's way to do a kind of a bad-looking trick to me, and it appears like he done it, too. So that's how it stands between Al Rankin and me."

And was this the way he described what her father had called an attempt to put the blame of a murder on his shoulders? She was staggered by this studious understatement. And there was a ring of truth about it that went home. For the first time a great doubt about Al Rankin entered her mind and lodged there.

"Then," she said, "as Al's wife I can only hope that the time will soon come when he can explain that away."

"I hope so, too," said the big man frankly, "but I misdoubt it. The point is, we've come to a pass where gun talk is a pile more likely than man talk."

Again that very simplicity of expression shocked her into belief. She began to feel suddenly that this was the reality for which she had been consciously seeking and never finding.

But she said coldly: "And why have you come to tell me these things . . . and you've come a long distance, Mister Lake?"

"Because," he answered calmly, "it came into my mind that you might have heard enough things from your father to think that you got hooked up with a yaller hound."

"Do you think Al Rankin is that?"

He paused, lost in thought. "No," he said, "I ain't sure of it. Not quite."

"And why do you wish to find out what I think?"

"Because," he said, "if you was to think that way, it'd

come in handy for me to go out and blow off the head of this same Al Rankin."

She could merely stare at him. "Mister Lake, I don't suppose I should listen to you, but you have helped Mister Rankin . . . and you do seem to feel that you have been wronged. But . . . do you realize that you are talking to Al Rankin's wife?"

"Lady," he said, "it's something that I can't forget."

"Do you actually expect me to ask you to go out with a gun to find my husband?"

"I ask you to talk frank to me, like I'm doing to you," he said.

"And suppose that I don't give you this mad commission?"

"Then it's up to me to go out and get to Al Rankin and see that he's safe and sound and clean out of the hands of the law which is tryin' tolerable hard to reach him, I figure."

"Of all the strange men I have ever known or heard of," she said slowly, "you're the strangest, Mister Lake."

"Me? Strange? Not a bit. I can tell you everything about myself in half a minute . . . everything worth knowing, that is."

"Then I earnestly wish that you would."

"Plain cowpuncher, lady. Does that answer?"

"Cowpuncher? But there are all manner of cowpunchers, aren't there?"

"No, they're mostly a pretty lazy set, take 'em by and large. They punch cows because they'd rather ride than walk. Not very clean in the skin, seeing the kind of a life they lead, and not a terrible lot cleaner under the skin, seeing the life they lead. Off and on they sort of smell of their work, you might say. They happen onto the range sort of casual, most of 'em, and they happen off the range sort of casual, most of 'em. They drink considerable, and they cuss considerable. Some of 'em dies in their boots and is glad of it, and some of 'em dies in their boots and is sorry for it. Religion they ain't bothered a pile with. Past they ain't got. Family don't bother 'em none." He paused to pick up the fragments of facts that might have strayed from his attention during this strange recital, and then he looked up to her faintly smiling face. "And there you are, lady, with a pretty fair picture, taking it by and large, of Bob Lake. Will it do?"

She knew by the very bitterness of his smile that he was not understating this time, but really striving to give her a literal portrait of himself, as he was, so that she might not be led astray hereafter in her estimation of him. With all her heart she admired that fearless honesty.

"I think," she said gently, "that you've named all the things about yourself that don't count a bit, and you've deliberately left out of account everything that really matters."

He bowed profoundly. "Lady, I never figured on having the last word with you, even about myself."

She could not help smiling. And then she stopped and wondered at herself. It was the most serious day of her life, and here she was forgetting the seriousness and centering only on this odd man — this stranger. What was coming to her husband all this time? "If I asked you," she said at length, "you would go out to help Mister Rankin?"

"I suppose," he said gloomily, "that I would."

"And will you tell me why?"

"Because I done wrong by Al Rankin," he answered after another moment.

"Wrong to him? How?"

"Speakin' man to man, that's a thing I can't talk about."

"But speaking man to woman, Mister Lake?"

"All the more reason."

At that it became absolutely necessary for her to know. Of course, she guessed quite distinctly, and she knew that she was walking on dangerous ground. But what woman could have done otherwise?

"It's a mystery," she said. "And . . . I'd like to know. How in the world could you possibly have wronged Al Rankin?"

"By envyin' him, Missus Rankin. When the sheriff took him off the train, I was sitting behind you, and I wished that he'd never come back . . . I started in hoping that he was done for. Well, that sort of thing is poison. So I jumped off the train to make up."

"Do you know that there are no other men like you, Mister Lake?"

"Millions of 'em, lady, but they don't let themselves go. Well, they ain't any real reason why I should horn in here. You're going back home with your father?"

"I'm not. I'm staying here."

He blinked and then looked earnestly at her. "Stay here and wait for Al?"

"Exactly."

"What you've heard about him, don't turn you ag'in' him none?"

"Not a bit."

Bob Lake sighed. "You're sure fond of him," he replied. "Well, that lets me out."

He picked up his hat, and she knew perfectly well that the moment he passed through the door he would be out of her life and gone forever. It was a hard thing to look forward to. Between the lines of his blunt speech she had been reading busily for herself, and what she read was a romance so astonishing that it carried her back to her days of fairy stories. Out of those pages all this seemed to have happened — a fairy tale turned into the ways and days of the 20th Century. A strange combination of Faithful John, Mysterious Prince, and Wandering Knight — there he went out of her life.

"Wait!" called the girl faintly.

He paused.

"A little while ago you made an offer. You said you would try to help my husband, if I asked you to."

"I did."

"You meant that?"

"Lady, are you going to take me up?"

"Ah, now you want to withdraw?"

He came back to her. "Listen," he said, "you think it over careful. Think it over a whole pile. But, if you need me, say the word. It ain't an easy thing to do, Missus Rankin. But, if you start me, I'll stick with it to the finish."

"But don't you see that there are no friends who will help him now? He's alone. Nothing but enemies around him. Mister Lake. . . ."

"You don't have to plead," said Bob Lake. "Tell me straight what you want me to do."

"Find him," said the girl, "and keep him safe."


IX


## "AL SLEEPS IN HIS BOOTS"

Out of Everett, Al Rankin rode hard, cursing in spite of his newly gained liberty. He had been on the point of running back into the room after shooting Smiley. That was his plan as Lake had afterward seen. He would come back, appearing surprised at what he found, and the gun on the floor would convict Bob Lake. He hated Hugh Smiley for various reasons; he hated Bob

Lake as a man of evil generally hates those who have found him out. The very fact that his life had depended on the romantic generosity of a stranger was abhorrent to him. The time might come, perhaps, when Bob Lake would boast of how he kept no less a person than Al Rankin from the halter.

For all these causes Rankin wished both Smiley and Bob Lake out of the way. And he had cunningly contrived it so that one blow might destroy both without bringing even a breath of suspicion upon his own head. Only one thing foiled him, and that was his own inaccuracy with the revolver. Had he thought twice he would have aimed for the head — it was far surer. But the bullet through the body had not taken the life instantly — it had left enough breath in the lungs of Hugh Smiley for him to cry out the name of his murderer, and Rankin, running back into the building, had heard that cry and recognized the voice. At one stroke all of his plans were ruined.

He hurried out of the jail again, and, rounding the corner at the hitching rack, he chose with a single glance the best of the three horses that were tethered there — a rangy bay with legs enough for speed and a wide expanse of breast that promised staying qualities. He had no time for a longer examination and threw himself hastily into the saddle. A moment later he was galloping swiftly out of Everett.

From the moment he swung onto the back of that horse, he became a thing more to be shunned than the guilt of a dozen murders — he became a horse thief. There is an old maxim west of the Rockies: "It takes a man to kill a man; it takes a skunk to steal a horse." Al Rankin knew the maxim well enough. He knew various other things connected with horse thieves and their ways. And yet here he was on the back of a stolen horse.

Crime had been for Al Rankin a temptation like liquor to

129

other men. If he had been born poor, he probably would have found sufficient excitement in the mere work of earning a living, which is rarely dull in a cattle country. But Al Rankin had never known the sting of breaking blisters on the inside of his hands. He had never known the pleasure of earned money, whether in the making or the spending. His only joy in life had come out of matching his wits against the wits of others and his speed of hand and straightness of eye against theirs. The trouble with Al was that he was different from his fellows. He despised his victims, and, when a man does that, he is past hoping for.

What tortured him with shame now was not that he had attempted to destroy his benefactor, Bob Lake, but that the obscure crime of killing Coy so long ago should have led to such complicated consequences. Of all the acts of his life that was probably the least blameless, for Coy needed killing if ever a man did. But out of that death the train of consequences sprang. It was that killing which had determined him on leaving the mountains for a time. That departure sent him into the life of Anne Sumpter. And Anne Sumpter led directly to the break with Smiley's daughter which in turn had worked back to put him in peril from Smiley himself. And to get even with Smiley he had now definitely enlisted against himself the enmity of the first man he had ever met whom he had definitely respected — that man was Bob Lake.

He was in fact, though he would not admit it, not a little afraid of Lake. Not that he would have feared a test of physical strength or a gun play man to man, but there were qualities in Lake that he did not understand, and whatever men do not understand they fear and hate. With all his soul Rankin hated Bob Lake.

He drew up the bay on a hilltop and looked back at Everett, a sprawling, shapeless shadow. By this time they knew that he was a horse thief. By this time the posse had started after him. He shook his fist into the night at them and spat in his contempt. In a way, there was a sort of fierce pleasure in knowing that from this time forth the hand of every man would be against him, his hand against every man.

Murderer and horse thief! There was a fine ending for Al Rankin, son of Judge Rankin. But he would fool them. For how long? Coldly there stepped into his mind the memory of other men, cool, confident, clever, experienced, who had from time to time passed outside the law. One by one they always fell. One by one their brief careers of wild living had ended with a wild or a wretched death. Some confederate enraged or bribed to betray them — but he, Al Rankin, would have no confederates. Other thoughts came to him.

"Curse resolutions," he said softly to himself. "I'll play the game the way it comes to me, and the boys that get me will pay a full price." And then he went on.

Another thought came to him and made him spur on the horse. For the first time in many hours he had recalled his wife. Again he cursed into the night — cursed Bill White and dead Hugh Smiley and his daughter and the interloper, Bob Lake. This was their work, he decided. He hardly knew Anne Sumpter — that name came to him more readily than the new one. He had sought her out because, when he went into her home town, she had been the attraction. He had wanted her because it seemed that everyone else wanted her. To his self-centered point of view she would have been desirable for this reason alone. And, indeed, he had not stopped to learn more about her. He had instantly concentrated upon learning how to win her. He had stepped into her home. He had studied her environment. He had quickly learned that she loved the West for its rough freedom, and he had exaggerated all these qualities in himself for her sake. It had from the first been a great game. He enjoyed it because he felt that he was deceiving her with consummate skill. Not once had he allowed his real self to come to the surface until that moment when he was saying good bye to her on the train to follow Bill White. Then for a moment the ugly inner self cropped up to the surface, and the sudden whitening of her face had been the result of his speech.

*But bah,* he concluded at this point in his reflections. *I'll fool her again. I'll fool her all her life. She ain't got the brains to see through me. I'll have her thinking I'm a martyr before she's two days older.*

It was very necessary that he should educate her to this belief in him now that he was a wanderer. She must be his base of supplies. She must be ready to send him succor of money and supplies from time to time. She must be the rock on which he was to build his safety and happiness. And again he cursed. It was surely an irony of fate that compelled him to accept a woman as a partner — he who had never had partners of any description.

Now, in the very beginning of his duel with the law, he found himself without any of the essentials. He had not a sign of a weapon except his pocket knife. He had very little money. It was necessary at once to strike to his base of supplies and get both money and weapons. As a matter of fact, it was the direction which he would choose. His cleverness was known. Ordinarily Bill White would have guarded the home of a man he wanted in the hope that the criminal would head toward it for refuge. But dealing with Al Rankin, the canny sheriff would probably never try such simple methods. He would attempt something complicated — some smart deduction — and Al Rankin would baffle him by doing the simple thing.

He decided to strike from the south toward the home town, making a wide detour and traveling in a loose semicircle so as to keep within a region of easy trails. In this manner he came down into that region where the deep and narrow gorge, which began near Greytown, spread out into a wider valley with tillable ground in patches here and there. It was near to his home in a matter of miles, but he had never been in that exact region before. The lowlands of the farmers were not exciting enough to attract Al Rankin. He was glad of this fact now, because it gave him a chance to harbor safely without much fear of being recognized. The first thing he did, when he reached that valley, was to head straight for a crossroads hotel and put up his horse for the night.

It was very bold, but he counted on two things. First that the news of his crimes and a description of him might not have been spread as yet. Second that he would never be expected and looked for so close to his home. It would be generally surmised that he would strike out for distant regions.

All went as smoothly as he could have wished. There were not, apparently, more than four or five men staying in the hotel that night, and he saw not a single face that was even remotely familiar. He put up his horse in security, ate his dinner with the five men before him, and then went up to his room.

But the scheme had not been as simple as it seemed. The moment he was alone in his room he began to worry, for he realized that he had stepped out of his natural character. Ordinarily he would not have favored these yokels with a single word more than orders for food. But this night he knew that he had been exceedingly affable, making himself laugh at their jests, even venturing a few stale jokes, and putting himself out to be agreeable. Was it not possible that he had been so unnatural that they would suspect something? Might they not be putting their heads together downstairs this very moment?

He heard a loud burst of laughter downstairs, and his skin

prickled. What if that laughter was at his expense? His pulse quickened. With soft steps he stole about his room and took stock of his surroundings. There was fortunately one easy exit that he could use in case of need. There was a shed beside the hotel, and the roof of it joined the side of the main building a couple of feet below his window. It would be easy in a pinch to slip out the window and down this roof, and then drop lightly to the ground.

Having noted this, he breathed more easily, and, returning to the door, he examined the lock. It was a stout affair, and there was besides a strong bolt on the inside. This he shot home and felt fairly assured against a surprise attack. But he dared not take off his boots, when he lay down on the bed. For the first time the meaning of the phrase "dying in one's boots" came home to him with all its force.

In the meantime, how should he sleep? Finding himself fast approaching a stage of hysterical excitement, he shrugged his shoulders, turned on his side, calmly assured himself that he was frightening his mind with silly fancies, and closed his eyes, determined to find sleep until the dawn. Then one day's march would bring him home. The closing of his eyes automatically induced drowsiness, and he was on the verge of falling fast asleep, when he heard a soft tapping at the door.

It brought him off the bed and onto his feet in the middle of the floor with one soundless bound. What could it mean? He slipped to the door.

"Who's there?"

"A friend. Let me in, Al."

"What news?"

"Danger, Al . . . and hurry."

# X

## "RANKIN'S ESCAPE"

Were they attempting to lure him out with this stale pretext? He decided to take the gambler's chance which he loved above all things. The moment he had drawn the bolt he leaped back and landed noiselessly far to the side where an enemy would never look for him on first entering. On one point he was certain. If there were the glint of a gun in the hand of the man who entered, he would fling the open, heavy pocket knife that he now held in his hand. That was a dainty little art which he had picked up in odd moments from an Italian friend.

But, when the door was pushed open, a big man strode in and at once closed the door behind him again and secured the lock and the bolt. There was no glimmer of a gun in the darkness.

"Where are you, Al?"

"Who are you?" asked Al Rankin.

"A friend."

"What name?"

"One you won't want to hear. But first, to show you I'm here in good faith, take this gun."

Something in the quality of the whisper that he heard brought a wild surmise to the outlaw, but he dismissed it at once as an absurdity. Then in the darkness he made out the butt of a weapon extended toward him. He clutched it eagerly; it was dearer to him than the touch of the hand of any friend had ever been. It meant safety. It meant, at least, a glorious fighting chance against odds. At once his heart stopped thundering. He felt that he was himself again.

"I'm going to light the lamp," said the stranger, feeling his way toward the bedside table and taking off the chimney with a soft chink of glass. "When you see my face, think twice before you jump."

A sulphur match spurted blue flame between his fingers, the wick of the lamp was lighted, and, as the chimney was replaced, the room brightened. Al Rankin found himself looking into the eyes of Bob Lake. Only the warning that had been given him before — and, in addition, the fact that Lake stood with his arms folded, his hands far from his holster — kept the outlaw from a gun play.

"You," he exclaimed softly. "You . . . Lake!"

"I'm here," said Lake dryly.

"You've come for an accounting, eh?" asked Rankin fiercely. "You can have it, Lake, on foot or in the saddle. With fists or guns or knives. I'm ready for you."

"You're a kind of man-eater, ain't you?" Lake sneeringly retorted. "But I ain't here for trouble. Besides, you got enough on your hands."

"Trouble?"

Lake pointed significantly at the floor.

"Those blockheads downstairs?" Rankin in spite of his mocking tone changed color.

"Those blockheads know who you are," said Lake.

"The mischief!" He set his teeth over the next part of his exclamation. "I had the idea of it," he muttered. "I should have jumped, when the hunch first hit me."

"You should have," assented Lake calmly. "There's a reward out."

"A reward!" Rankin felt his skin prickle.

"Who offered it?" he said huskily.

"The gent whose horse you stole. Sid Gordon."

"How much?"

"Three thousand."

Al Rankin cursed as the perspiration streamed out on his forehead. He knew what three thousand dollars as a reward meant. In that hard-working community, where a man would labor all month for wretched "found" and fifty dollars a month, how many hard riders and sure shots would turn out on a trail that ended with three thousand dollars — sixty months' savings — a fortune to most of the men he knew. The country would be alive with those who pursued him. His hand closed hard on the handle of the revolver.

"They heard of the reward? But how did they locate me? They don't know my face down this way."

"There's a description of you and of your horse. Bill White wired it all over the country and the amount of the reward. Maybe they figured the way I did . . . that you'd come back home this way."

"They knew I'd come home?"

"The first guess was that you would, the second that you'd be too clever to make that move . . . but there was a third guess that you'd count on them figuring you for the foxy move. I made that third guess, and they's a pile of men around here that's smarter than I am."

"They told you downstairs that I'm here?"

"It's all they're talking about. They wanted me to join in with 'em. I told 'em I didn't give a hang about rewards. What I wanted was sleep. So I came up to my room. Then I sneaked out to yours."

"How many are there? Have they sent out for help?"

"No, they don't want to split the reward up too much. They figure they're strong enough. There's the landlord and five others. Two of 'em are pretty handy in a fight, two ain't much, and one is yaller. I could tell it by the twitching of his hands."

"Six to one, ain't that enough?"

"Sure. But six to two ain't so bad."

"Six to two?"

Rankin crossed the room with a long light step. He had never walked like that before. He had never talked like this before. But now loud sounds had become abhorrent to him. They prevented him from listening to what was going on outside the room. They kept him from marking and interpreting every creak, every rustle of the wind in the old building.

"Now, Lake," he demanded in that new, soft voice, "who in blazes are you, and what's behind all this? Who are you? Where do you come from? How do you figure in on me and what I do? What made you save me at Everett? What's brought you down here, pretending to play in on my side? Can you tell me? Do you think I don't know that you're trying to trick me so's you can turn me over to those skunks downstairs? Out with it!"

"I'll out with it," answered Bob Lake. "It's the girl, Al. Not you, you dirty, sneakin' coyote. Not you, you treacherous, man-killing, life-stealin' hound! But it's the girl. Keep your hand away from your gun. You're a fast man with a gun, Al. Maybe faster'n I am. But I'd kill you. There ain't any shadow of a doubt in my head. I'd kill you, if it come to a pinch. And why I don't kill you is because the girl loves you. I ain't going to have her face hauntin' me. If keepin' you safe is going to make her happy, safe you shall be, if I can make you."

"Fairy stuff," said Rankin, but he stepped back. There had been a conviction in that steady, low-pitched voice that was still thrilling him. "Now what's your plan?"

"A dead simple one. First we switch bandannas. Yours is

138

blue and white . . . fool colors. Mine is red. Then gimme your sombrero for this Stetson. We're about the same size. They won't look close, and they won't see much by this light."

He tore off the big bandanna as he spoke and tossed it to Rankin, and then he took Rankin's and knotted it about his throat.

"You go right downstairs, Al, hummin' to yourself, and don't speak to nobody. Head for the stables. They'll think that you're going for somethin' you forgot in your saddlebags . . . somethin' *I* forgot, I mean. When you get in the stables, saddle my horse. It's the big gray, and it's a sound horse, if there ever was one. Then saddle your own horse . . . Gordon's bay. Take that horse out behind the barn and leave him there. Will he stand with the reins throwed over his head?"

"Sure he will."

"Then leave him there like that. After you've done that come out the front of the barn with my horse, climb on him, and lope off up the road, up the valley. You can break through, and before morning you'll be at your home. Keep off the main trail. They'll be watching there for you, but they won't watch at your house. Now, get out!"

"Lake," began Rankin, "after what I've done to you, this. . . ."

"Don't talk," cut in Bob Lake. "When I hear you talk, Rankin, it sort of riles me. I ain't doin' this for you. I'd be glad to see you planted full of holes or swingin' from a tree. That's where your happy home had ought to be. Get out. I'm sick of your face."

"All them kind things," murmured Al Rankin, "I'll remember. Someday I'll pay in full. S'long."

Without another word he adjusted the Stetson on his head and slipped softly out of the room. His first steps were soundless, but then Lake heard his heel striking heavily and caught

139

the burden of a tune the outlaw was humming. It was very good acting, but would someone downstairs see his face and halt him? Bob Lake waited breathlessly. Any moment there might be the report of a revolver. But the moments passed. There was the clatter of a back door swinging shut, and then, peering out the window, he saw a shadowy figure move toward the barn through the starlight. It was outlined distinctly against the whitewashed wall of the barn and then was swallowed in the blackness of the open doorway. The first step had been successfully taken.

Next he studied the shrubbery opposite the window. He had heard them say that this was the point at which Rankin, if alarmed, might attempt to break out, and two of them — the landlord and another — were posted yonder among the trees, keeping a vigilant watch on that window.

Yet through that window he must attempt to escape. For it was two-thirds of his plan to make them think that he was Rankin and to draw their pursuit after him. That would give the outlaw a clear break up the valley and toward his house. It would give him a chance to see his wife for the second time since their marriage, equip himself with plenty of funds, supply her with the location to which she should send him further relief, and, in short, give Al Rankin a flying start in his career of outlawry. Later, no doubt, the Rankin estate could buy off Gordon and the heirs of Hugh Smiley, and the prosecution would be dropped. Then Rankin could return and, accepting a short term in prison, could make a fresh start in life.

All of this was perfectly plain, but the difficult thing was to make that escape from the window. To attempt to pass down through the house would be madness. At this point in his thoughts he saw Rankin bring the gray out of the barn and climb into the saddle. Someone spoke to him from the hotel, and he returned a loud and cheery answer. There was no doubt that the fellow had plenty of nerve. But what if he had again betrayed his benefactor? In that case, even supposing Lake ran the gamut and reached the back of the barn in safety, it would only mean that he would be run down later on by odds of six to one. The thought made him cringe closer to the wall.

In the meantime, the tattoo of the departing horse sounded fainter and fainter in the distance and finally died out altogether. Then very softly Lake pushed up the window to its full height. Fortunately, there was no protesting squeak. He passed his legs through the window and sat on the sill, making ready for his start. They would not see him against the black square of the window; not until he began running would they note him.

He waited. The longer he delayed the farther away Rankin was riding, and the closer he drew to his goal. The longer he delayed the more this keen cold of the mountain air would be numbing the arms and fingers of the watchers who sat as sentinels yonder in the dark. That same cold was eating into him, and finally, for fear it should numb his own muscles, he determined to make the break for safety. It was no longer a game. If he were found in the clothes of Rankin, even though he were discovered not to be the wanted man, his shrift on earth would be short. What was the punishment for assisting an outlaw? If he were caught, it would be by a bullet that would ask and answer all its own questions.

He slipped completely out of the window and rose and lowered himself until his leg muscles were unlimbered. Then, crouching low so as to make a less important mark against the gray of the house, he started running, aiming his flight at the lower and farthest corner of the roof of the shed. The first step betrayed him. He had not counted on that and had hoped to cover most of the distance to the edge of the roof before he was noted by the watchers, but with the first fall of his foot the dry shingles crashed and crackled beneath him with a sound almost as loud as the report of a gun.

His alarm was answered by a yell from the shrubbery. Two bits of fire flashed like great fireflies, and at the same instant two deep reports came barking through the night. There was an ugly, whining whisper beside him. He knew that sound, and by its nearness he knew that expert marksmen were shooting.

He raced on with the smashing of the shingles beneath him, the yells of the sentinels beyond, and now a rapid fire of shots. Rifle shots, he supposed, by the depth of the tone. Yet he reached the corner of the roof before something swept across his forehead like the cut of a red-hot knife, moving at an incredible speed. There was no pain, but a stunning shock that cast him off his balance, and he floundered forward into thin air.

Only by luck he landed on sprawling hands and knees instead of on his feet. And that fall gave him a new lease on life. The marksmen had seen the fall, and now, ceasing fire, they ran toward him with yells of triumph.

He was up on his feet and racing away again like the wind. He saw them drop to their knees, heard their cursing, and once more the sing of bullets whipped around him. But this time the surprise had unsteadied them, and they shot wildly.

A moment later he had turned the corner of the barn, and one breathing space of security was left to him. But the horse? Had Al Rankin done as he was bidden, or had the selfish devil gone off without a single thought of the man he left behind him? That heart-breaking question was answered an instant later. Whipping around the farther corner of the barn, he saw the form of a tall horse, glimmering under the stars, and on

142

his back he recognized the bunched outlines of a saddle.

He reached that saddle with a single leap, and, sweeping up the hanging reins, a second later he was rejoicing in the first spring of the horse as the spurs touched his flanks. That very first leap spoke volumes to Lake as to the animal's running power. A fence shot up before them out of the night. Before he had well noted it, the horse rose and took it splendidly, the lurch of the jump hurling Lake far back in the saddle.

Yells and bullets came from the direction of the barn, but they were random shots. He shouted his defiance back at them and fired his revolver foolishly in the air. For they must know his direction. They must know that he was fleeing not up the valley toward the Rankin house, but across it toward the higher mountains. For that would give Al still further respite and make him certainly safe.

New sounds began behind him. He swung low in the saddle and listened away from the hoofbeats of his own horse. It was a steady drumming. The pursuit had already begun.

## XI

## " 'WRONG — ALL WRONG!' "

Twenty-four hours perceptibly changed the outlook of Paul Sumpter. He had an eye of not inconsiderable shrewdness for men, but with him men and money were inextricably entangled. He had been a banker on a small scale all his life, and property to him had an almost human appeal. The broad face of a meadow with a furrow turning black behind the plowshare was to him like beauty in a woman. A dense stand of yellow wheat with the wind rattling through it was a perfect symphony.

His opinion of Al Rankin began to change insensibly before he had been in the house a full hour. In the first place, it seemed a shame that the owner of such a property should be so evil. And that thought fathered the next, which was that the young fellow might not be entirely evil, and this in turn gave rise to the idea that there might be explanations. He had begun by insisting that Anne return with him to his home. He ended by blushing, when he remembered the folly of his advice.

Let it not be thought that the heart of Paul Sumpter was no larger than his money bags. He was a generous man. But he had thought in terms of dollars for so long that, like many a rich man, an oil painting could be actually beautiful to him because fifty thousand dollars had been paid for it and the pedigree of a Thoroughbred became an entrancing study because its appeal to the bank account was so intimate and real.

He would have been the first to denounce such an attitude, but unconsciously he had come to feel that poverty was a sin. Naturally wealth became a virtue. He was very humble about himself, because his own affairs in money were very moderate.

In a word Paul Sumpter, having denounced Al Rankin and all that appertained to him, looked out the window and beheld the noble pine trees marching up the mountains — timber to build a whole city — and the violence of his rage abated. He turned from the window, and his heel, that was intended to crash against the floor, was muffled in its fall by a rug of exquisite depth. Sinking thoughtfully into a chair, its softness embraced him and wooed him to stay, while his fingers strayed idly over the delicacy of the velvet upholstery. When he sat at the table that night opposite his daughter — how far she was removed by the noble length of that table — it

144

seemed to him that her beauty acquired a new luster from the beauty of the silver and the shimmer of the glass. From the luxurious depths of a chair, a little later, he expanded his hands toward the blaze of a great fire and accepted with sleepy pleasure a long and black and thick cigar that his daughter brought him in a fragrant humidor. He noted the white turn of her wrist as she lighted that cigar for him.

"By heaven, Anne, dear," he said, "you were cut out for the wife of a rich man. And what's more," he added, drawing strongly on the cigar, and then pausing to let the smoke waft toward the ceiling, "what's more, you've found him. You waited, and you found him."

Wrinkles of amused understanding came at the corners of her eyes. She knew him and understood his frailties. Sometimes it seems that a woman loves a man actually on account of his faults. Saints are usually loved by posterity alone. Paul Sumpter was by no means a saint, and Anne, knowing it, gained her power over him by never letting him see that she understood. Nothing is so ruinous to domestic peace as that. When a family man feels that his native mystery has vanished, he cringes behind his newspaper.

"I suppose I have," she said, and went back to her chair so that she could indulge herself in a smile while her back was turned. Her face was perfectly grave, when he saw it again.

"Just now," went on Paul Sumpter, "things look a little blue. But we'll have them out of that. Oh, yes, we'll straighten affairs. There are ways."

She remembered his mingled indignation, despair, and rage earlier in the day. And again the wrinkles of mirth came around her eyes. Her father did not see; he was watching the cigar smoke mount in fat, blue-brown wreaths.

"What ways, Dad?"

"Ways of money with men. Al has followed a foolish . . . er

145

. . . impulse . . . and has broken the law. What's the law? Men! What do men listen to? Money! Who has the money? Al has it. There you are."

He smiled beneficently on her and waited for admiration. And he received it. It was always her habit to slip in the little verbal pat on the back whenever she could.

"It sounds wonderful, Dad, but is it possible?"

"Of course, it's possible. What's against him? The Smiley family . . . that's all. Aren't they poor as rats? Five thousand would make them swear their souls away and bring them weeping with joy to Al Rankin. Then there's Gordon, you say? Tush! I go to him and give him some straight talk . . . 'Boy made a few mistakes, but he's good at heart. Wants a new start. Just married. Ready to settle down. I'll answer for him. Besides, here's the value of your horse plus the reward you offered.' I guess that would hold Mister Gordon, whoever he is. Suppose the case comes to trial? No evidence . . . no weeping relatives of Smiley to appear. A yokel of a district attorney against a real man of the law such as I could get. Why, girl, don't you see how it will come out?"

"But there's one other . . . the only living eyewitness . . . Bob Lake."

"He didn't see the shot fired," said her father. "If he wants to talk, can't he be bought off as well as the others? Tut, he knows which side his bread is buttered on. What other reason has he for working for Al now?"

"Oh," sighed the girl. "You think he's like the rest?"

"Why not?"

"I wonder."

"But there's no use worrying about him. He's already with us."

"You don't think I'll have to leave here and go home, Dad?"

146

He flushed a little. "I was excited when I said that. Hadn't a chance to look over the ground of the case. Needlessly excited, my dear, that's all. Now, don't worry. If Al can only be kept out of danger until we have this thing straightened out. . . ."

"He will be kept out of danger."

"You're so sure?"

"Bob Lake will see to it."

"Yes! Remarkable fellow! I'll see to it that he's rewarded."

"How?"

"With money, my dear. How else?"

"Do you really think that money would do for him?" Anne asked her father.

"How else, then? Do you think he's working for us for nothing?"

"I don't know," replied the girl. "I don't know."

For it had started a train of thoughts that had run through her brain too often of late. What would be the result for Bob Lake? At the idea of a money reward she shivered. Of course, she would have to prevent such an offer to him. Before she had finished that thought, there was a swish of a door swung swiftly open, and she looked up into the face of her husband.

There followed without a word spoken an instant of hurried movements. Her father ran tiptoe to one door and closed and locked it; she did the same for another; and Al Rankin tended to the one through which he had entered.

She came back slowly, a little timidly, waiting for him with a smile and with gentle eyes. He had not a glance for her.

"First," he said, "money! I need the coin."

"Certainly, my boy. How much?"

Paul Sumpter had drawn out his fat wallet. It was snatched from his hand and pocketed by the outlaw. Sumpter stared blankly at his own open hand.

"That'll do for a while," said Al Rankin. "I'll tell you where to send more. Now a gun!"

"You have one in the holster."

"I need two. One might jam on me, and then where'd I be? I need two!"

"Al," asked Sumpter, "you're not going to fight?"

"What do you think? Lie down and let them grab me? Not me! This is a game, and I'm going to play it." He threw his clenched fist above his head and laughed in silent exultation. "What's happened?" he continued, firing the question at them like a shot. "What's been doing around here? And where are the servants? That rat-eyed Charley . . . where's he?"

All vestiges of a smile had been brushed from the face of Anne Rankin, and all softness was faded from her eyes, and they were now hard and steady. Al passed close to her as he went around the table, and she shrank back, but this he did not note.

"Nothing has happened. They haven't been near the house, but I know they're watching the approaches. How in the world did you get through?"

"Night before last. It was a squeeze, but I made it. What's that?" He whirled, his teeth showing under a lifted upper lip. There was a far-away sound of a door closing. "Try . . . try the hall. Look out!" he commanded.

The command was directed to Anne, but she did not stir. Her father covered the embarrassing part of that moment by going himself to obey the order. He unlocked the door, peered out, and turned back into the room, forgetting to lock the door.

"Someone must have gone out. There's not a soul or a sound in the hall."

"All right."

Anne raised her head. "You've met Bob Lake?" She pointed to his bandanna and the Stetson hat that he wore crushed onto the back of his head.

"You're sharp-eyed, ain't you?" he asked. "Been looking pretty close at this Lake fellow, and he at you? The idiot! Well, don't forget that I'm watching you both."

There was no avoiding or explaining away the pointed ugliness of his voice. It brought a stifled exclamation from Paul Sumpter. But the girl smiled in an odd manner, and she met his eyes with a steadiness which in another than his wedded wife might have seemed contempt. He turned, fumbled in a cabinet, and brought out a second revolver, looked to its mechanism, and then laid it on the table.

"You met Bob Lake," she went on. "What happened?"

"Him?" He tossed up his head and favored her with a wolfish grin. "The skunk tried to play the crook with me."

"The fiend," said Sumpter softly.

"The fiend he is," asserted Al Rankin calmly. "But I paid him his dues. He ran onto me in a crossroads hotel . . . found me in my room. Then he went down and warned the people that I was there and came back to me."

Anne had sunk in a chair where she sat very erect, her fingers clutching the arms until the knuckles whitened.

"The dirty dog," breathed Paul Sumpter. "Anne, I knew there was something behind that cur's actions. I'll have him skinned alive for this and run out of the country, if there's a law in it."

"There ain't any law for gents like him," said Rankin. "He's too smooth to get caught."

"Go on," said Anne, strangely without emotion. "Tell us what happened after that?"

"After that? Well, when he come back to the room, I gave him a look. The hound smiled too much to please me. I

149

waited a minute. Then I asked him point-black what he was up to. What d'you think he did?"

"What?" asked Paul Sumpter.

"Went for his gun!"

From the corner of his eye he became aware that Anne was smiling a mirthless smile, and the sight disturbed him a trifle.

"Great Cæsar!" said Sumpter. "And what did you do?"

"Didn't waste a bullet on him. I knocked the skunk head over heels."

"Good. I'd have given a thousand to see you do it."

"Then I tied and gagged him and took his hat and bandanna, and with that I managed to get away. The others thought it was his outfit and let me pass . . . there wasn't much light. And that's all there is to Mister Bob Lake."

"I knew it!" said Sumpter, striking his fist into his open palm. "Something in the face of that fellow that I distrusted the first time I saw him."

"You think pretty good . . . backwards," replied Al Rankin. "Point is I got clean away from him."

"Wrong," said a soft voice behind him. "All wrong, Al."

He whirled. The door into the hall had been opened silently, and Bob Lake stood in the arch. His revolver was at his hip, pointing at Rankin.

## XII

## " 'PLUMB HOLLOW INSIDE' "

Instinctively Rankin made one impulsive clutch for his revolver, but an imperative jerk to the side of Lake's weapon discouraged him.

"Don't do it, Al," said Lake. "I told you before I'd had a hunch that I'd blow your head off one of these days, and now I got an idea that the time has come."

"Sumpter!" implored Rankin.

"Stay where you are, you thick-headed fool," said Bob Lake. "And you, girl, stay where you are. I'm watching all three of you. You're wrong . . . the whole bunch of you."

Anne was on her feet.

"It shows that playing square don't count and don't pay. I'm a fool to bother with you, but first I'm going to get the truth out of this hound, and then I'm going to wash my hands of the whole gang of you." He stretched back to the door, and with his left hand, feeling behind him, he turned the lock. "These walls are tolerable thick," he said, "and I don't think that a rumpus here would get much notice in the house. Rankin, you and me has got to have it out here. Understand?"

Paul Sumpter had backed up step by step against the wall as though an invisible hand shoved him, and, even when his shoulders struck the wall, he still wriggled as though he hoped to work his way through it.

"Now," said Bob Lake, "I want that gun you got there, Al. I want it bad. No, don't hurry. Move slow, Al, move slow. Pull back that hand of yours like you was liftin' a hundred pounds instead of a gun. Then bring the gun out careful . . . mighty careful . . . because, if I got to complain, this gat of mine'll do my talkin' for me. That's right. Now take it by the barrel. There you are. No flips, Al. Nothin' fancy. Just shove that gun of yours onto the table. And now we're nearly ready."

Al Rankin was trembling like a man with ague, and he raved at the others. "Sumpter . . . Anne . . . are you tongue-tied? Give a yell. Get somebody in here."

"There ain't going to be any noise," stated Bob Lake.

"There ain't going to be a whisper. You figure on that, Sumpter. You figure on that, ma'am."

She made a little motion toward him, but once more he failed to see, and certainly he failed to understand.

"Now," he continued, "since I've started in preaching, I'm going to finish the sermon. I'm going to tell you what's wrong with you, Al. You're like a kid that needs a thrashing. When a kid don't get the whip once in a while, he goes wrong. He gets wild. He turns bad, but maybe he ain't quite as bad as he thinks. One taste of the whip would straighten him out and bring him to time. Well, Al, that's the trouble with you. You need the whip. And I'm it. I'm the whip!" Then he shoved his gun back into his holster. There was a slow gravity about this that was more impressive than any burst of violent action.

"I'm going to lick you, Al," went on the cowpuncher slowly. "I think you're a better man than I am with a gun. But what are guns for? Cowards. Cowards, Al, like yourself. Yaller hounds, like yourself, gents that practice till they're perfect and then go out and pick a fight. Fight? No, it ain't a fight, it's a murder, when a gent like you picks on an ordinary 'puncher. Fists are what we were meant to fight with, and fists it's going to be today. I know you're a fast one with your hands, Al, but what I'm going to trust is the muscle that come out of labor. You see you're a gentleman, Al, by all accounts. I'm a cowpuncher, plain and simple. And I'm goin' to bulldog you the way I'd bulldog a yearlin' . . . if I can. Now step up and put up your hands. Unless . . . you'll tell this lady what was the truth of the last time I met you?"

The alarm had been gradually fading from the face of Al Rankin. As Bob Lake said, Al was fast with his hands. Careful boxing instruction had trained him, and he knew how to use his great strength to the greatest advantage. Now he smiled with savage satisfaction.

152

"Why, you fool," he said, "I'll bust you in two! Tell 'em the truth? I've already told 'em the truth."

On the heels of that speech he leaped in with a left arm that shot out with the precision of a piston and thudded squarely on the jaw of Bob Lake. The weight of the blow carried him before it and drove him back until his shoulders were against the wall, but Al Rankin, instead of following, made for the table where his gun lay. To his astonishment the girl intercepted him like a flash. She snatched up the heavy weapon and leveled it at him, her eyes on fire with anger and excitement.

"A fair fight, Al Rankin. That's all he asked from you, and he'll have it."

The beast came up in the face of Rankin as he glared at her. He would have sprung in to wrest away the gun, but a merciless coldness in her bearing told him she meant what she said.

"You've swung over to him, eh? I'll attend to you later on. You. . . ."

He had to whirl before he had finished the sentence and meet the rush of Bob Lake. For the first blow had stung the cowpuncher rather than dazed him, and he came in now furiously, a terrifying figure. The bandage around his forehead was thickly stained. The jar of the first blow had opened the shallow wound where the rifle bullet had skinned across the flesh of his brow, and now a thin trickle went down his face.

Al Rankin, wheeling, smashed out with both hands, and both hands struck the mark. The weight of the punches held up Lake, but in he came again. A lightning side-step made him charge into thin air, and, before he could change direction, a heavy blow behind the ear knocked him sprawling.

He was badly dazed by the fall, and Al Rankin whining with beastly satisfaction caught up a heavy stool and swung it

153

around his head. That blow would have ended the fight and Bob Lake, but the shrill voice of the girl cut in on Rankin.

"Drop it, or I'll shoot you, Al. Drop it and fight fair, or I swear I'll shoot!"

He aimed a curse at her, cast the stool away, and sprang in on Bob Lake, who was rising slowly to his feet. He came in rashly. Sure of his man he paid no attention to his own guard, and the result was that Lake, lunging low with the full power of his big body behind the blow, drove his fist fairly into the ribs of the other. The impact sounded heavily through the room, and Paul Sumpter groaned in sympathy.

Al Rankin was not too much hurt to side-step, but this time Lake did not rush blindly. Instead, he followed his man slowly with a bulldog steadiness, and he dealt out bone-breaking blows with either hand, swinging full-arm punches, four out of five of which were blocked by the skill of Al Rankin, but the fifth blow went home with cruel effect.

He was taking terrible punishment in the meantime. The cutting, darting fists of Rankin battered his face and played a tattoo on his body, but still Lake came in like a tide with a re-sistless force.

There was dead silence in the room except for the impacts of the blows and the panting of the fighters. Paul Sumpter cowered against the wall in terror, but the girl stood erect, swaying a little, following the battle with a fierce interest as though she gloried in it. And the revolver was never lowered in her hand.

There was a short, half-stifled cry from Al Rankin. He had smashed both fists fairly into the face of Bob Lake, and yet he had failed to stop the rush of the latter. The sneering con-tempt and confidence with which Rankin began the battle had changed to a wild-eyed fear. His own strength was failing him, but the strength of Lake, built on the ranges, remained.

It grew with the taste of battle, apparently. If ever he came to close quarters, the end would be near.

Al Rankin sensed it, and he used every trick he knew to keep away. If it had been the open, he might have succeeded through his lightness of foot, but the walls of the room confined him. Finally, he leaped aside from a swinging blow, and, as he leaped, his shoulder struck the wall. He sprang back, and his shoulders struck against the corner. He was fairly trapped, and now Bob Lake came lunging, head down, arms circling, and caught his enemy under the armpits.

The minute those bear arms circled him the last strength left the body of Rankin. He remembered a fight he had once seen — a fight that he had egged on. It had been like this — bulldog against wolf. And finally, when the bulldog cornered his man, the ending had been horrible to see — a hurricane of short blows that battered the body and face of the wolf to a shapeless pulp. No quarter, either. Al Rankin gave up.

At the very point where Bob Lake had expected the crucial test, he found a form of putty in his embrace, and then the harsh scream of terror from Rankin's lips — "Help!"

He jerked his hand over the shoulder of the man and crushed his hand against the lips. The wild, horrible eyes stared at him — the plea and the terror of a cornered beast. Bob Lake shook himself free with a snort of disgust. Rankin, that support suddenly removed, was cowering against the wall.

"I knew it," said Lake. "I knew it. Plumb hollow inside . . . a bluff. A yaller quitter. Look at him!"

He stood back so that the others could see the better, and Al Rankin crouched and shuddered. His eyes flashed here and there, seeking escape and finding none — finding disgust even on the face of Paul Sumpter, his gaze reverted to Lake.

"He . . . he'll kill me," said Rankin. "Anne . . . Sumpter . . . take him off."

"If she asks me," said Bob Lake slowly. "Otherwise, I'm just beginning on you, Al. Down on your knees and beg her to call me off."

To the horror of them all, Al Rankin dropped to his knees. "Anne . . . say a word. . . ."

She covered her face. "Bob Lake," she whispered.

And Bob Lake drew back. "It's the end for you, Al," he said with a certain amount of pity in his voice. "It's the complete end for you. You've been showed up, and your color is yaller . . . like a dog's. This is just the beginning of what's coming. The next gent that meets up with you, you'll buckle to. You'll be afraid. You can't help it. You'll be scared that he'll call your bluff the way I've called it. You'll take water going down the line. You ain't going to be hung because you ain't worth the price of a rope. Get up, Rankin, and git out of the house and never come back."

It was long after the divorce; it was long after Anne Sumpter Rankin had become Anne Lake. Bob Lake was a little less lean of face, a little less brown of hand. But happiness had kept the eyes of Anne like the eyes of a girl. They had gone to New York to celebrate the end of a prosperous season. Stepping out of a taxicab one night, they encountered a beggar, unshaven, thin-shouldered, thrusting his lank, white hand before them.

Anne Lake dropped a little shower of silver into it. She would have paused, for something in the beggar interested her, but her husband drew her on.

"But do you know," she said, "that I thought I recognized that face?"

"Maybe you did," said Bob Lake. "Maybe it was something you saw in a bad dream. Nothing more'n that."

# Stolen Gold

## A Reata Story

Frederick Faust's original title for this story was "Stolen Gold." Street & Smith's *Western Story Magazine*, where it was first published in the issue for December 23, 1933 under the byline George Owen Baxter, changed the title to "Reata's Danger Trail." This was the fourth short novel to feature Reata who had proven to be one of Faust's most popular characters. There would be seven short novels in all about Reata. The first of these, "Reata," appears in THE FUGITIVE'S MISSION (Five Star Westerns, 1997). The second, "The Whisperer," is to be found in THE LOST VALLEY (Five Star Westerns, 1998). The third, "King of the Rats," is to be found in THE GAUNTLET (Five Star Westerns, 1998). In this fourth story of the saga, Reata, having completed his three labors for Pop Dickerman, attempts now to set up a household with Miriam the Gypsy, only to be required again by Dickerman and the three henchmen Reata previously liberated to perform yet one more labor.

## I

### "THE HOLD-UP"

Dave Bates had the outside job. Next to Gene Salvio, he was the best shot of the three, but they had matched for the choice position, and the turn of the coin insisted that Harry Quinn should go inside with Salvio.

The outside job was the easiest, because, if the two inside men were both shot up without being able to complete the robbery of the bank, Bates could slide away undetected. But if the two came out with the stuff, he had his share of the trouble. Also, he had to watch the main door and see that, if a disturbance started inside the place, no sudden rescuers poured in from the street, no men with guns in their hands.

The day was still and very hot. It was ten in the morning, when there is just enough slant to the sun to give it a fuller whack at the body. There was not a horse, not a wagon, not a man, not a dog, or even a chicken in the crooked little main street of Jumping Creek. The sun was making itself felt, and the wooden and canvas awnings bravely stretched out their arms and threw a gentle shadow down to the ground. The heat of the day was enough to make one, at a stroke, understand the whole nature of the people who live south of the Río Grande. It made one want to sit still and trust time.

But Dave Bates could not trust time. He had to trust, instead, to his two partners inside the bank, to the two revolvers under his coat, and to the rifles that lay aslant in the saddle holsters under the right stirrup leathers of three of the saddles.

The other two horses would not be backed by men. They were on hand to carry a heavy load, and the load would be gold, if all went well. A powerful canvas saddlebag hung on each side of both saddles.

When Dave Bates thought of the ponderous, unwieldy nature of such a metal as gold, he cursed the stuff and wondered why a bank had to be loaded down with that stuff, instead of light, crisp, new, delightful banknotes? And his lean face, that looked as though it had been compressed in a mold to half of the proper width, twisted crookedly to the side. Then he glanced up toward the mountains that, in the distance, flowed away into the pallor of the skies. Of course, that was the answer, and out of the rocky sides of those mountains the gold was worked and the ore ground and washed, and so, in driblets, the precious stuff was brought down to Jumping Creek.

Well, as soon as the work had been finished, Dave Bates hoped that they would get out among those mountains. And he reached a hand under his coat and touched the handle of one of his Colts, already well warmed by his body. Then he drew himself up to the full of his five feet and five inches, and expanded his scrawny chest. The two guns were what made a man of him. People could laugh down a little fellow like Dave Bates, but they could not laugh down his guns.

What he prayed was that Gene Salvio would not be too hasty with his weapons. Guns are all very well, but they ought to be used with discretion. Otherwise a fellow had blood on his trail. Invisible blood, perhaps, but nevertheless damning. In a wide and careless country like the West, many crimes are forgotten. They wash away. But murder sticks worse than soot. Dave Bates knew all about it, and now he remembered the savage eyes of Gene Salvio and wished that he, not Harry Quinn, had walked into the bank with Salvio. He might be a stronger influence to keep Gene in check, if a pinch should happen to come. In the meantime, the seconds went by, with gigantic strides, measured by the pounding of the heart of Bates.

And then it came, like the crash of two mighty hammers brought together, face to face, or like the sudden first stroke of a booming bell — a gunshot in the bank. And then a voice screaming out. It might be a woman; it might be a man. Pain unsexed the sound. No, it was the scream of a man. No woman would cry so loudly.

Words came babbling through the screeching. That was the voice of Gene Salvio, snarling, raging, threatening, and then came three more revolver shots in rapid succession — just the way Salvio knew how to fan them out of his gun.

The street had been empty a moment before. Suddenly there was life in the shadows, here and there. Then someone shouted: "The bank! They're after it!" Men came on the run. They came from up the street and down the street. They came with naked guns, glittering in their hands.

Dave Bates thought what an easy life robbers have in other parts of the world. But who would choose a life of crime in the West, where men go armed and know how to use their weapons almost as well as though they had to live by powder and lead?

Like two counter waves the men of Jumping Creek rushed toward him. His heart shrank in his body. He wanted to run. His queer half face grew longer and smaller and twisted more to one side.

Instead of running, he remembered that code which he had learned long years before. A bad code to live by, but a good code to die by. Stand by your fellows in crime, and never let them down. That code had brought him through many a dark moment and stained him black enough. Now it made him step suddenly back from the horses with a gun in each hand.

Inside the bank, the screaming had died away to a deep, pulsating groan. Footfalls were scuffling in there.

Bates shouted: "Get back on your heels, all of you! Drop them guns and hold back. Watch lively now!" And he fired a bullet just over the head of a chunky man with gray hair and a black mustache.

The two advancing waves of armed humanity wavered, halted, and then swayed back and forth for a moment, uncertainly. If a single leader had sprung out now, to give the men new impetus, they would have closed over Dave Bates with a single rush, and he knew it. He even saw one about to act — a slender, tall youth with a ridiculously bright Mexican outfit on him. This fellow wavered less than the others. He began to crouch a little, with a wild look in his eyes.

Dave Bates drove a bullet into the ground at his feet and knocked dust over his boots as high as his knees.

"I'm watching you *hombres*. Back up!" he shouted. "I'm goin' to let a streak of light through some of you."

Suddenly the tall young man stood up straight and pressed back. He had had enough. He wanted to be a hero. He wanted desperately to be a hero. He wanted desperately to be brave, but his courage had not quite hardened in his breast. He was just a year or so too old or too young. Who could say?

The whole crowd gave back on either hand, and then Salvio and Harry Quinn came out, staggering with the weights they carried.

Gold — they were staggering under weights of gold!

Harry Quinn was a strong man, but he grunted as he heaved up a chamois sack and dumped it onto one of the empty saddlebags.

Someone in the crowd — well back toward the rear — yelled out: "Are we goin' to be bluffed out by three thugs? Come on, boys! All together. One rush and we got 'em! They're cleanin' us out of all our cash!"

The crowd was stirred by that appeal, but it was not stirred enough. The sight of Dave Bates, as he kept his body swinging a little from side to side, was too disheartening — the sight of him, and his lean hands that held the guns with such familiar ease, just a little above the height of the hip, his

161

thumbs resting on the hammers. He could turn loose a torrent of lead from those weapons, and each man, as the little figure swayed, felt the dark muzzles of the guns draw across him like knives. The vast emptiness of death yawned at them from the little round barrels of the Colts.

So they hung there, in suspense, willing to be brave, but held back by the lack of a dashing leader. One man able to take one step forward would have loosed a double avalanche capable of smashing the life out of that band of three, but no man dared take the single step.

The two extra horses were loaded — well loaded. And more of those small chamois bags were dropped into the saddlebags on the horses that would have to carry riders, also.

"Ready!" snapped the voice of Gene Salvio.

"Ready!" said Harry Quinn.

Gene Salvio leaped into the saddle on his black horse. How beautiful all those horses were, well chosen for strength and for speed. But far better-looking was Gene Salvio, as he sat in the saddle with laughter on his lips and the devil in his eyes. Men shrank away from him. They looked down. They did not want those eyes to single them out, because they saw that this man was ready and willing and eager to kill. They could see that gold was only an excuse. It was blood that the fellow really wanted.

Dave Bates and Quinn mounted in turn. Salvio was unencumbered on the black. Both Harry Quinn and Bates led one of the extra horses. They moved forward.

Gene Salvio said: "You fellows get on ahead. Go slow and steady. And keep looking into their eyes. Mind the windows and the doors, too, but mostly mind the windows. Go on ahead. I'll take care of these gents behind us."

Admiration warmed the heart of Dave Bates. To be sure, Salvio might have been a little too ready with his guns, back there in the bank, but he was also the fellow to push them safely through the crisis that he had helped to bring on by his rash bloodthirstiness. Watching the windows — that was a good idea. Of course, there might be men at any of these windows, and the doors, too, were open mouths out of which the dragon danger might rush at them.

He heard Salvio shouting: "Stand back there! You in the black hat . . . don't move your hand like that ag'in! Give us room through here, or we're going to take room, and the room we're going to take is going to be vacant for a hell of a while after we're gone!"

It was well expressed, thought Dave Bates. There was really a brain in the head of that fellow Gene Salvio.

The crowd, in fact, was bearing back. As the robbers went through the street, there was silence around them, but there was a shrill murmur ahead of them and a growling murmur behind them. Men in that crowd began to shift their eyes from one face to another, trying to find that most needed thing — a leader, a man to cry out a single, right word. And still there was not a voice raised. Still there was only that same muttering, that helpless, groaning sound which only a crowd can make.

Then some of the cleverer heads, foreseeing that it would be hard to start the fight in that humor, broke away from the crowd and went for horses.

The end of the main street came under the eyes of Dave Bates. He looked out toward the foothills and the great mountains and felt that he was safe with his portion of the loot. Then he heard the beating of hoofs here and there on the outskirts of the town, and then flying down the narrows of the streets, and he knew, with a grim pull at the corners of his mouth, that the trouble was only starting.

# II

## "THE PURSUIT"

The noise of the horses was almost enough to make Dave Bates call for action on his own part, but he knew well enough that it was best to leave decisions and commands to the outstanding man of the party, and that man was certainly the famous Gene Salvio. So Bates said nothing but, like his companions, kept two steady guns turned toward the crowd.

He had never done anything like this before. To face a gang in this manner was very much like facing a vast, a dangerous, but a witless monster. If it knew its strength, it would be heedless of the small harm that could happen to it and would instantly take revenge. For what would be the death of two or three of its members — to the rest of the crowd?

By a pretense, by a sham, they were holding back the others. And, in that way, they came to the cluster of trees around the bridge at the end of Jumping Creek. There Salvio at last gave the word, and, with a rush, they galloped their horses around the curve, and thunder boomed from the planks as they rushed over the bridge.

A storm of bullets followed them. The bullets crackled like hail through the trees, whistled like invisible, incredible birds through the air. By the thickness with which they flew, the numbers of the crowd could be estimated, but already there was a rising shoulder of ground that gave the low-stooping fugitives shelter, and now they could sit erect, well down the winding road.

Dave Bates looked back at the saddlebags that jumped at the side of the led horses. There must be five hundred pounds, or thereabouts, between the pair. And another hundred pounds of the gold had been given to each rider. Say almost eight hundred pounds of gold nuggets and dust! It was not a very difficult bit of arithmetic to work the thing out. Somewhere around a hundred and eighty-five thousand dollars, at least. Split back one third to Pop Dickerman who had suggested the job and who had fixed the cashier in order to find out when the greatest available sum would be in the safe of the bank. That left about a hundred and twenty thousand. And this carved up into forty thousand bucks per man. Forty thousand dollars — and all in gold!

There was an ache in the head and a pull across the eyes of Dave Bates that had come there from facing out the crowd so long. This ache began to pass away. He wanted to laugh. He saw that Gene Salvio and Harry Quinn were already laughing. They were good fellows, thought Bates. Quinn was something of a brute, at times, and Salvio was always something of a wildcat. But in a time of necessity you want a man who knows his job and can do it. This pair knew their work, and they could do it. The heart of Bates swelled.

He did not even have to be troubled about the rather dim worry of having robbed poor men. The miners had been paid. There were only the great, million-headed corporations to consider, and to Dave Bates they were not worthy of consideration. He felt, almost, that he had honestly earned forty thousand dollars. Other men had found it and grubbed it. He had earned it by endangering his life.

As they pulled up the road, Salvio swung into the lead from the rear, and, when they came to a cross trail, Salvio without hesitation took the dimmer way, forcing his horse up steep rocks along the slope of a hill. This seemed a dubious policy to Dave Bates. The point of it, however, was clear. Far behind them could be heard the hoofs of many horses, rolling like the rolling of drums, and it was probable that the blind mob of riders from Jumping Creek would pour heedlessly up the wider road, looking for no sign, heads high to catch a glimpse, around a bend, of the three riders and the five horses that they wanted. Therefore, instead of heading straight on toward the mountain wilderness that would give them sure covering, Gene Salvio intended to dodge the first rush of the pursuit, save the strength of the five horses, and angle off at a new direction, even though the mountains in this quarter were farther away.

In fact, when they got over the head of the hill, Salvio actually brought the horses back to a walk. Considering the necessity which spurred them all forward, this seemed to Bates like standing still. He would not complain about it, however. To complain, in a time of need, of what is actually being commanded by the leader, is a foolish thing, as a rule. However, it was all right to ask questions about the past.

"Look here, Gene," he said. "What happened in there? You started the shooting?"

"Aw," said Salvio, "there was a fool of a red-headed kid. I never seen a redhead with any brains. Their hair is so hot that it burns their brains dry. You know how it is. Well, this redhead was hanging around. Kind of like a chore boy. After I'd got the gun on the cashier, the redhead pulls a gat out of a drawer. I let him have it. A funny thing . . . I aimed for his head, because I wanted to put him out quick. It's better to put 'em out quick, in a time like that. Just a wound don't do so much good. They gotta flop and stay down, dead. That sort of discourages the rest of the boys a little. Well, redhead seen the trouble coming, and, while he swings up his gun, he puts a hand out before him. Imagine trying to ward off a bullet, eh?

Anyway, that slug of mine went right through his hand and his wrist.

"The funny thing was that it *did* seem to turn my bullet a little. It just ripped along the side of his head, and he falls down and starts moaning over his hand. And then he starts screeching. You could've heard him in the street."

"You could've heard him in hell," said Dave Bates sincerely. "He sure raised the hair on my head, and he raised a crowd, too."

"You handled that crowd fine," said Harry Quinn.

"Yeah, you done your job," remarked Gene Salvio, who rarely praised others.

"Then you turned loose three more," said Bates.

"That was for the cashier," said Salvio. "Pop Dickerman, you remember, said for us to cover him up pretty good, if we could manage it. So, since I'd already heard the crowd gathering, I thought that a little more noise wouldn't do any harm, and I turned loose on the cashier. Like I wanted to drop him. I put three bullets in the air, and he curled up on the floor and died . . . he was scared to death, pretty near." Salvio began to laugh, rather guardedly.

And in fact, the trees that so slowly retreated around them seemed to be looking down gravely, watchfully, disapprovingly upon the trio of robbers.

Then, far behind them, on the other side of the hill, they heard the men of Jumping Creek go by like a storm. They listened, looked at one another, and then grinned.

"The gents that stay inside the law, they don't seem to have very good brains in their heads," said Salvio. "Ever notice that? They're always wrong."

"But when they're right, they hang a lot of gents from the trees," suggested Dave Bates. For his own part, he did not like crowing until a job was well finished and the danger gone.

167

They came down off the slope and turned up through a pleasant valley that ran near the railroad line. In the distance, they could see the flash of the wheel-polished rails with the sunlight running on them like swift water, tinted blue. The trail was dim. They left it and took the straight way up the valley. This was still a longer way to the higher mountains and security, but, again, it would save the horses. And Dave Bates knew the value of fresh horses in any pinch. His admiration for Salvio was growing every moment when, from behind, they heard a horse neigh.

The three robbers looked suddenly at one another.

"What could that be?" asked Harry Quinn, scowling. He stared back over his shoulder. Then, with a groan, he pointed.

Bates saw the picture that came out of the trees behind them. There were a dozen men, all with rifles, all riding hard, and at the head of them journeyed a tall man with a face so thin that his features stood out in a relief of highlights and shadows, even from this distance. He rode on a small, mouse-colored mustang, that looked more mule than horse. It took small strides, but so many of them that it easily kept in the lead. This man now turned and waved to his companions, and then pointed ahead where the robbers were in full flight.

Well, it was bad luck that somebody among the men of Jumping Creek had guessed that the fugitives might take the way over the short trail, uphill. However, this would be the point where freshness of horses would tell. Goodness of horses would tell, too, and the one thing on which Pop Dickerman never spared money was the sort of horseflesh with which he provided his missionaries of crime.

All five animals legged it valiantly, and in an instant it was clear that they had the wind and the foot of the pursuit.

They swerved along the edge of a marsh. They sped up a

slope. They twisted through a denseness of trees. And then, suddenly, Salvio in the lead drew rein so hard that his horse stopped on braced legs, the hoofs plowing up the ground.

"There's somebody ahead!" he called softly.

Then Bates heard it, too. Right and left, as though spread out in a long line, he heard horses coming. He heard the shrill, penetrating squeak of saddle leather, and the far-off murmurs of voices. He could see clearly what had happened. The men of Jumping Creek had divided. Half had taken the rear trail of the robbers; half had swung around the hill and blocked the robbers in their advance of the valley. Now they were blocked as neatly as though they had been cooped in a box!

## III

### "THE MARSH"

They could turn left — up the staggering face of a rocky hill, treeless, bare, open to a sweeping rifle fire. Or else they could turn right into the stench, the mud, the puzzling mists and vapors of the marsh. Gene Salvio took the only possible course. He swung the black horse to the side and struck right into the marsh, and, as Bates followed, last of the three, a sudden uproar of voices, a sudden crash of rifle fire, told him that he had been seen.

That made their chances one point worse. He liked to estimate chances. When the crowd gathered in the street of Jumping Creek, their chances of getting away had been about one in three. After they cleared out of town and escaped the first rifle fire, they had chances of two to one in their favor.

When they put the high hill behind them and swung up the easy grade of the valley that contained the railroad, they had chances of four to one in their favor. Even the sight of the pursuit in the rear only decreased their chances by a point. Then that encounter with the unseen line of riders, blocking their way, beat them down to the bottom. They had one chance in five, as they turned into the marsh. They were seen, and they had a chance in six.

Salvio called, with inimitable cheer: "We'll get to the railroad, and we'll gallop up the ties and laugh our heads off at those fools!"

Bates looked forward and saw Salvio riding his horse out of a depth of thick, green slime that mantled the fine creature from the ears down and altered its color completely. Salvio was the fellow with the heart and the brain. Of course, that was the trick. To reach the railroad, and then to rush down the open way at full speed, out of the marsh, and then to cut either to one side or to the other — that was the thing, that was the thing. The heart of Dave Bates rose in him. Ah, what a thing a brain is in a good man! You can have your good men, if you want; Dave Bates wanted a man with a brain; he wanted a fellow like Gene Salvio.

The marsh was a horror. It was black water and green wood. And firm, grassy ground turned into a horrible muddy wash through which the horses broke. But they floundered on, keeping right behind Gene Salvio — who had the knowing brain.

They held on. Presently the foulness of the marsh, the thickness of the trees that made a hot twilight, here, in the middle of the day, gave way to glimpses of light, and suddenly they were out on the side of the railroad grade, with Gene Salvio already cutting the wires of the big fence.

Two strands had hardly clanged apart and whipped back

under the clippers of Salvio, when voices shouted to the side, and Dave Bates had a sight of a tall man with a face as thin as starvation, riding a little mouse-colored mustang out from the edge of the marsh. He had found a solid way across the marsh — there was hardly a bit of mud above the hocks of his mustang.

Bates, as he backed his horse violently, saw the stream of armed men break out behind that leader. Bates snatched out his right-hand Colt and opened fire slowly, accurately, intent to kill. He wanted to kill that tall man. He wanted to kill that mouse-colored horse. He had a strange feeling that, if he could dispose of either of them, chance would swing back to the robbers.

He steadied his gun for the third shot, when he saw something flash in the hand of that rider. The gun spoke. Bates's right-hand gun, his old favorite, was knocked out of his hand and into a pool of black, stagnant water.

He grabbed his bruised hand between his chin and his breast and rode back through the trees, spurring his horse deep. He uttered no complaint. He was not disheartened by pain. He simply knew, calmly, that the chances were suddenly a hundred to one against them. Some people might have the frankness to admit that they had no chance at all.

Salvio's gun was barking behind them. Voices shouted everywhere, everywhere, everywhere. Human voices talked from the ground, out of the sky. It was very true, that which Bates had said. He thought of it again. When the dummies, the honest people, *do* win, they hang lots of thieves from convenient trees.

With his numb hand — it seemed otherwise uninjured — Dave Bates led the way. His horse seemed to know something, and he let it have its head. Presently, it plunged into water up to its belly. That water shoaled away to knee depth.

It forced its way into a hedge of thorny brush, regardless of the stickers. Bates found himself on dry ground — a little ridge that stood up in the center of the marsh. He was glad of that. If they had to die, it was better to die on good, clean ground. As he checked the horse, which stood panting, he saw something slither off into the water, almost soundlessly. He looked the other way. All his nerves gave a great leap, and then he had the sense of falling rapidly. He was not meant for the confinement of marsh ground. This bit of clean earth, and the bit of clean, blue sky over it was all he claimed. The rest was a wet hell.

Harry Quinn came up beside him. Harry's face was gray, and his mouth was pulled back from his yellow teeth, as though he were lifting a great weight, every muscle dragging at it.

"You fool, what you stopping for?" Harry Quinn asked, and pushed his horse straight past. In a moment he stopped, however. He seemed to be listening to the voices that shouted close at hand or murmured far off. "Yeah," he said, "I understand." He dismounted and sat down on a rock. He was still sitting there, rolling a cigarette, when Salvio broke out of the marsh.

Salvio said: "You rat, Quinn . . . are you ratting on us? Jump up and stamp on that smoke. Get down there at the other end of the dry land. I'll take the middle. Dave, you take this end. Shoot at anything you see. They think they got us, but we're going to show them a few tricks. Shoot at anything . . . and shoot straight. Hey, Dave, did that *hombre* get you?"

"He lifted the gun right out of my hand. That's all. I'm all right," said Dave Bates.

"Get off your hoss then, and stand watch," ordered Salvio. Bates obeyed.

They put the horses — and the gold — in the central

cluster of brush that covered the middle of the little island. Then each man sank away in a chosen place of concealment, waiting for the approach of the enemy.

But there was no approach. Bates could hear voices shouting close up, or muttering far away. But they never turned into visible humans among the trees of the marsh. For his own part, he had a nest of rocks out of which he could look to three sides; Salvio was taking charge of the center of the island, and his back.

Those voices to which Bates listened were bright with joy, ringing with the certainty of triumph. And Bates could understand. A hundred to one chance — for their lives. The gold? Well, there was nothing to that. It was simply a weight. It was worthless. It was worse than lead that could be shot out of a gun. Well, they could shoot gold out of guns, too. Bates grinned as he had the thought. Then he heard a high-pitched, nasal voice. It was not loud, but it prodded through the silence of the nearby marsh like a needle, and into Bates's brain.

"Boys," said the voice, "we know that you're in there on the island. But it ain't any good. You're in there, and we got you. What we wanta know is this . . . d'you wanta come out?"

There was no answer.

Want to come out? Of course — but there would be other things to hear.

The nasal voice went on: "We got you snug, and we got enough men to fence in this whole marsh and keep it fenced. You can live for a while on frogs and snakes. That's all right. But after a while, you'll get kind of sick of the mosquitoes, and the marsh water is sure hard on the stomach. What I'm saying is . . . why not come out now, the way you'll have to come out sooner or later? We'll give you a fair break. You didn't kill nobody. And if you march out of there now and

173

turn in the stuff you stole, you'll have a better chance with the jury. That there jury is goin' to be made up of some of the men out of this party, most likely. And that jury will recommend you to the mercy of the judge. You been and done a good job, but you lost. Now pay, and pay quick, or we'll sure raise hell with you."

The speech ended, and Bates listened for the answer of Salvio.

Presently Salvio called out: "What's your name?"

"Steve Balen," called the nasal voice.

"Are you the gent that rode the measly little mouse-colored bronc'?"

"That ain't a lookin' hoss, but it's a ridin' hoss, partner," said the nasal voice. "Yeah, I'm the man you mean."

"Then the devil with you!" called Salvio, and followed his words with a shot that flew crackling through the woods.

Very cheerfully the voice of Steve Balen replied: "I don't blame you, brother. If I was in your boots, I'd hope to hang on to the finish. I didn't want to come and yarn with you like this here, but I figgered it was my duty. What I aim to wanta do is to string you up by the neck, the three of you, and I reckon we'll have the chance to do that before the month is out."

That ended the parley.

Dave Bates was still staggering under the impact of what he had heard, when he made out the muffled voice of Quinn, which was saying: "Hey, Gene, you ain't gone crazy, have you?" The voice came closer, repeating: "Gene, you ain't gone nuts, have you?"

Bates went to join the conference. It took place in the central cluster of shrubbery, near to the horses. "They're giving us a chance, and you go and chuck it away!" said Quinn.

Salvio was very calm and restrained. He merely said: "You

boys can load your stuff onto your hosses, if you want, and go out and give yourselves up. I ain't doing it, that's all."

"Hey, Gene, what's the sense?" asked Quinn.

"You tell the dummy," said Salvio to Bates, after staring for a moment at Quinn.

"They got hanging stuff on Salvio," said Bates, nodding his head.

"They ain't got hanging stuff on me," said Quinn. "Come on, Dave. We'd better get out."

"Get where? Into jail for eight, ten years?" asked Bates.

"Better jail for eight, ten years than hell forever," said Harry Quinn.

"Sure," said Salvio. "Go on and get out." He stood by the black horse, patting its wet shoulder, sneering at them both.

Well, perhaps it was better to go to hell — in brave company.

Bates said: "We started this job with three men. We're going to wind it up with three men, I guess, Harry."

Harry Quinn threw out a hand in an eloquent gesture and started to exclaim in protest. Then he checked himself suddenly. A realization came into his eyes. "Oh, I see," said Quinn. "Sure, I didn't think of that at all!" He seemed to be vastly relieved, and said to Salvio: "What about a smoke, Gene?"

"Sure, kid," said Salvio, and smiled.

Quinn was a lot older, but Salvio had a right to call him kid, if he wanted to, thought Bates. Quinn was not very bright, but he meant well. He'd do the right thing, when it was pointed out to him. Quinn built a cigarette and lighted it, and smoked it with enjoyment.

It was very hot. Sweat began to run on all their faces, and the smell of the marsh was heavy and sick in the air. Out of the distance they could hear more horses pounding up the valley, or down it. Reinforcements were coming. The men of

Jumping Creek would make a party out of this. Even the boys would sneak away from home with some old .22. It would be a great thing, for the men and for the boys. Bates could put himself outside, in their boots, and he almost smiled as he thought of it.

A mosquito bite sent a thrill of cold down the back of his neck. He struck the place with his hand and brought the hand away with a splotch of blood on it. The mosquito was a small smear of nothingness.

"You take a mosquito," said Harry Quinn, "and it can drink its weight in blood, eh?"

"Sure," said Dave Bates.

"Look it," said Quinn. "Suppose that a gent could drink his weight in booze without passing out cold. That'd be the life, eh?"

Salvio was walking up and down slowly, his hands clasped behind his back, his head bent, and a little veil of mosquitoes trailing unheeded behind that head. Dave Bates listened to Quinn, but his eyes and his mind kept following the leader, step by step, blindly hoping.

## IV

## "HIDDEN GOLD"

The sun had been sliding slowly down the western sky until, now, it no longer struck the island with its direct light that merely served to show the vapors that rose from the marsh so thickly that breathing seemed more difficult. Then Gene Salvio paused in his walking.

He said: "They're pulling up more men around us all the

time. They're waiting for three men and five horses to try to charge out through 'em. They'll be expecting us in the middle of the night. Well, we'll beat 'em on all those counts. There'll be no horses with us, and we'll go now."

"Wait a minute," protested Harry Quinn. "Can you carry about three hundred pounds through this kind of a marsh?"

"We're not carrying out the stuff," said Salvio.

"Hey! Leaving it with the hosses?" asked Dave Bates.

"Leaving it inside that tree," answered Salvio. "Shift it into that hollow trunk, boys."

He set the example and started carrying the small, chamois bags to a tree that grew two strides from the end of the island, thrust out of the black water of the marsh. It was almost dead. Only one branch showed green, and this was turning yellow. There was no gap in the side of the trunk to indicate that it was hollow, but, when Salvio pulled himself up to the crotch, he was able to drop the bags he carried into the interior. They were actually heard to splash in the slime at the roots of the tree.

"How'd you know that it was holler?" Harry Quinn asked admiringly. "You got X-ray eyes, Gene?"

"I tapped ag'in' it, when I was coming up to the island," said Salvio. "Rush the stuff inside the tree. It'll wait there for us, I guess."

"I dunno," said Harry Quinn. "It could wait there for a long time, for all of me, the way I feel now. I been feeling my share of it hanging around my neck all this time."

They got the stuff inside the tree. After the first few bags had fallen, the others dropped without bringing out that splashing sound. There was simply a dull, heavy, thudding noise, and presently the last of the gold had been put out of sight.

"Let 'em try to guess where the stuff is now!" said Dave

Bates, gloating. "Just let 'em try to guess. Why, Gene, that's the best idea you ever had. But how'll we get through those *hombres* all around the island? There's still daylight!"

For an answer, out of the distance, a number of rifles suddenly opened fire. The bullets could be heard crackling through the woods, then the echoes rang for a moment, and there was the silence of the marsh again.

"There's a mite of daylight," agreed Salvio. "But it'd be hard to read fine print by it, and it'd be hard to see faces very clear. There's so much daylight that they're not going to expect us to try to come out, and there's not enough daylight to make them very sure of us if we do. They're shooting at shadows already. Come on, Dave. Come on, Harry. We'll see what we can find."

"You remember that they all had a chance to have a good look at us," suggested Bates.

"Yeah. They had a good look at us in the bright of the sun, setting up there in the saddle on our hosses. They ain't going to see us the same way now." He went down to the edge of the filthy water, deliberately picked up a film of slime, and trailed the ugly green of it over one side of his face. "That ain't pretty," said Salvio, "but it'll make a difference."

Without a word, the others imitated him, smearing slime here and there on their clothes, on their faces. Then they followed Salvio across the island, and slowly through the slime and water that sometimes rose higher than their knees.

Salvio went very slowly to avoid making noise. The others came exactly in his wake, and presently he held up a hand. Before them rose a narrow ridge of brush.

"They're out there beyond the brush," said Salvio. "Lemme have a chance to talk to 'em, and then you fellows do what I do. Understand? Lemme think for you, and you do what I do."

178

"I'm ready," agreed Dave Bates, putting his life readily into the hands of the leader.

Salvio pushed through the brush, rather noisily. "Hey, hello!" he called.

"Who's that?" answered a voice in the near distance. "What fool is that callin' out so loud?"

"Maybe it's one of 'em," suggested another.

"Hey," called Salvio, "is Balen around anywhere?"

"Who wants him?"

"Pete Bennett. Me and Charlie and Chuck, we've found the easy way to the island that Balen wanted to get at."

"It's too late to go in there now. It'll be pitch dark before long."

"Look it here," said Salvio angrily, "what've we been wallering around in the slush for, if Balen ain't going to use what we've found out for him?"

"Shut up talking so loud and come out."

"Sure," said Salvio. "That's fine for you *hombres* that been staying on dry land all the time. But what about us that been wallering?" He stalked forward through the brush, calling over his shoulder. "Come on, Chuck! Come on, Charlie!"

"Not so loud!" cautioned the other speaker.

"I'm pretty nigh fed up with the whole business," said Salvio, as Bates and Quinn came on behind him.

Beyond the bushes there was another bit of shallow marsh. They crossed this toward some trees under which a number of men were in plain view, except for the increasing dimness of the light and the intervening vapors of the marsh.

"I got half a mind to pull out of the business," Salvio was saying as he advanced into the group. "Dog-gone me, if I ain't spent!"

And, to the amazement of Bates, Salvio threw himself right down among the others, on the grass.

Bates took that example and plumped himself down on a stump, resting his face in his hands, as though exhausted. He saw Quinn settled with his back against a tree, his head also hanging. Then he could hear the man who seemed in charge of this section of the line saying: "Well, I didn't know that Balen sent anybody into the marsh."

"I wish *I* didn't know it," answered Salvio. "I sure had enough marsh. I'm going to have the smell of it in my nose for the rest of my life. And I'm dead beat. Anybody got a drink on him? Anybody got a flask?"

There was no answer to this, and Salvio fell to muttering.

A fellow came up beside Bates and said: "Dirty work in there, eh?"

"Yeah, and damn it," said Bates.

"I wouldn't've thought that Balen would've sent nobody into the marsh," said the other.

Bates said nothing. He merely groaned as with fatigue.

Then he heard someone saying: "Here's Balen now."

Bates stood up. He saw that Quinn was rising, also, but that Salvio, strange to say, remained stretched on the ground, face down, arms flung wide, as though worn out with labor.

"I'm going to see if I can find me a drink of something," said Bates to the man beside him.

"Say," said the other, "you look like. . . ."

He stopped his voice suddenly. Bates went on into the brush with cold snakes working up and down his spine.

What did he look like? In another moment he would show all those fellows what his back looked like when he was running as fast as his legs could carry him. Off to the side, he saw Quinn moving away, also.

"Here, Balen!" called a voice. "Here's a gent to make a report to you."

Bates paused on the farther side of the brush. He could

look through and see Salvio rising. Not twenty steps away were a string of tethered horses, which might mean liberty for them. But Bates would not desert his leader, even though Harry Quinn was already striding toward that group of mustangs.

"Wait a minute," Salvio said quite loudly. "I'll be back in a minute. I want to get something out of my saddlebag, and I'll be right back."

And there was Salvio, stepping unhurried toward the horses. Bates made haste to turn in the same direction. He only risked one glance behind him to see, in the half light, that the man with whom he had been talking was now seriously debating something with two other men, and pointing after him. The same worms of ice began to work again in the spinal marrow of little Dave Bates. He walked right up to the first horse of the group as he heard Balen saying : "Find a way through the marsh? I never told any man to. . . ."

A big fellow jumped out from nowhere and grabbed the arm of Dave Bates.

"Hey, whatcha doin' with my hoss?" demanded the stranger.

Salvio stepped right up behind the big cowpuncher and clinked the barrel of a gun against the base of his skull. The man dropped like a falling sack.

"Fast, boys!" said Salvio.

They swept into the saddles, each of his chosen horse.

"Cut the other ropes. Cut the ropes and drive the bronc's with us!" commanded Salvio.

"Stop 'em!" yelled the ringing voice of Steve Balen. "You day-blind owls, you've been and let the three of 'em walk right through you! Shoot! Get the hosses down . . . anything to stop 'em!"

But the knives of the three already had slashed right and

181

left at the tethering ropes, and now with busy quirts they beat the horses into flight.

Guns began behind them.

Dave Bates distinctly heard the sound of a rifle bullet bang into the head of a horse running beside him. It was a noise like the impact of a club. The horse went down in a heap and turned a somersault. And then the whole covey of horses and the three riders crashed through the underbrush and stormed up the valley.

Behind them, there was such a yelling, such a frenzy of hysterical rage, that wild Indians could not have raised a greater tumult. Men were still firing from back there. Pounds of lead were vainly searching the air, but, with every moment, the fugitives sped farther away toward safety, and, with every moment, the night was thickening the air. Salvio had been right. It was the moment of the most treacherous light in all the twenty-four hours of the day. To look down the avenues of the trees was like looking into deep water.

Life was being given back to the three of them, and Dave Bates felt that he was enjoying separately and specially every breath that he drew.

They drew out of the valley and up a steep hill, on the shoulder of which Salvio drew rein and let the horses breathe.

"Gene," said Dave Bates, "you done that as well as anybody in the world could've done it. You sure saved our hides . . . that nobody else could've done!"

"And what about Reata?" asked Gene Salvio angrily. "You're always sayin' that he can do anything. Could he've done what we three just done?"

"He couldn't've done no better. It was a great job, and you did it all the way through, Gene," said Bates.

And Harry Quinn heartily agreed.

## "AT RUSTY GULCH"

Later, the three heard the loud river of the pursuit turn aside out of the valley, heading back, no doubt, toward the main road, and that gave the fugitives a chance to jog softly on through the night. Harry Quinn even suggested that they should turn back and try to get at the gold they had left behind them, but Salvio would not listen to that.

It was night now, he reminded them. Fires would be lighted here and there. By lantern light, people would probably begin to search the marsh to look for the buried treasure, because everyone must have known that the three fugitives could not possibly have taken away any great percentage of the stolen gold. Bates had two or three pounds in his pocket; that was all they had taken with them. Balen would be at the island, working hard to find the hiding place. No doubt it was because Balen was back there with part of his men that the rest of the crowd had taken the wrong trail. Be that as it might, the three had their skins whole, and they could be grateful for that.

Salvio said: "But maybe we ain't through with a pile of trouble. That Steve Balen, he acted and he sounded to me like a gent that would stick tighter than a corn plaster. We'll get to Pop Dickerman and find out what he's got for us in his old brain. He's always got ideas."

"Yeah, he's always got ideas," said Dave Bates, "and we've always got the blood to bleed for 'em."

All through that night they journeyed on patiently. And in

the first thin gray of the dawn they raised the dim outlines of Rusty Gulch and, finally, of the high-backed barn in which Pop Dickerman lived, on the edge of the town.

They put up the horses in the shed behind the house barn. Then they went to the back door of the place, and Salvio knocked three times, paused, knocked twice again.

"Do it ag'in, louder," said Harry Quinn. "He can't hear that."

"You don't wanta forget that he's a rat," said Salvio. "He can hear everything."

"He ain't coming. There ain't a squeak on the stairs or along the floor," complained Bates.

"Sure there ain't," said Salvio. "What would a furry-faced rat like him be making a noise for?"

A moment later a voice said, behind the door. "Go around to the big room. I'll open up for you gents there."

"You see?" muttered Salvio to his companions, as they went around to the side of the old barn. "You gents can see Pop Dickerman every day of your lives, but you ain't never going to get used to him."

"Sure we ain't," agreed Bates. "Poison is hard to get used to, too."

There *was* a poison about the air of the place to those who knew it well. Few people knew the junk peddler as well as did these three henchmen of his. The knowledge of most was limited to the big piles of rubbish that rusted and slowly consumed the outer yard, or to the more valuable stuff that was piled on the floor or hung from the rafters of the mow of the barn. They knew these things, and the skill of Pop Dickerman in driving bargains, and the buzzard-like instinct which led him to appear on the scene the instant that a home was about to be broken up. But his three men could have talked out whole books of information concerning this practiced and consummate fence. They knew his far-spreading knowledge, the underground wires by which he kept in touch with numerous scenes and opportunities for crime which he farmed out, at a high price, to his favored few criminals. They knew scores of his personal idiosyncrasies. But also they were constantly aware of a wall which barred them away from a great intimacy with the strange fellow.

The sliding door was noisily unlocked from the inside and pushed back. They saw the tall, stooping silhouette of Pop Dickerman and the whole room vaguely illumined by a single hanging lamp that was suspended from a central rafter of the mow and cast just enough light to make the nearer heaps of metal work and crystal on the floor glow, and all those great bundles of assorted junk that hung down at the ends of ropes and chains. Some of them were always turning slowly, winding and unwinding.

Before he went inside, Dave Bates looked up at the spectacle and muttered: "Like dead men hanging in rows, Pop. I always think of dead men hanging in rows."

Pop Dickerman made that gesture of his, ten thousand times repeated and always in vain, that attempt to smooth down the fur of whiskers and hair that covered his long face almost to the eyes.

"Maybe it's a kind of a prophecy, Dave," he said. "Maybe it's kind of like a lot of mirrors, and you see what's goin' to happen to you." He slid the door home behind them, the wheels that supported it running soundlessly on the track overhead.

Bates merely said: "You ain't funny, Pop. You ain't hardly ever funny, except when you don't know it."

The three of them gathered under the hanging lantern, and they threw themselves down on the various chairs and couches that were always standing at this point. They were

185

continually changing, as one housewife or another found things here that were to her taste for the furnishing of her home. Only one article remained always, and that was the legless divan on which Pop Dickerman himself sat cross-legged in heelless slippers that were forever seeming about to fall from his feet. He took his place there now in the familiar attitude and lighted and commenced to suck at the water pipe that was his chief consolation. It made a faint bubbling sound that was not unmusical, and a heavy perfume began to spread through the air of the strange old barn.

"So it was a bust for you, boys?" said Dickerman.

"What makes you think that?" asked Harry Quinn, rather angrily.

"Not a bust? You got the goods, but you didn't bring 'em back with you?" said Dickerman.

"They run us down in the marsh, this side of Jumping Creek," said Salvio. "You know the place?"

"Yeah. I know," said Dickerman. "So you buried the stuff, and then you managed to wriggle through 'em and come away?"

"How'd you guess that?" asked Salvio curiously.

"Because you look beat, but not all beat. You missed the money, but you kept your hides for yourselves, eh?" said Dickerman.

His husky voice continued with other words that were not quite intelligible. The sound of that voice made one expect to see the face of a man dying with years, but the bright, rat-like sparkling of the eyes was a continual denial of weakness. He was not a pretty picture in his soiled flannel undershirt, with one half of a pair of suspenders strung across his shoulder.

"We got off with our hides, and lucky," said Dave Bates. "Lucky because we had Salvio along to bluff a way through for us. I never seen a cooler or a smarter thing, Pop!"

"Yeah, Gene is cool, and Gene is smart, but that ain't

money in *my* pocket," answered Dickerman. "When you boys goin' to go back and get the stuff?"

Harry Quinn generally left the talking for his more clever companions, but now his heart was full, and speech overflowed. "Listen," he said, "there was seven, eight hundred pounds of gold dust, Pop. And the gents are going to be digging up that marsh for a thousand years till they find the money. And the whole town seen us, when we was riding out of the place."

"The town didn't see you, if you didn't do some shootin'," said Dickerman. "I know that town, and I know the way that it sleeps. That time of day, you shouldn't've had no trouble!"

"There was a red-headed fool in the place," said Salvio. "I had to plug him."

"Dead?" said Dickerman.

"No. Not dead. Just enough to make him holler."

"Good," said Dickerman. "It's better not to have 'em dead. A death trail stays red for a long while. The other kinds, they blot out pretty quick. A wind and a rain and a coupla weeks, and they're blotted out. But you boys wouldn't want to go back into that neck of the woods to get at the stuff?"

"Why should we wanta be lynched?" asked Salvio.

"Seven, eight hundred pounds of gold," sighed Dickerman. "Then who else can we get to salvage the stuff?"

"There ain't anybody," said Salvio. "Anybody that was smart enough to get at the stuff . . . would be crooked enough to keep it for himself."

Bates said: "Nope. There's one man."

"Who?" challenged Salvio.

"Reata!" exclaimed Bates.

"Reata? Reata?" said Salvio, in a jealous anger. "You'd think that he was a tin god on a stick, the way you gents talk about him. He's as big a crook as anybody."

187

"He's big, but he ain't a crook," said Pop Dickerman. "It's fun to him. Bates is right. But how would we get at Reata? He hates my heart. I ain't a clean enough kind of a man, the way I live, to suit Reata. Besides, the Gypsy gal has him."

"Are they married?" asked Bates.

"They ain't married, but they will be as soon as they get the house they're workin' on finished. They're buildin' it together. They're a mighty happy pair, boys! They've raked together a little money. They got their cabin started, and they're goin' to have a little land and start a small herd of cattle chewin' the grass."

"How d'you know all these things?" asked Salvio. "Been up there?"

"I got wires stretched around," said Pop Dickerman. "They keep me in touch. Yeah, and I think a lot about Reata. There's one that would've opened up a lot of money for himself and me. There's a fine, useful sort of a gent. There's an edge on Reata that would cut through chilled steel like butter, and it kind of grieves me, boys, to think that I lost him. So I just keep in touch a little. I dunno another man that could do the job of getting that gold back for us, except Reata. Them that could do it, they'd keep the loot. But Reata, you could trust him with your blood."

"That's the kind of a fool he is," said Salvio, sneering.

"Wait a minute, Gene," said Harry Quinn, scowling. "You're a damned smart gent, and you're a cool gent. But you and Dave and me, we all owe our skins to Reata."

Salvio's face darkened, but he said nothing.

Bates said: "It's the Gypsy gal that hangs up Reata. Pry him loose from her, and we might get him back to us ag'in."

"Pry him loose?" said Dickerman. "Aye, and I been dreamin' about that, too. How would you pry him loose? Kidnap her? He'd find her, if it took the rest of his life."

"Get *her* to give him the run," said Bates.

"Her? She loves the ground he walks on," said Dickerman. "A kind of a hard gal, she is, but she loves Reata."

"Suppose you made her think it was for his own good?" said Dave Bates.

"How could you make her think that?" asked Quinn.

"Wait a minute!" exclaimed Dickerman. He raised a grimy hand, commandingly, for silence, and then he said: "Don't speak, nobody. Bates has give' me an idea. Wait till it hatches out of the egg, and it's goin' to fly like an eagle."


VI


"REATA'S HOME"


Up in the Ginger Mountains, the three riders found their quarry. Reata had not picked out the site of his home very wisely. He had it at just the wrong distance from the town of Ginger Gulch. He had chosen a site where no wagon road passed into the town and, therefore, where all supplies would need expensive hauling. He had picked out a small valley with a small lake in the bottom of it like a little blue eye that always had, even in August, some white of snow to reflect as well as the deeps of the wide heaven. There were pine forests on the march up and down the sides of the mountains as far as the bald summits above the timberline. And in fact, there was everything that the eye of the nature lover could ask for, but very little to please the wit of a good cattleman. That valley would be a hot furnace in summer, and it would be an ice box in winter. Furthermore, there were plenty of trees and not enough grass.

The three men of Dickerman, perched like patient birds of

prey on a lofty mountain shoulder and looking down, day by day, upon the center of the valley and the little cabin that was growing there, took careful heed of all of these things. They commented upon the picture to one another.

Dave Bates, who had prospected the scene closer than any of the others, said: "They done only one sensible thing. They built the horse shed before they started on the house. But damn me, unless they get a hustle on them, they gotta live in the cattle shed, instead of the house, this winter. They ain't got it finished, and they ain't going to have it finished, even if they keep on working all day. You take Reata, he never was made for a worker . . . you take a Gypsy gal . . . was there ever one that ever was worth a hang, when it come to work? But I'll tell you what, that there Miriam is doing a damn' sight better than you ever would suspect. She does the licks of hard work, mostly, and Reata, he sets back and gives ideas."

"I was down there the other day," said Harry Quinn, "snaking up to the edge of the woods where I could watch. Each of them had hold on an adze, and they was making the chips fall off of the bellies of a couple of logs. But after Reata had hit a few licks, he takes a stop, looks around him, and rolls a cigarette.

" 'Hey,' says the gal. 'Go on and work, loafer!'

" 'You don't understand me, Miriam,' says he. 'I'll tell you what the facts are. I don't get ideas, when I'm swinging an axe all day long. But now and then, when I stop, things happen inside my head . . . I get good hunches.'

" 'What sort of hunches have you got now?' says Miriam.

" 'Well,' he says 'just for a sample, I've thought of damming up that creek, yonder, some day, and out of that we'll get the water power to work a sawmill, and then we won't have to go to all this hard work in fixing the logs for the house.'

" 'Are you going to build a sawmill so that you can build a house?' says she.

" 'The idea,' says he, 'is that afterwards we'll be able to ship out timber. There's a fortune in good, clear pine, right around here.'

" 'Sure there is,' says she, 'if you can get the mountains to open up so that we can ship the stuff out. It would cost the weight of those trees in gold, pretty near, to haul them from here to Ginger Gulch. And even after you got them there, what sort of a market is there for them? People can cut down enough timber in their back yards to build ten new houses apiece.'

" 'Miriam,' says Reata, 'I'm sorry to hear you talk like this. People that haven't a good faith in a thing, they're going to have the bottom drop out of whatever they're doing.' "

"Did Reata talk like that?" asked Dave Bates suddenly.

"Sure he did," answered Quinn. "And I heard him, and I saw him leaning on his adze, and smoking, and making big gestures, and the girl just standing back and sort of laughing at him with her eyes."

"If that's what's in the air," said Dave Bates, "then I've got the idea. Reata's going to make the trip into Ginger Gulch with the roan mare and a couple of mules. He'll be back tomorrow afternoon . . . and instead of going down to the village yonder, where she mostly spends the nights, Miriam is going to camp out at the new cabin and hold things down, you might say. Well, boys, listen to me talk. I got ideas. I need some help, but I don't need very much."

In fact, they found that the idea of Dave Bates was so neat, so full of wise invention and novelty, that even Gene Salvio, who was apt to be critical of all ideas other than his own, readily admitted the possibilities in this scheme. That very afternoon, as soon as Reata was seen to ride out of the valley and out of sight along the newly worn trail to Ginger Gulch, the three criminals descended to their work. They began at the cattle and horse shed, and they worked there for some time, before Dave Bates took his horse back through the woods, and came singing along under the trees, and so out into the clearing beside the lake.

It was so beautiful, down here in the valley, that Dave forgot all about the practical difficulties of raising cattle in any numbers on such a site. For the lake had a small beach of white sand and crystal quartz pebbles to set off the blue of the water from the green of the meadow. The small waves washed in on the shore rapidly, filled with light out of the west, for the sun was still above the western summits; and the blood of Dave Bates also began to rush and hurry with happiness. He felt that he could decide, on the spur of the moment, that this was the most beautiful spot in the world; he would not need to hunt any farther.

The girl was still making her axe ring against the log. The chips flew far as she wielded the broad blade of fine steel that gave out a bell-like note at every stroke. Even a strong man can easily grow exhausted by such work, but the girl, swinging the tool with exhaustless grace, made rhythm take the place of muscle. She was in a sleeveless jacket of brown doeskin, and she was as brown as the soft leather.

She was still working, when a mite of a dog ran out, yipping, toward the horseman, a slender little thing with a body as sleek as that of a rat, and a fuzzy face like a duplicate, in the small, of the head of a wire-haired fox terrier. Dave Bates had almost forgotten Rags.

The barking made the girl turn. She was looking straight into the west, so that she had to shade her eyes to see Bates clearly. Then she stepped back to where a good new Winchester rifle leaned against a sawbuck.

"Why, if it isn't old Dave! Hullo, Dave!" called the girl. "Glad to see you, old scout. Get down and rest your feet and tell me how's things?"

"Hullo there, Miriam," he said. "Things were never better."

He swung down from the mustang and advanced with his hand stretched out. Little Rags, in a barking fury, planted himself in the path, with bared teeth ready to bite.

Bates, inwardly cursing the little dog, had to pause, while he saw the girl throw one fleeting glance at the rifle. After that fractional hesitation, she came straight up to him and shook his hand with a firm grip. She always dazzled him a little. In spite of the ruddy bronze of her skin and the roughness of her clothes, she looked to him like the sort of a jewel that should be laid up in velvet. Perhaps, he thought, it was because of the deep blueness of her eyes under her black hair and lashes.

"How's every little thing with you?" she was repeating heartily. "Found any good fat beef to rustle lately, Dave? Any bank safes been open when you were going by?"

The nearness of that hit made him stare at her a bit.

"You look right up to yourself," he told her. "Stop that dog yapping, will you?"

She snapped her fingers. Rags jumped back and sat down between her feet, but still he growled very softly at the stranger.

"You know me, Rags," said Dave Bates. "You know me, boy. I'm a bunky of your big boss, ain't I? Don't you know me, boy?"

"Keep your hand away from him, or he'll take a finger off," said Miriam. "Reata put him on guard over me, before he rode into town, and Rags knows it's a serious job. Any old day, a dog-gone mountain lion might walk down here and take a pass at me, if it weren't for old Rags, here, ready to tear that lion to bits. Same way with men. Rags doesn't trust anything until his boss comes back and calls him off the job."

Dave Bates laughed. He sat down on the white of the log at which she had been chipping.

"You look fine," he said, insisting on that pleasant theme.

"Sure I look fine. Why wouldn't I look fine? Three squares a day for the old girl, and plenty of exercise to keep up her appetite."

"And plenty of Reata for sauce," said Dave Bates. "He keeps the world turning pretty fast, I bet."

"Yeah. You'd bet that, wouldn't you?" she said. "Full of rope tricks and fun, you'd think, wouldn't you? Babbling all day long, and telling stories about places he's been or ought to have been?"

"He's a great card," said Dave Bates.

"Sure he's a great card," agreed the girl. "The sort of a card that wins the trick in the poker game, all right. But up here in the mountains, he's more of a poet. He takes a lot of time off to fill his eye with the scenery. He has his dreams by day, and don't you ever doubt it, Dave."

"Good old Reata," said Dave Bates. "There's nobody like him. Kind of pleased with this spot?"

"He likes it a lot," she agreed. "But as I say, he's getting the soul of a poet . . . or a promoter. He likes the taste of this air so much that he'd like to bottle it and send it to his friends. He's built a great big hotel there in the meadow, right beside the lake, and he's filled it with high-class dudes, at ten dollars a day."

"I can see 'em down there, taking the sun right now, can't I?" said Dave Bates, staring from under his lean little hand.

"Yeah, that's easy. But do you see the bucket line that runs up to the top of the mountain, there?"

"No, I don't quite make that out."

194

"Look harder," said the girl. "That's for the guests to go up to the top of the mountain and enjoy the view. And maybe you saw the big fences all around the water divide?"

"I must've seen them," said Bates.

"That's because Reata has made this place into a preserve," said the girl, "and, when the dudes take a walk, they find a lot of tame deer wandering around ready to eat sugar out of their hands. The bill for cube sugar is one of the big items over there in the hotel."

"Yeah, I bet it is," said Dave. "But outside of the tame deer and what not, and the hotel, and all of that, what are you and Reata going to live on?"

"I don't know," she answered. "And I don't care, what's more. If I can once get him to pass the old ring onto my finger and say, 'I do,' a couple of times in front of a preacher, I don't care what happens, after that."

"You like that *hombre,* all right," said Dave Bates.

"Yeah, I'm a little queer that way," she said.

"There's nobody like him," insisted Dave. "But when does the marriage come off?"

"As soon as the house is finished. He's proud, Reata is. Many a time he sits out here and shakes his head and says that he can't marry me till he has a home to take me to."

"Maybe he says that many a time while he sits out here and watches you work?" suggested Bates.

"Many a time," she agreed, "but what do I care? You know the old boy, Dave. He loves work the way a cat loves wet weather. I suppose we'll eat more beef than we raise. But that's all right. It's a good old world, if you've got it on a rope."

"And Reata has the rope," said Bates. "What's his real name, by the way?"

"I'm to find that out the wedding day, for a present," said Miriam. "But what brought you sashaying down the mountainside, singing so sweet, Dave?"

"I came up here to see Reata," said Dave.

"You're not going to, though. Reata's away in town. He won't be back till tomorrow. What's the matter, Dave? Has Pop Dickerman got another job too big for his boys to handle? Is he sending out a hurry call for Reata?"

Bates blinked at her shrewdness. "This time it's a friendly turn to do Reata," he said. "You wouldn't think that rat of a Dickerman, or three roughs like me and Gene and Harry Quinn, would travel very far to do a fellow a good turn, would you?"

"Yes, you'd travel a ways," said the girl. "How good is the turn?"

"I see it's no good at all," said Bates. "You've got him nailed down, and he won't move."

"You want to move him, do you?"

"I want to keep him alive," said Bates calmly.

## VII

## "THE ROAR OF A GUN"

The quiet of Dave Bates's voice gave his words the necessary solemnity. He saw the brightness of her eyes narrow at him.

"Go on, Dave," she invited presently. "It must be a big idea. Why not sell it to the weaker half of the family-to-be?"

"It's not any good talking to you, Miriam," he told her. "Sure, you're fond of Reata. You're so dog-goned fond that you've about anchored him. And the waves are going to tear hell out of him, when the first storm comes up. And the storm is coming now."

"What kind of a storm?" she asked.

Bates shrugged his shoulders as he answered: "They're going to get him, Miriam. They got him located, and they're working on him already. I've said too much already. But as long as you asked, I had to tell you."

"You think he ought to move away from here?"

"I do."

"Where?"

"Anywhere. Just keep moving, or the wave'll drown him sure."

"Who's in the storm?"

"What's the good of going on?" said Dave Bates. "You know how it is. Reata is a clean-bred one. There ain't a better fellow in the world. I owe my skin to him. I'd be two times dead, except for Reata. But while he was helping me and some of the others, he sure stepped hard on a lot of toes. There's gents been getting together that want his scalp, and they're going to have it, if they can. But . . . oh, well, what's the use?"

"I sort of think you mean what you say," answered the girl.

"Do I? You bet everything down to the spurs that I mean it," said Bates. "But what's the good of talking? Anyway, he's pretty smart . . . he may beat them, no matter how many they are."

"Dave, you've got to talk out," she commanded.

"It's no good talking out," he declared. "You've got Reata anchored here, as I said before, and this is where he's got to stay. Maybe I can come over and hang around for a while and help a little. I don't know. Depends on how much rope old Dickerman will give me."

"There're going to come up here and try to cut down Reata? Is that the story?" she asked.

"Quit it, will you?" said Bates. "I've talked too much. But

197

. . . well, Reata means a whole lot to me. Well . . . show me around the place, will you?"

She hesitated, her face dark with thought, before she said: "All right, I'll show you. There's two things to see. The cabin and the shed. Take the cabin first. Those uprights are the cabin uprights, old son. Those beams are the cabin beams, and, when we get the logs laid, we'll have walls around it, and, when the roof goes on, we'll have a roof on our little cabin. See?"

"Sure. It's a great idea." Bates chuckled. "Let's have a slant at the shed, then."

She walked over with him.

"A sliding door, and everything," said Dave Bates, putting his hand on the finger slot, and pulling back. The natural way would have been to lean a shoulder against the door and walk it back, but he had the best reason in the world for not doing that. As the door opened to the width of a yard, a gun roared, and a huge charge of shot whistled out through the gap.

Bates, with a yell, sprang back, a gun flashing out into each hand.

"Get back to the house!" he yelled at the girl, and raced promptly around to the rear of the shed.

But when he reached the spot, he found the girl turning the opposite corner, her face wild and set, and a lean, dangerous-looking .32 revolver in her grip. She could use that gun, and how efficiently she could use it, Bates knew perfectly well. She stared about her at the trees that advanced right down to the rear of the long shed.

"They're inside! We got 'em!" shouted Bates.

"Wait a minute," said Miriam calmly. "There's the gun that did the trick." She pointed at a single-barrel shotgun of large bore that was strongly propped up against a sapling, its muzzle projecting through the rear wall of the shed, having been pushed through a large knothole. "That's it," said Miriam. "And there's the string attached to it. You see?"

"I don't make it out? What do you mean?" asked Dave Bates.

She was pale, but very steady. She gave Bates one long, searching look, and then her doubt seemed to leave her.

"I guess it's news to you, all right," she said. "But coming right on top of what you've been telling me, I thought for a minute. . . ." She did not tell what her thought for a minute had been, but led the way around to the front of the shed.

Bates grabbed her as she started to go through the door. "You don't know what hellishness is fixed up inside!" he said.

"There won't be anything more," she declared. And she slipped away from him into the interior.

There was nothing to be seen except the long line that ran past the ends of the stalls and connected with the front door. The pull of the door traveled back to the trigger of the gun. It was the simplest and almost the oldest species of deathtrap in the world.

"Now I get it," said Bates, muttering the words hardly aloud. "Suppose that somebody put his shoulder against the sliding door to walk it open, the way most folks would . . . ? But who would've been the first one to open this door ordinarily, Miriam?"

"Reata," she said faintly. "Reata, when he comes back from town. He'd put Sue up in here and turn the mules loose to graze."

Bates left her, rounded the shed, and took the shotgun out of the brace. It had been his idea, but Gene Salvio and Quinn had executed it perfectly. He was proud of himself, and he was proud of them. Two heads are better than one, and three pairs of hands are the best of all.

When he went back, he found the girl sitting on the log

199

beside the lake, absently stroking Rags, who lay beside her. The great shadow of the biggest western mountain, streaming palpably through the clean mountain air, had fallen across her and half the lake so that the waves made only a dull glimmering as they kept rushing in toward the shore.

The sound of them pleased Dave Bates. He saw that he was winning, and he determined to say nothing more.

The girl looked up at him. "Have you got the makings of a cigarette?" she asked.

He proffered them to her, and she twisted up a smoke in short order, and accepted his light. Breathing the smoke deep, she blew it out again in wisps.

"It tastes good . . . but a little dizzy," she said. "First smoke I've had since Reata took control."

"He doesn't like to see a girl smoke. He's funny, that way," said Dave Bates. And he began to guess, grimly, what this breaking of the prohibition might mean to the future of the girl and Reata.

"Yeah. He's funny, that way."

She pointed toward the shed, without herself looking in that direction, and Dave Bates stared down at the perfect brown modeling of that arm.

"He wouldn't have looked so funny . . . with that load of buckshot through him."

"It was big. I heard it whistle," said Dave. "I guess it would've tore a hole through a tree, all right. But maybe Reata wouldn't've got it. Maybe something would've happened. . . ."

"Shut up, Dave!" she commanded.

She closed her eyes, smiling very faintly. He could see that she was sick with pain, but she took it like a man, quietly, digesting the poison.

"I've got to cut him loose," she said finally.

"What you mean?" asked Dave Bates hastily.

"You know what I mean," she told him. "I've got to do what you came up here to make me do. I've got to cut Reata adrift."

"You can't," said Bates. "You can't tell him to leave the place. He's crazy about you, Miriam. He'd never give up marrying you."

"Wouldn't he?" she asked sourly. "You don't know me, partner. You don't even half know me, yet. Oh, I'll cut him loose. I'll make a free man of him." She was silent again, with the same sick, grim smile on her face, and her hand went gently over the sleek back of Rags.

"Now I guess I get what you mean," said Bates. "You mean you're going to pretend that you're tired of him, or something like that?"

She shrugged her shoulders.

"You can't do it," said Bates. "You love him. You couldn't live without him. You. . . ."

"I'd soon be living without him, if a pound of buckshot was socked into him," she said.

He bowed his head, as though to this convincing argument he could find no possible rejoinder. "I'm sorry," said Bates at last. And, in fact, there really was a measure of regret in him. He needed Reata. Dickerman needed Reata. The whole crooked gang needed that fearless and cunning magician's touch in their affairs. And yet Bates was sorry for the girl. "You tell me how I can help. Tell me what to do," he pleaded.

"I'll tell you what to do. Get out of my sight!" she exclaimed.

# VIII

## "MIRIAM PLAYS A PART"

When Bates was gone, she went slowly about the place, all that evening. In the middle of the night she sat up in the mountain cold and breathed the sweetness of the pine trees until the breath of them was like music to her, and the trees filled her eyes. The next day it was the same thing — and she went from spot to spot, staring, filling her eyes with the many pictures for the last time, until every curve of the mountains, of the lake shore, was fixed in her mind like so many human faces.

Reata would not be back until the middle of the afternoon. He would come down that slope, racing the roan mare, yelling like a happy, wild Indian, and the mules would be left to wander slowly along at their own gait, behind him.

She wished that she could have a longer interim before he returned. She wanted to have longer to steady herself for the part that she had to play. She wanted to school herself more, and build up her resistance. However, that day ran on heedlessly, swiftly, like the last hours of a condemned prisoner in a death house. And when the time came, she was in place and taking the part that she had decided on.

She had dug out some tobacco and wheat-straw papers from among the things of Reata, and, when she heard the long, echoing whoop and then the clatter of hoofbeats coming down the rough of the trail, she was posted beside the lake, seated on that log where she had been working when Dave Bates appeared and darkened the world for her. She made her cigarette, and was smoking it calmly when Reata came whooping into view from among the trees.

She usually met him, running. He would catch her, and she would leap, and so they would finish the trip to the front of the cabin. But today she merely turned and waved a hand at him.

She saw him check Sue abruptly. The long, ugly, unmatchable roan machine fell at once to a trot, then halted nearby. Rags flew into a passion of delighted welcoming, so shrill that it darted needles through the brain.

Reata stopped that demonstration with one harsh word. Rags slunk at the heels of his beloved master.

The girl kept herself smiling, calmly, impersonally. She tried to reduce that brown face of Reata to a mere picture in which she had little interest. She tried to forget that the gray eye could burn with yellow fire, and all the quick, electric nature of this man whose like was not in the world. A hand was gripping her heart, but she kept on smiling, and, as she smoked, she blew the thin cloud into the air.

He leaned over her. She turned up her face, as one submitting to a kiss, but he stepped suddenly back again.

"Hell's broken loose, eh?" he said.

She shrugged her shoulders.

"Where?" he asked. "Around the place, or just inside you?"

"Just inside me," she answered.

"Quiet hell?" he said.

"Yes."

"That's the worst kind," answered Reata.

He sat down on a stump opposite her. Even in his sitting and his rising, he was not like other men, but there seemed to be in him springs of steel strength. She looked at the broad shoulders and the strong neck and the high, fine poise of the head. He was all strength above and all wiry speed below.

"Maybe it's the worst kind," she agreed, looking out over the lake.

"Stop smiling that way," commanded Reata.

"Yes, my lord," she said, and kept on smiling, although every bit of it hurt.

"Smoking, eh? Just to show that the rebellion goes deep?" he asked.

"Oh, you know," she answered. "Kind of got tired of things."

"What things?"

"Oh, everything." She waved at that scene around her.

"And me?" he asked.

She shrugged her shoulders again. There was a frightful desire in her to fling herself at him and pour out words and weep. For his own sake she had to go through with this efficiently.

"I see," said Reata, making his voice very bright and cheerful, so that she recognized the steel in him for the thousandth time. He could do it, of course. If she could smile at disaster, he could laugh at it. "You have the old hunger, eh? Want to go back with the Gypsies again? Want to see old Queen Maggie and get the whiff of her big black cigars? All of that?"

"You know, when a fellow gets bored, there's not much to say about it, is there?"

"No, I don't suppose so," said Reata.

He kept sitting up straight on the stump, looking directly at her, while she looked out past him at the scene from which she would soon be cut off. It seemed to her that every line of the thing cried out eternal happiness to her.

"Let's be logical. Let's go sashaying right through the details, if you don't mind."

"I don't mind," she answered.

"Take it like this. The mountains . . . they're lonely. If a girl is left up here . . . twenty-four long hours . . . she's bound to be lonely. You know, Miriam, I suggested that you should go back to the boarding house, down there in the village."

"I know. I thought I'd try the place out, though."

"You've been feeling it come up in you for a long time, eh?" he asked.

"Well . . . ," she said.

"Don't mind me. I want to get at the inside of the truth, if you'll tell me."

"Talking won't be much good," she declared.

"I won't persuade you," said Reata. "Not a quarter of an inch. I'd rather burn my tongue out by the roots than say one word to persuade you."

"Thanks," said the girl flatly. And she hated the rude, ugly meanness of that single word. After all, she had to make him despise her. That was the only way to cut deep enough.

There was a bit of a pause, because that single word had hit him hard. But after a moment he went on: "The mountains are lonely, eh? Well, we could change that. We could go to a town, or to a city."

"And live in a dirty flat, eh? No, it's better to have shanty life in the open than shanty life in a town."

"Put it that way, then. The worst thing has been I. Is that it?"

"Oh, I don't know," said the girl.

"Try to speak it out. I'll take it."

"No, you wouldn't have a broken heart." She sneered. She could see that sneer eat at him like an acid, also.

"My heart won't break. It may bend a little, but it won't break," he said.

"Of course not! There are a lot more girls in the world. I know that."

"Of course, there are," he said, with that deadly good humor.

"And there's the other side of it," she went on, with careful brutality.

"Yes, that's true. A lot more men. I think you've always looked over my head a bit."

At that, she laughed. It was a thing she had felt that she would be unable to do, but the exigencies of the rôle supplied, suddenly, the strength that she needed for the acting. She was able to laugh, and then to say: "Yes, quite a bit over your head."

After that he remarked: "Well, it's the finish, all right. Mind you, I'm not whining, and I don't want to do any persuading. I'm just saying this . . . and I can be proud, too, even if it damns me . . . but I want to say that I'll do anything. Anything that'll help to put things back where they used to be."

"What could you do?" she demanded.

"I'm a lazy hound. I know that. I've sat around here and built castles in the air. I suppose you've even done more of the work around here than I've done. I'm sorry about that. I think I could change it. I really think that I could change myself for you."

"Sure you could. For a week. Then you'd be the same tramp that you've always been."

"I want to kill you, somehow, when you say that," Reata said softly.

"Do you?" asked Miriam sweetly, the devil in her eyes and her smile.

"Because I start thinking of a lot of things," said Reata. "I start thinking about all sorts of things such as . . . well, the way you've sat and looked at me, up here . . . the hours we've had . . . good, clean hours . . . the cleanest in my life. I've been thinking that the world was all made of blue and gold, and you the middle of it. That's what I've been thinking. That's what. . . ." He jumped to his feet.

"Go on," she said. "Finish the speech."

"All right," said Reata. "I'll finish it. If you've been double-crossing me all this time, playing a part like a sneaking little actress on a stage . . . why, it's high time for us to split up."

"All right, chief," she said. She began to make another cigarette.

"But I can't believe it, Miriam," he said. "I feel as if you'd have to change, even if I touched you . . . and. . . ."

"Try it, honey," said the girl. And she put back her head and smiled lazily up at him.

"Miriam," said Reata, "you're only a. . . ."

"Say it," said the girl.

"No, I won't say it. I won't think it. It makes me sick."

"Want me to say just one little thing?" she asked.

"Say whatever you please."

"All the way through I kept remembering, but only lately it's been beginning to grind on the bone. I mean, what *you* are."

"Say it, Miriam," he urged.

"A dirty little sneak thief and pickpocket," said the girl.

She looked down suddenly. The world was spinning. She knew that she was maintaining the sneering smile, but she also knew that one touch, one breath, one word would shatter the last of her brittle strength. She had struck her last blow.

Well, it was enough.

"All right," he said. "I've been a sneak thief and a pickpocket. All right. You've a right to say that. It just seems sort of rotten . . . but that's all right, too. I'll sashay along. I'll take Sue. The rest of the stuff . . . oh, it may be worth something. The mules . . . the Gypsies would like to have 'em, and you

207

can load 'em down with the portable junk. So long, Miriam."
He stood over her. His voice remained clear and easy. "You
know," he continued, "if you were what you look like to me,
I'd get down on my knees and eat dirt for you. I'm going to
get out fast, so that I can keep a bit of what I thought you were
in the back of my mind. I hope I never have to curse my soul
with the sight of your face again."


## IX


## "REATA'S ENTERTAINMENT"


When Reata rode the roan mare over the trail again, he was
heading south, and he went by a clump of trees out of which
three pairs of human eyes watched him with interest.

"White and smiling," Dave Bates said, as the rider passed.
"Boys, didn't that gal do a good job on him? She turned his
stomach, and she slapped his face, and all he wants to do now
is to find a nice little hot piece of hell so that he can break it
apart and scatter it where it'll do the most people the most
good."

"He's going to do that same thing, and he's going to do it
quick," said Harry Quinn. "And what a lot of hell he *could*
scatter around, if he made up his mind."

"Oh, I dunno," said Gene Salvio, who seemed to be
burned by the praise of other men, and physically marred by
it. "All he's likely to do is to get a slug of lead under his ribs.
Don't forget that the fool won't never carry no gun."

"It's a pretty fast hand that can beat him with guns," said
Quinn, "if he's in striking distance with that reata of his, and
anything up to forty feet is his meat. Don't forget that. Don't

forget all the tough gunfighters that have gone to hell on account of Reata. Don't forget the damnedest man that was ever on this earth . . . I mean Bill Champion, if you got any doubts."

"He robbed me of my chance at Champion," growled Salvio.

"He robbed you of a chance to push daisies. Come on, boys," said Bates. "We better cut along behind him and see where he goes."

Reata went as far as the first town. It was not much of a place. Three roads ran together in a mountain valley, and that was enough excuse to make a bit of a village sprout up.

Reata went to the saloon and looked over the crowd. They were big men, strong men, fierce men. They were true mountaineers, of the sort that swung axes in lumber camps, and fight with hands or knives or guns for the fun of the thing. And there was a sprinkling of hardy cowpunchers in that lot, their Colts bulging under their coats.

He could not have picked out a better crowd for the purpose that he had in mind. He wanted hard rock on which to grind the hard, rough steel of his temper to a fine edge.

He took his rope out of his coat pocket, where the forty feet of that slender line of rawhide and mystery slumped into a not too bulky knot. He unraveled a knot or two with a gesture, and he began to make that rope perform for him.

The men at the bar turned and looked at him and grinned. The men at the tables along the wall grinned, also. Other men came from the back rooms, leaving their card games for a little time and staying till they forgot the course of their play.

For they saw that lithe reata jump snake-like into the air. They saw it twist and turn as though possessed of its own brain and messenger nerves and obedient muscles. They saw it roll in a double and a single wheel on the floor. They saw it tangle and untangle in the air, making swift, melting patterns that kept dissolving into one another.

"And look at here!" bawled a voice, over a round of brisk applause that came in the middle of the act. "What is that stuff all good for, except to make the kids laugh?"

Reata smiled pleasantly on the big man with the big voice. This was no common lumberjack — this the pale face of a professional gambler and the wide, thick shoulders and brutal jaw of a prize fighter.

"It makes gentlemen take off their hats to the music," said Reata, and the next instant the snaky loop of his reata had jerked the hat from the head of the big man. Once in the air, the good Stetson stayed there. It was sent spinning to the ceiling. It was caught before it reached the floor and driven whirling upward again. In the narrow, encircling arm of the rope it darted toward the window, out through it, and back again, and finally it was deposited, once more, on the head of its owner, although a good deal awry.

At this feat of legerdemain, a loud roar of pleasure burst out of the chorus of those wide throats.

And beyond the window Harry Quinn muttered to Salvio: "Look at the yaller devil in the eyes of Reata. He's looking for trouble, and the big feller is going to give it to him."

Reata, at the end of his show, had taken off his hat, and now he was passing it, making a little bow to each man in turn. And a veritable shower of wealth poured into the hat. Quarters were the smallest coins. And there were dollars, too. One man took a whole handful of silver out of his coat pocket and chucked it into the hat, while the others cheered.

But when Reata came to the pale-faced man, that angry gentleman made his contribution by kicking the hat out of Reata's hand. The silver sprang high into the air and rained down in a wide, bright shower. At this jest, the big fellow laughed uproariously.

The others laughed, also. The rougher the jest, the better they were fitted to appreciate it.

Reata, however, laid the flat of his hand along the cheek of the chief jester. The noise of the blow was loud. The spatting sound of it wiped out the loud mirth instantly, and left men staring, wide-eyed. It was apparent that the big fellow was a very well-known man.

He proved it now by whipping out a Colt and shouting: "Dance, you rat!" He plowed one furrow in the floor with his first shot. Then the gun hand was gripped by the supple, iron-hard loop of the lariat. The fingers were crushed flat out by that pressure. The Colt itself was jerked into the air, caught by Reata, and flung out the window.

The gambler, with a low moan of exquisite rage, hurled himself straight at Reata.

"The poor fool," said Harry Quinn, almost in sympathy.

But exactly what happened to the gambler, no eye in the room was swift enough to decipher. Certainly he missed the head of Reata with his long, driving punch, very scientifically delivered. Then he seemed to stumble even on the smoothness of the floor. He kept on stumbling, and, as he went past Reata, his feet flew from beneath him, and he landed flat on his face. There is nothing so discouraging as a belly flop even in the soft of water, but on a wooden floor it certainly shakes the spirits out of a man.

When the gambler got to his feet, there was a deafening yelling all around the room. Men were whooping and leaping in the ecstasy of their content. So the big man charged again. More warily, this time, with the straight left, jabbing in front of him to prepare his way. But if he moved more slowly, Reata sprang like a cat, and barely seemed to touch the gambler, who swerved once more, and fell again, flat on his face.

This time he sat up, sick and dizzy, and he found the noose of that pencil-thin lariat around his throat.

"Get up," said the voice of Reata, "and pick up all that money you spilled a while ago. Get up, but don't get any higher than your hands and knees, because it's better for dogs to keep on all fours. Hop to it, because, from the look of you, stranger, I'd like to take you apart and see what's inside the case."

The gambler was disheartened. It was plain that, if he picked up that money, he would be shamed for the rest of his days. On the other hand, he felt that he had been involved with a hurricane against which he was helpless. But if he could not win with his own unaided hands, there were others who could help him. Three men had just come out of the gambling rooms at the back of the saloon. These three, the victim now picked up with his eyes, one by one.

Then he said: "I'd just like to see you make me do it."

This was to Reata, and the gambler tried to scramble to his feet. A flying loop of the lariat caught him and jerked him forward on his face once more. It was a massacre, and the crowd yelled, because massacres were what it liked.

But here a cold, snarling voice from the back of the room said: "Stranger, stick up your mitts and drop that rope of yours!"

Reata felt the presence of that leveled gun before he turned his head. He had wanted hot water, but perhaps this was a little higher temperature than he needed to find. And then, just behind him, through the open window of the saloon, two glittering pairs of Colts appeared, looking large as cannons to the startled eyes of the men inside.

"You fellers back up," said the voice of Harry Quinn. "Reata, come out through the front door. We got the skunk covered. Come on out. The three of us is all here, waitin' for you!"

"Come out?" exclaimed Reata. "Like the devil I will. You fellows come inside, and the drinks are all on me!"

Gene Salvio went in first, stepping lightly, head high, a gun ready in each hand, and the gunman at the back of the room faded away, guiltily, softly, from view.

Harry Quinn followed. Dave Bates was the last, because he had kept watch from the window till the last minute.

A thick silence embraced the saloon, till Reata called out: "Set 'em up, bartender. There's plenty of money on the floor, and it's got to be turned into whiskey before I get out of here. Open up your throats, boys, and pour the stuff down. My partner, there, on the end of the rope, he aims to get the money for us off the floor. Start in, dummy, and make the collection, and don't miss a dime!"

The gambler had tried three times, and he had failed. Three times was enough for him. Therefore, he proceeded with the work that Reata had directed, and went on his hands and knees, with a groaning soul, to do the labor. He knew it meant the entire West was closed to him from that moment forward, unless he chose to be followed by grins and muttered comments wherever he appeared. But, for that matter, there were other parts of the world. And certainly the West would be better without him. So he continued his work of gathering the silver, and the bartenders busily turned the money, as bidden, into whiskey, so that the entire crowd was whooping and shouting long before Reata walked out of the place, followed by his three companions.

When the cool air of the night struck his face, he found that whiskey and excitement had not, after all, diminished the grim aching of his heart, and the world was as empty as it had been when he turned his back on that blue lake in the mountains.

However, a man must meet his obligations. And there was an audience here.

He said to Salvio: "Gene, I owe something to all of you fellows. Just what am I going to do about it?"

"Owe us something?" Salvio said. "Not a thing. We owe our hides to you, partner!"

"Forget it," said Reata. "I want something to fill my hands. Any of the three of you know what I can do to put in my time?"


# X


## "AGNES LESTER"

The marshes along Jumping Creek belonged to the estate of Colonel Percival Lester, but even if they had not, he probably would have taken charge of the organized search for the stolen gold of the Decker & Dillon Bank, because Colonel Lester — although his title was entirely complimentary — liked to find himself at the head of large numbers of men. Nothing pleased him more than to be revealed in riding boots and breeches, extending his arm and pointing with a riding crop as with a sword. His English outfit, contrasting with the sloppy casualness of the dress of Western riders, was like a uniform, distinguishing the leader from ordinary men.

The bank, of course, had offered a thumping big reward to the man or men who could find the hidden money, so that there was a hearty crowd of volunteers. However, the work had to be done on the colonel's land, and, therefore, he had the right of excluding any man he did not wish on the premises. The only fellows he could imagine excluding would be fools refractory to his will. For the rest, the bigger the crowd the better, so that he could mount his finest horse and let it swagger slowly and proudly from point to point.

The colonel did more than direct the labor. He supplied the mule teams and the wagons and the tools for the moving down of earth and broken rock until a road had been built across the shallows of the marsh to the island in the center of it. For it was obvious that the island was the place where the three robbers must have buried the gold. They had remained there for a number of hours. Certainly they would not simply have thrown the treasure into the oblivion of the mud and water of the marsh.

So the island was searched. It was a hard job, because it was chiefly rock and full of crevices, but the colonel supplied plenty of blasting powder and drills and double jacks, and the work went merrily on. Since everybody in the county could not be employed, the first fifty men were used, every morning — the first fifty to appear at dawn. The colonel arranged this, and everyone admitted that this was eminently fair play. When the gold was found, the reward from the bank would be equitably divided among all the fifty. Even at that, each man would receive a tidy sum. In addition, the colonel hired and paid from his own pocket two armed guards who kept watch on the island every night.

The whole range had to admit that the colonel was an extremely public-spirited man. His high-fangled riding outfit was forgiven. He was quite the man of the day, and, when he went by with a severe preoccupation on his handsome face, the men would pause in their work, for a moment, and nod good-naturedly toward him before they spat on their hands and resumed their toil. For he was, in fact, as fine a looking fellow as you could wish to see, with his big forehead and regular features and neat mustache. His jowls hung a bit — that was all.

This afternoon his daughter, Agnes, had come down to watch the work, and with her rode her fiancé, Thomas Wayland. If anything could have improved the good humor of the colonel, it was to have sight of this couple. He had faults to find with his daughter. To be sure, she was a very pretty blue and golden girl, but she lacked the poise, the dignity of mind and carriage which, he felt, should be inherent in every Lester. However, Tom Wayland more than made up for the defect. In lands and hard cash, the Waylands were to Rusty Gulch what Lester was to Jumping Creek. Tom Wayland was as tall as the colonel; he bore himself with an air of haughty aloofness that even the colonel could not have improved upon, and, like the colonel, he distinguished himself from the ordinary run of ranchmen by wearing, always, a very neat outfit of English riding togs. He was to marry Agnes Lester this same year, and, as the colonel looked at the pair, he was reinforced by his conviction that a necessary aristocracy, a highly bred and highly educated leisure class, the brains and the culture of a nation, would soon be growing up in the West. For the colonel thought of himself as a bright torch that illumined a portion of the barbarous darkness of the land, and he would hand on that torch to Tom Wayland.

It was a little unfortunate that his daughter did not love Tom Wayland, but, after all, children rarely know their own minds. How can they? He saw that it was, of course, far better for him to select her life mate, and he was glad that he had established, in his household, such a discipline that it would never enter her pretty little head to go against his will in any matter of importance.

So the colonel ranged slowly up and down the little island, overseeing the work, silently taking charge, occasionally extending his arm of authority and pointing out something with his riding crop. He had almost forgotten about the gold, to tell the truth, and he would have been rather shocked if he had known that one of the fellows who toiled here knew perfectly well where the treasure could be found.

That was Reata. When he had asked Salvio and the rest to find something for him to do, Dave Bates had explained the thing very briefly. There *was* a thing for Reata to do. Down there in the marsh by Jumping Creek was a lot of gold that had been buried, a long time ago, in chamois sacks. Lately, people had begun to hunt for the stuff, but they were laboring at the hard rocks of an island in the marsh. As a matter of fact, that gold was hidden in the hollow trunk of an old tree situated near an end of the island. Why didn't the three of them go and get the stuff? Why, unfortunately, their faces were all known to the people of Jumping Creek, and not known favorably. If they went down to the marsh while the hubbub of the hunt for treasure was on, they would be promptly nabbed and put in jail. How had they come to know about the location of the treasure? They had just picked up a hint. Why not wait until the present search had failed, and the noise had died down? The trouble was that, when the island definitely was proved not to be the hiding place, the search would extend farther, and the first man who tapped that tree would be aware that the trunk of it was hollow.

Afterward, Salvio had drawn Bates aside and told him that it was folly to let Reata go without revealing to him the entire truth. But Bates answered, with a snarl: "Yeah? You think that he'd touch the stuff, if he knew that it was stolen money?"

"He'll hear about the robbery of the bank before he's been down there long," said Salvio.

"He'll have the stuff before he's had a chance to hear much," answered Bates.

That was why Reata was on the ground with nothing on his mind, except the very difficult task of getting the treasure away, and he was glad of the difficulty, because it prevented him from letting his thoughts drift too often back to that valley among the Ginger Mountains and the picture of Miriam. She was back with Queen Maggie and the tribe, by this time, he told himself. She was happy to be free. She was delighted with the old existence, and, when she thought of Reata, she yawned and shrugged her shoulders.

So Reata drew deeper breaths, and swung the big twelve-pound double jack in swifter, harder-striking circles, while his partner turned the drill slowly in the hole. There was no love of labor in Reata, and yet he persisted unweary-ingly in his hammering, for those stringy muscles, that robed his shoulders and his back and tapered down to wire-like ten-dons at his wrists, were so full of power that even the wielding of the twelve-pound jack was a simple matter to him. The heaviness of the work acted as a cure to his mental sickness. He did not even look up from time to time to mark the passing of the colonel in charge, and never raised his head higher than the body of the huge brindled mastiff that stalked up and down behind his master. As for Rags, he lay curled up in the shadow of a rock near Reata.

And then, as the dull drill was jumped out of the hole and a sharp one was put in its place, Reata stood back to breathe more deeply and wipe the sweat from his face. And it was at that moment that he saw Agnes Lester. He saw her not dimly, not vaguely and far off, as he told himself that he would always see women through the rest of his life, but she came in-timately into his mind with the freshness of something never beheld before. She was a new point; she was a beginning. He did not compare her with the dark beauty of Miriam. They were not comparable. He thought that Agnes Lester was as beautiful as an angel. For angels are blue and golden in their loveliness, surely. Who would paint a brunette as one of the songstresses of heaven or as one of those radiancies among the clouds that saints and martyrs have a special permission to see? No, if a brunette is to be an angel, she will certainly not appear ministrant in the summer half of the future life.

But Reata was not thinking about brunettes. He was not thinking about Miriam. He was stepping out of this life, out of this world into — well, into a rosy dawn where all that is noble and true and beautiful and good is not a prospect, but an accomplished fact.

Perhaps Reata was a bit on the sentimental side. Certainly a fellow whose heart was broken by one girl should not be snatched up into a seventh heaven by the mere sight of another. Such changes are not heroic. They are not noble. As a matter of fact, Reata looked on Agnes Lester not as a woman at all, but as a divine being with just a taste, let us say, of sweet mortal femininity about her.

Then he remembered something else. He had seen that face before. He had seen it in the back of the watch that he had purloined from the vest pocket of big Tom Wayland, who rode yonder. Think of such a noble gentleman as Tom Wayland pasting the picture of "his girl" into the back of his watch. But that was what Wayland had done, and, when Reata had opened the watch, he remembered how even the photograph of this girl had moved him to such a point that he had gone into the rodeo crowd once more and restored the watch to the pocket of Mr. Wayland. In that very act of restoration he had been caught; he had been chased; he had been jailed.

Well, that was long ago, and since then the hunting down of Bill Champion had made Reata free of the law and wiped out his past and made people willing to forgive a certain illegal lightness in his fingers. But it seemed to Reata that there had been a fate behind the whole thing. Otherwise, why should he have seen the picture of the girl in the back of that watch? Why should Wayland have done a thing so cheap, common, and out of character as to put the picture in the watch case, except that fate intended Reata to see her image? And now he was seeing her in the flesh.

"All right! All right!" said the man who held the drill impatiently.

Reata missed the head of the drill entirely with the next blow, and his partner grunted. "Hey . . . what's the matter with you, kid?"

Reata would have found it difficult to say what was the matter with him, unless he were able to burst at once into verse and music.

Music of another sort started just then. For the big mastiff that haunted the steps of Colonel Percival Lester had just spotted Rags, and, being without a sense of humor and trained for nothing but battle, the huge dog let out a growl that was like the harsh rumbling of thunder, and hurled himself at the little mongrel.


## XI


## "THE COLONEL'S DOG"

Imagine a huge fist grasping at a floating bit of a feather, always so hard that the wind of its own motion knocks the feather away. It was like that, when the mastiff charged at Rags. He came on with his mouth a great red gulf, but he kept champing his teeth on nothingness as Rags dodged from this side to that, letting the monster miss him by fractions of inches.

Work stopped. Men gathered around to shout with delight as the mastiff charged, missed, recovered, lunged again and again, wildly slashing at the air as he went by a target that he knew he could hardly get a tooth into. And always Rags waited for the charges with pricking ears, with little head cocked a bit to one side, and with bright eyes and wagging tail, as though he were sure that this was only a game out of which he could receive no harm. He waited until the red gulf was actually just upon him, and then he jerked himself to this side or to that, until the great mastiff, fairly baffled, stood back and howled out his rage.

Rags, at the same time, got behind his master's legs. He was a little tired of playing with death, perhaps, and, therefore, he went into the shadow of his god on earth, his all-powerful being, out of whose hand nothing but kindness and protection flowed. Having reached this shelter, little Rags stretched himself comfortably and turned a regardless eye upon the final charge of the great mastiff.

Colonel Percival Lester was not happy. Nothing in the world annoyed him so much as an attack upon his dignity. And the dignity of his very horses and dogs was a part and a portion of his own dignity. It was a personal reflection upon him, therefore, when the crowd bawled out its applause for the little dog and its mirth because of the mastiff's misses.

"Major takes the mongrel for a rat . . . no wonder he's trying to get hold of it. Take that mongrel off the island. Get it out of the way!" thundered the colonel.

Before anyone could do this, however, the mastiff was charging. And when Reata saw that the little Rags no longer intended to continue the sport, but was serenely trusting everything to him, Reata took from around his hips, where it was hooked up like a belt, the many folds of his rope. The big mastiff, Major, was intent on charging straight through the fence made of the skinny shanks of this man. But as he came gloriously in to make the kill, a double fold of a thin line, slenderer even than the clothesline in the back yard, a jumping pair of noosed half hitches dropped over the yawning muzzle of Major and jerked his jaws shut.

His charge he halted on skidding feet. He turned to tear to pieces this stranger — for Major was a guard dog in every sense of the word — but another swift loop of the reata caught about his legs and tumbled him on his side. He lay there, struggling, while the crowd shouted with delight, loudly and more loudly.

The colonel was stifled with rage. But he knew that he had seen a very good exhibition of skill on the part of this sinewy, young fellow with the brown face and the gray eyes. And there was nothing he could say. A man cannot be blamed from defending himself against the attacks of a huge and savage beast like Major.

The colonel, being silenced, was choking. If he could have commanded the lightnings of heaven, he would have brought down a special and a blazing vengeance upon the heads of Reata and Rags at that moment. But he could only choke, and choke, as Reata loosed the mastiff from those humiliating bonds, that sinuous bit of rope that looked no larger than twine to the eye of the colonel.

Reata having loosed the great dog, Rags came around and sat down in *front* of the feet of his master, so assured was he of the defensive power that inhered in the very shadow of the great man. And at Rags — no, only at Reata, now, came Major, slavering with red-eyed rage. He was met by a dart of that rope as inescapably swift as the striking of a snake. The noose caught one forefoot and the neck of Major. It jerked his foreleg up against his throat and caused him once more to

222

topple head over heels, while the crowd fairly howled with delight.

Agnes Lester, touching the arm of big, handsome Tom Wayland, said to him: "Tom, how can *any* man be so wonderful with a rope? I'd as soon have a bear at me, as Major in a rage."

Tom made no answer. She might as well have touched a stone. In fact, she saw that Tom Wayland was rigid with a pale-faced wrath that exceeded even the wrath of the great Colonel Lester.

The colonel was shouting out something, but it was a lost, a wordless sound, in the great tumult of the happy crowd. Men forgot the heat of the sun in their ecstasy over this improvised entertainment, the more so when they saw Reata actually setting the formidable dog free for a second time.

But mastiffs, no matter how big they are, have brains. Major had an extra supply of them that enabled him to see when he was licked. When he got to his feet this time, he went skulking off with his tail between his legs, and took down-headed shelter in the shadow of the colonel's horse.

Could anything have been worse for the colonel than to see his favorite dog thus shamed and disheartened publicly? Was it not as if that paralyzing rope had actually fallen upon his own dignified limbs and constricted them to helplessness?

And there stood little Rags, in perfect dog parlance, laughing his small and silent laughter at the huge dog that was discomfited. If the colonel could have only the least shadow of an excuse, he would have seized upon it with rejoicings.

And behold, a good excuse was thrust into his hands. For Tom Wayland, recovering from his pale-faced rage, now pushed his horse up beside that of Lester and exclaimed not what was in his mind, not that this slender, blond-headed, deft-handed scoundrel had twice laid his lordly bulk heavily upon the ground, but these words: "Colonel, why do you have such a man as that on the place? That's Reata! That's the rascal who was jailed in Rusty Gulch as a pickpocket. I caught him snaking my watch out of my pocket!"

These words were shouted out so loudly that every pair of eyes was sure to hear it. But Reata cared nothing about what the rest might think. They were all men, and among men he could soon prove that he was as hardy as the hardiest — he knew the ways of winning their respect. However, before a woman he would be helpless, and that was why his glance went instantly to the face of the girl.

It was a very striking thing to her to see the head of the stranger suddenly turn in this way, and to feel his gray eyes fixed upon her with something like fear widening them, and with a flush coming into his face. It was as though this formidable fellow, who could handle Major like a mere harmless puppy, could be destroyed in turn by a mere lifting of her hand.

It was such a compliment as even queens rarely receive in the whole of a throned life. It required one full second for the paying, and it was given in silence, like a salute.

No one noticed her. She was glad that all eyes were fixed on Reata. But even if her own father had been staring at her with a forbidding eye, she could not have helped smiling at Reata.

He could not smile back. Not at her, without impertinence that would be too public. But she saw him straighten. She saw him smile, in turn, at Colonel Lester himself.

The colonel was shouting: "Pickpocket? Why isn't he in jail? Isn't there an officer of the law around here? Where's Steve Balen? Steve is a deputy sheriff. Balen, come here and do your duty!"

Tall Steve Balen came slowly through the crowd. He was

taller than the rest by a head, and his shoulders stooped a little as though he were trying to shrink himself down to the dimensions of ordinary men. He was almost as narrow as he was long. Only his hands were of the proper size, and those hands were specially fitted, on occasion, by the big handles of his pair of Colts. He wore a gun on either thigh, strapped low down, just under the grip of his dangling hands.

When Balen came into the inner circle, the colonel was repeating: "How does a rascally sneak thief come to be here among honest men, Balen?"

Steve Balen pushed back his hat and scratched his head. "Are you Reata, partner?" he said. He looked at the slender rope that was magically recoiling in the slim fingers of Reata and saw his answer there. Then he added: "Sure, Colonel Lester, they had something ag'in' Reata up there in Rusty Gulch. And they chased him, and, when he was about to get away, he seen this here snipe of a dog in the river and rode in and saved that dog from drowning, and got himself in jail. And he sawed his way out of jail, and, later on, it was him that trailed down Bill Champion, and got two bullets through himself. But he killed Bill Champion in that fight, Colonel, and the governor thought it would be a good idea to pardon him. The law ain't got anything ag'in' Reata . . . not now."

At that speech, Agnes Lester was so delighted that Reata saw her smile as a shipwrecked mariner might see the rising of the glorious sun.

Why should she not smile, when she had seen her man transformed from a sneak thief into a hero? And did he not belong to her by that special right of possession that only beautiful women understand — those who can distinguish between lip service and a tribute that has come from the heart?

The colonel was shouting: "Get off my place! Get off my

225

land, Reata . . . if that's your name. I won't have scoundrelly pickpockets on my place! Get off, and take your rat of a dog along with you! Take him away, some of you. Tom, herd him off the land! An outrage . . . among honest men . . . a sneak thief!"

Tom Wayland was never given a job more to his liking than this one. He closed instantly on Reata, and with a gesture of his whip he exclaimed: "You heard the music. Get out, Reata! Move along there! Some of you fellows get hold of the man and hustle him along."

None of those "fellows" chose to lift a hand. There was a range of mountains between Jumping Creek and Rusty Gulch, and, therefore, they did not know a great deal about what happened around the other town. But every man jack of them had heard, vaguely, the terrible legend of Bill Champion, and every man knew that Bill Champion was dead, fallen like some heartless, terrible prehistoric beast that had survived by an anachronistic freak of chance into the age of a weaker and a lesser human race. And this was the man who had sent Bill Champion to the long account? This slender fellow whom half of them outmatched in size and in apparent strength? They would sooner have hustled a lion in his native wilderness; they would sooner have hustled a tangle of rattlers with their bare hands. Only Tom Wayland, malice in his handsome face, crowded his horse close to Reata and urged him on his way.

Reata turned and faced him. A good many men were able to see the yellow come into the eyes of the smaller man as he said: "Don't hurry me, Wayland. Don't come within twelve steps of me, in fact!"

That was all he said, but it was enough. Tom Wayland reined back his horse as though a wild beast had started up under its nose. And Reata, without haste, with happy little

Rags leading the way before him, went on his way with a slow step.

He went straight toward the girl and pulled off his Stetson from his tousled head. He had to face straight toward the sun now, in order to see her, but he had the eyes that can look into the sun without being blinded.

He stood beside the head of her horse and said: "Some day I'd like to come and do a little explaining. May I?"

"Yes," she said. "I want to see you again."

Reata walked on, and she saw Tom Wayland sitting motionless on his horse, at a distance, glaring at her with terrible eyes. He had not heard the words, but he had seen the smile with which they were uttered. Well, let him see. Let her father see. Let all men see whom she had favored. Sometime the brown face and the gray eyes would appear before her again, and she would be glad, either by day or by night.

She actually turned in the saddle, shamelessly, and looked after that retreating figure, and watched the light step as he rose on his toes like an Indian runner, and saw the little dog bobbing in front of him contentedly. She saw, with flattering eyes, another scene — a man pursued, and a little dog struggling and lost in a smother of white water. And she saw the rider rush his horse into the current. Well, thief or no thief, she knew that she had seen a man, this day.


XII


"THE TREASURE"

Reata, from the side of an overhanging hill, looked across the marsh as the day ended, and saw the thick mist rising from the

227

wet ground, and saw it take on a ghost of the sunset color. His fingers idly pulled at the fuzzy ears of Rags, who lay asleep on his knees, and the awkward-looking roan mare he could hear plucking at the dried grasses among the tall brush behind him. But what he really saw was like a double photograph, one printed above the other — he saw dark Miriam, and this blue and golden girl. All that he knew was that the pain was gone from his heart, and that, in its place, there was a strange excitement, and a stranger peace.

He saw the workers troop away from the island. He saw them get on horses or into buckboards and go rattling back toward Jumping Creek. He saw the proud colonel giving final directions with extended arm. He saw Percival Lester at last ride off, accompanied by big Tom Wayland and the girl. Then quiet and the twilight gathered over the marshes, and Reata called the mare with a whistle.

Her bridle hung from her saddle horn. He put the bridle over her head. A cheek strap seemed to tickle her, and she rubbed her head with fearless freedom against his shoulder. He swore at her gently and jerked up a hand as though to strike. She merely pricked up her ears at the gesture and then nibbled at the sleeve of the raised arm.

Reata laughed. "Sure," he said, "I'm only a bluff!"

He walked down the slope, and the mare walked after him. When they came to the narrow roadway that the colonel had expensively built as far as the island, Reata took from a saddlebag a rather odd feature of his equipment, four moose-hide, padded overshoes that he now tied over the hoofs of the mare, and with that gear on her, she went ahead as silently as a moccasined Indian.

This was a hunt. The half-bowed body of her master told her that, and she had been taught how to step with flexed knees, softly, when there was hunting at hand. Little Rags, also, sneaked on ahead. He was better than a searchlight, for showing danger in the way. His body was very, very tiny, but it seemed that his sense of hearing and sight and smell had been correspondingly enlarged to strike a balance between him and others of his race. His master trusted him implicitly, and, when Rags stood still in the dimness of the starlight, Reata paused, also. Then he went stealthily ahead through the fringe of trees that shrouded the inner portions of the island. Rags went with him cautiously. The mare, at a gesture, had been anchored behind them in the darkness. A whistle would bring her in, when she was needed.

From between two tree trunks, Reata could see the fire that the guards had built. They had made it small. One of them was cooking. The other walked on guard very like a soldier, with his rifle over his right shoulder.

The darkness was thick. The rising mist gave the air almost the dinginess of heavy fog. No stars could be seen now. There were only the splintered, golden rays of the firelight, obscurely lighting the little island. And there, close to the farther end, Reata could barely see the outlines of the tree in which the treasure was actually planted.

Well, there were two armed guards between him and the taking — but neither of them was a Bill Champion. He unloosed the reata that still was around him like a belt of many strands. The fellow who was cooking over the fire could be attended to later on. This one who walked on guard — well, he could be made the first victim and then the bait, perhaps.

The man came near, walking his round close to the covert of Reata. He walked briskly, a man with all his senses about him, a chosen man who was ready to do his part even if there were plenty of fighting involved in it. But with all his wits alert, how could he see the snaky line of the reata as it sprang into the air? There was the thin whistling sound near his ears,

229

and then the invisible noose gripped him, jammed the rifle against his breast, crushed his arms to his sides.

He was jerked straight back against the trunk of a tree with an impact that knocked the breath out of him. And before he was thinking, before he was capable of movement again, a bit of strong twine had lashed his hands behind his back and around the tree trunk. He could not possibly be more helpless, now.

At his ear, he heard a voice whisper: "Call in your partner. Call him over here . . . or I'll slide a knife under your ribs."

Reata could have laughed at the thought of using his knife in that way, but it was a device good enough to make the prisoner obey his will, no doubt. He shook out the noose of the reata again.

That silent weapon, why would not other men use its silent power instead of the fatal noise and the blundering inaccuracy of firearms?

"Harry!" shouted the prisoner.

The man bending by the fire jumped erect. "Aye, Pete?" he called.

"The devils have got me! Give the signal . . . they've got me! Give. . . ."

A jolting blow from the fist of Reata silenced him. Harry, by the fire, snatched a brand from the blaze and with it lighted a fuse that dangled by a tall, big-headed rod that stood by the fire. Then Harry ran for the roadway.

Reata went after him, running low and swift, his rope ready in his hands. But behind him he heard a loud explosion. From the corner of his eye he saw the heavy-headed rod shoot up from the ground, trailing a shower of crimson, bright sparks behind it. High up in the air flew the thing, and Reata, groaning, understood. It was a signal rocket, and it would bring men swarming from all directions to the rescue.

He no longer ran after the fleeing guard. A whistle served to bring Sue swiftly toward him. As for the second guard, he had done his mischief, and there was no need in bothering about him. With fear at his heels, he would run fast and far.

Reata looked up and saw a burst of wild red fire in the middle of the sky. It steamed downward almost to the tops of the trees before that fire went out. Then the report came dimly down out of the sky, and echoes spoke the same sound softly from the hillside. It said to Reata, first loudly and then over and over again: "Hurry! Hurry! Hurry!"

He got to Sue, opened the narrow pack behind her saddle, and pulled out of it a strong axe. Then he waded into the water to the hollow tree. The first blow of the axe sheared through the thin rind of the tree. In a moment he had ripped the side open. Then he had to dive his hand into the cold muck and slime of the marsh inside the rind of the dead trunk. When his fingers touched the chamois leather, it seemed to him that he had grasped a water snake's slippery sides. He began to lift out the small sacks. There were twenty-two of them, according to Salvio and the others. And each one was, indeed, a weighty little burden of treasure.

He called Sue and loaded the first lot into the saddlebags. She could carry three hundred pounds of that burden at a load, as well as himself. It was not fair to ask her to lug more through the treachery of the marsh where she might sink at any moment, out of his power to aid her. He loaded her with eight of the bags. Then he mounted, put little Rags on the special place that he had arranged in front of the pommel, and waded the mare through the water.

To go back by the dry road seemed now the better solution of the problem, but he would have to make three trips. And before that, perhaps the rescuers would be pelting out from the town, out from the neighboring ranches. That fellow

Lester, he would be sure to turn out, gallantly, at the head of all of his armed cowpunchers, and perhaps the Lester ranch house was not so far away. Hurry, hurry, hurry!

He would follow his first idea. He would get out to the level of the railroad track. He would then hide two-thirds of the treasure somewhere up the track. The remaining third he would carry away on Sue's shoulders and his own.

In the meantime, it was dirty work getting through the slime. Once the water rose to his knees, and Sue was almost submerged, but she was presently on better footing, and now she took him out to the back of the railroad fence, where the glimmering barbed wires stretched far away to either side. His wire clippers rang on the strands. They flew back with a ringing sound, and he rode out onto railroad property. That was when he saw the tool that might make the rest of his work easier. Of course, Colonel Lester had managed to borrow from the nearest station a hand car on which some of the supplies could be transported to the marsh. And there it stood, derailed, at the bottom of the embankment. Well, what had brought supplies could be made to carry gold away.

## XIII

### "REATA'S RIDE"

He was out of the saddle at once, and hefted the thing from one side. It was murderously heavy. A heavy coiled chain on top of it did not decrease the weight any. He started to drag the chain off, when it occurred to him that here was a chance to use the power of Sue. Instantly he had the chain looped from the front axle of the hand car to the two stirrups of Sue. Those stirrup leathers

232

were strong, and they would hold. He put his own shoulder to the rear of the hand car and called to the mare.

She walked the hand car straight up the embankment. The wheels clanged against the high rails and stopped her. He found a stick and pried the wheels over the top of the rail. It took another minute of anxious sweating before he had the hand car settled properly on the tracks, and then, to his dismay, it began to roll slowly back.

He understood. He had forgotten that there was a heavy grade here, that climbed as far as the throat of the pass which opened darkly, yonder, through the mountains. There it began to descend with even greater angles. Suppose, then, that he loaded the car and sent it shooting with the grade? Well, in that case he would have to whiz through the station yard at Jumping Creek and, as likely as not, he would find the way blocked, or else the light car would be switched off on a siding and come to a crashing halt.

No, he had to labor up the grade, if he could manage it. And were the stout sinews of Sue there to assist him? He blocked the sliding wheels of the hand car with the stick he had found, loaded the eight sacks onto the car, and hurried back through the marsh. Rags he left with the load.

Halfway back to the treasure tree, he wondered why he was there, wading through the foulness of the marsh. Well, he had wanted something that would fill his hands, and, of course, his three friends had found something for him.

For the first time he asked himself how they could have known so surely where to find the stuff? There were a thousand questions he should have asked, if his wits had been about him on that night. But, now that he had put his hand to the job, he would carry it through while there was still blood in his body. Only, supposing it wrong, what would be the thought of him in the mind of that girl he had seen this day?

He reached the tree. The voice of his prisoner sounded cheerfully from the island.

"You back there ag'in, brother? You sure knew where the stuff was, all right! Goin' to flag a train and load it all on?"

Reata said nothing. He was fishing up the dripping sacks, and with them he loaded the mare again and made his second trip, to be greeted with a silent ecstasy by Rags. It had taken time to teach Rags when his voice was permitted to come shrilling out of the air of either day or night, but it was a lesson that the little dog never forgot.

For the third load — it should be the lightest of the lot — Reata returned to the end of the island, and again his prisoner was voluble.

"They're goin' to be along on your trail before long, brother," he said. "And maybe you're goin' to have a necktie party before the sun comes up. Maybe you're goin' to dance on air, after all."

"Maybe," said Reata. He had fished the twenty-second bag out of the muck and loaded it into the saddlebag. He added: "You can tell 'em that I headed off toward the tracks with the stuff. Why shouldn't I rap you over the head before I go?"

"Why shouldn't you've slid that knife between my ribs the way you promised?" responded Pete instantly and insolently.

"I don't know why," said Reata.

"I'll tell you why, brother," said Pete. "I dunno your name, and there ain't been light enough to see your make-up. But I know what you are . . . you got nerve enough to steal, but you ain't got nerve enough to kill. I'm goin' to send 'em on your trail, and then. . . ."

There was a picture in the mind of Reata of the gray stallion of Bill Champion leaping from the edge of the cliff into the empty air, and of the gigantic Champion drawn out beside the horse at the end of the lariat.

Well, he knew how to kill well enough, and he was almost tempted to put in practice a little of that art at the expense of Pete, who was bawling: "Listen! They're comin' now! They're comin' now!"

Reata, straining his ears, could hear it very well. It was not the rapid-fire pattering of his heart. It was the rattling of hoofs of horses that were coming at a dead gallop over hard ground.

Reata turned the mare and urged her desperately through the marsh. To save himself, that was still easy enough with the speed of Sue at his command. But to save the treasure, also? That was the question.

He thought that voices were calling to him out of the damp odors of the marsh as he rode through from the island. He passed the gap of the fence. He rode up to the hand car and fastened the saddle leathers once more to the double end of the chain. Then he mounted the hand car and gripped the handle to pump it forward.

From the raised position of the railway embankment, he could hear clearly the pounding of many hoofs that turned off the valley trail and took the narrow road that the colonel had built into the marsh. That self-assured scoundrel of a Pete would be telling them, in an instant, exactly the direction in which Reata had ridden through the marsh.

Reata called to the mare, she strained ahead, and he began pumping at the big handles where eight men could find a grip to sway up and down and shoot the car along the tracks, but up this grade there was no shooting to be done. There was only constant and heavy laboring to get the heavy machine rolling at all, with Sue taking most of the burden. She walked; she jogged; she got into a shambling trot with her head down and her weight pulling steadily at the load behind her. She worked as faithfully as though she had been trained at draft labor, or to the plow. So, very slowly, they worked up the grade, with Reata straining like a giant at the reluctant pumping handles, and the heavy wheels of the car clinked over the joinings of the rail sections.

Now and again he turned his head and strained his eyes back toward that point where he had issued from the marsh, and far back there, most vaguely seen through the mist and the night, he saw the riders begin to spill out onto the railroad. He could hear them better than he could see them. He could specially hear them when they began to whoop, and then came up the track after him like so many yelling devils. There was no hurrying possible, for him. He was working his utmost, and he was giving the mare all that she could do.

In the meantime, those shapes behind him grew out of the mist, grew taller, more distinct, and the rolling noise of the hoofs was a weight upon his very soul. Still, he struggled with the pumping handles, and, looking up at the great black mass of the mountains that drew back toward him, he told himself that he would never come to the top of the grade.

But at that moment he felt the speed of the mare increase to a full trot, while the handles began to swing up and down more rapidly and more freely in his grasp. He understood, then. He had actually topped the rise, and now there was a down slope to aid him just as the up grade had been a frightful handicap to overcome. The mare would be a hindrance now, instead of a help. He leaped forward off the hand car, uncoupled the dangling chain from the stirrup leathers, hurled the chain down beside the track, and sprang back onto the hand car. Even without his work at the handles, the car was running along at a good pace, and, when he added the swinging weight of his body, it began to jump ahead with a swifter and a swifter impulse.

236

He could not tell whether he still had a ghost of a chance. The mare was running now, at the foot of the embankment, keeping even with the car, and not far behind her came the shadowy troop of the men of Jumping Creek.

"Faster, men, faster!" shouted a voice which he recognized as that of the colonel. "Balen, open fire on the scoundrel! Balen, start shooting!"

That fellow, Balen, he would not be one to miss. And perhaps he had a good target in the form that swayed up and down at the handles of the car.

A rifle clanged, and a bullet hummed with sickening speed close to Reata's head. Then he felt the swing of a curve take hold on the wheels of the car. The black shoulder of the first mountain gradually thrust out and shielded him from further attack, for an instant. At the same time, the strength of the grade took stronger hold on the car. Moreover, there was suddenly cursing from the pursuers. They were finding rough going for their horses, no doubt, on the slanting foot of the embankment.

The car was shooting now at great speed. As the rails straightened out after the curve, it seemed to Reata that he was rushing down a long flume that narrowed in the distance before him. And the thin glimmer of the tracks diminished to a faint sparkling, probing the darkness of the pass.

More guns crackled behind him, but he did not hear the winged noise of the bullets. Off to the side, he saw even the roan mare losing in the race against him. How badly beaten the rest of the horses must be, if Sue was falling behind.

He was traveling now at such a round rate that the car rocked dizzily at every curve, but still he strained at the handles as they jerked up and down. It was flying speed. The wind of that going hurt his eyes, dimmed them, so that the light which he saw far ahead was at first a dull thing that had no meaning to him. Then he heard it, the faint roar thrown off the flat face of some distant cliff, the sound of a locomotive as it labored at the grade.

He could have laughed, when he thought of being trapped in this manner. Now, on the very verge of shooting away to freedom, distancing all pursuit on this mechanical charger of his, his way was blocked not by intention but by chance. He applied the brakes. A square-shouldered pile of ties not far ahead was his goal, and he worked the brake so that the hand car screamed to a halt beside the pile.

He leaped from the car, shouldered one of the heavy ties, and thrust the end of it under the front of the hand car. The ground was trembling, he thought, with the approaching vibration of the locomotive and its long train of cars, or was it only the humming sound of the rails that seemed to pass into the ground under his feet?

He heaved. The heavy car swayed. He heaved again, and the hand car lurched up, toppled, and rolled down the embankment.


## XIV


## "DOWN THE CLIFF"

The broad glare of the headlight of the engine, as it pulled slowly around the curve below him, showed Reata the lay of the land. Up to his right there was the steep, erect mass of the black mountain. To his left, a hundred-foot cliff, or something more, dropped sheer down to the narrows of the valley beneath, and at the very foot of the cliff there was a little shanty.

Two or three of the gold sacks slipped over the edge of the

height, slithered down its forehead, and then dropped away from sight. Reata instantly thrust the rest of the bags in the trail of the first ones.

He could see, behind him, the flying form of Sue as she tore along the side of the track, but he could not use all her speed and her honest heart, now. He needed, rather, wings to get him off that height of land before the dim troop of shouting riders behind the mare came swarming up to the rock.

Instead of wings, he had the reata, and he used it. As the full glare of the headlight of the train flashed out at him from around the curve, he was already fitting the open loop of the rope around a projecting point of rock.

Swinging over the ledge, he found himself hanging opposite a concave face of the cliff with a narrow ledge a dozen feet beneath him, and the pounding wheels of the train set up a vibration that he thought he could distinctly feel in the rope from which he hung.

Rags was curled on one of his shoulders, with teeth fixed into the collar of the master's coat. Above him, Reata heard the anxious whinny of the mare. Well, she would find her way. It would be as hard to lose her in the mountains as to baffle a wolf, and she would discover some trail back to her old quarters at Rusty Gulch. He need not worry about her or fear that any other man would ever come close enough to daub a rope on her. He slipped down to the very end of the doubled rope, and found his feet resting on the ledge. A shake of the lariat loosed it from its hold above. By the same process he lowered himself from another crag, a dozen feet, and then found a short distance down that he could climb. But still again, at the very bottom of the rock, he had to use the rope for a last time across a sheer concavity of fifteen feet.

They had reached the edge of the cliff above him before he was down there on the safety of the level ground. He could hear their voices growing dim as they spoke behind the edge of the cliff, or booming loud and clear as they leaned out over nothingness, to wonder what had become of their quarry.

He heard the voice of Steve Balen calling: "Some of you ride up the track. You'll come to a place in half a mile or so where you can work back down into the valley. Go hell-bent, boys, and we'll try to get down this cliff while you're going that way!"

The roar of hoofs began again from the line of railroad track. Reata, pulling down his rope from the rock above him, stood on the level of the valley floor and saw a man come running out of the back of the shanty, carrying a lantern.

Reata ran forward through the bushes and encountered the stranger under the spread of a low tree, calling as he came. "Douse the light, partner!"

The man from the shanty knew how to obey orders quickly. He jerked up the chimney of the lantern and put out the light with a single breath. So in the thick of the darkness Reata came to him. Over their heads the high, nasal, penetrating voice of Steve Balen was calling: "You down there! Don't give no help to that feller! He's a thief, and he's wanted by the law. Hold him up. Grab him and hold him for us!"

"Hey," murmured the voice of the shanty man, "looks like I got good company droppin' out of the sky tonight."

He was so perfectly calm that Reata instantly took heart. He said: "They're hounding me pretty close, partner. But if you can saddle up three or four of those horses in the corral for me, I'll pay you a forty-pound bag of gold coin for them and your time. Does that sound good to you?"

"Brother," said the man of the shanty in the same unemotional voice, "I'd sure sell my soul for five hundred dollars in hard cash. Come along, and we'll slam some saddles on them mustangs."

In the shed they got the saddles, and in the corral they rapidly got saddles and bridles onto four horses. Then, on the run, they swept the mustangs to the foot of the cliff, where Reata rapidly loaded saddlebags with the loot.

Above him, he could hear the noise of the manhunters descending. He could hear them shout to one another. A revolver spoke three short, deep notes. The bullets thudded into the ground nearby, but under the cliff there was not even starlight to show the hunters how to shoot at their quarry. They only knew that he was down there almost in touch of their hands, but still a chasm of dark distance kept them away.

Reata, as he worked, was saying quietly to the man of the shanty: "I pulled a gun on you. For fear of your life, you had to do what I told you to do. You had to saddle the horses. You had to ride away with me the minute the horses were saddled and loaded. Understand? Hop on that horse next to mine, and ride hard, because I can hear the other half of these lads from Jumping Creek coming down the valley."

Those other men from Jumping Creek came like mad, in fact, for out of the distance, from the face of the cliff where Steve Balen and his men were working out a perilous descent, they could hear occasional gunshots, and the loud, pealing voice of Balen himself urging them on. The tired horses from Jumping Creek charged valiantly to get to the vital place, but, as they drew near, through the bushes, dim and shadowy, they saw two riders moving; they saw four fresh horses galloping, stretched out straight with speed.

For a few jumps the hunters kept up the pursuit. Then they pulled their guns and opened fire. But weary men with bodies and nerves shaken by long riding cannot shoot straight. And the trees that made a broken screen for Reata and his companion soon thickened between them and the pursuit. Rapidly they drew away. There was no sound of beating hoofs behind them. They were able to draw their horses back to a steady canter, and presently this gait got them into view of a single riderless horse that moved ahead through the night at a trot. Looking closely through the darkness, Reata made out a saddle on the back of the mustang.

A sudden hope made him whistle the call that Sue knew. Instantly the horse ahead of them swung about and came at a gallop to him. It was Sue. He knew the long, low outline of her now, and even little Rags began to murmur a whining welcome.

"Hey," said the man of the shanty. "How'd you learn to whistle hosses to you like bird dogs, stranger? You teach me that, and I'll lay off working."

Reata, pulling up his horse and stopping the cavalcade, dismounted and took the saddle on Sue. "What's your name, brother?" he asked.

"Pie Phelps," said the other. "What's yours?"

"You wouldn't want to know it, would you?" asked Reata.

"Nope. Sure I wouldn't. Come to think of it, knowing your name wouldn't do me no good."

"The night was so dark, and you were so scared," said Reata, "that you couldn't tell what I was like. Is that right?"

"You just looked sort of average to me," said Pie Phelps.

"Hide out this bag of stuff," said Reata. "It's not stolen. It was hidden away on the land of Colonel Lester, that's all. And he had the neighborhood under guard. But you have as good a right to it as the next fellow. However, you'd better hide the stuff and let it ripen for a while. I wouldn't go back to that shack again tonight, if I were you."

"I sort of hanker to sleep out under the open sky, anyway," said Pie Phelps. He took the chamois sack and weighted it in his hands. "All gold?" he asked in a low voice.

"All gold," said Reata. "So long, and good luck to you."

"Good luck? I've got it already in my hands," said Phelps. "I've got enough good luck to turn it into a ranch and a cattle herd. So long, stranger!"

Reata headed up the narrows of the valley on Sue. Four loaded horses followed him, and he saw the standing form of Pie Phelps fade into the night to the rear.

XV

"THE WIND-UP"

It was the next night, just when the dusk had faded into the complete darkness, before Reata came down out of the hills with his cavalcade. He had the twinkling lights of Rusty Gulch to guide him, but, when he reached the high-backed house of Pop Dickerman, he halted his animals just inside the south gate of the junkyard and tied them to the hitch rack which stood there. Afterward, he tapped at the kitchen door.

Beyond the shutters he could make out the dim glimmerings of a light, so that he knew someone must be in the room, but it was some moments before the door was pulled a few inches ajar and the husky voice of Pop Dickerman asked who was there.

"Reata," he said.

The door was instantly jerked wide. "You, Reata? All alone?"

"Yep. Alone."

"Come in, old son," said the rat-faced man. "It's all right, boys!" he added loudly.

A door on the other side of the room was opened by Harry

Quinn, with Salvio and Dave Bates behind him. They waved gloomily at Reata.

"Had to give it up, Reata, did you?" asked Salvio. "I told these *hombres* that it wasn't no one-man's job. There was too much of it, even if you ever got a chance to lay your hands on it."

"He had his try, anyway," said Pop Dickerman. He was eyeing Reata keenly. "He had his try, by the look of him."

"What look?" demanded Salvio grimly, as Reata took a chair and built a cigarette swiftly.

"Like he'd had his fun," said Pop Dickerman. "What would it matter to Reata, if he didn't get his hands on the gold? What would seven, eight hundred pounds of gold mean to Reata, if he could have his fun, eh?"

This bitterness left Reata untouched.

"Did you even get a chance to lay a hand on that holler tree?" asked the gloomy Salvio

"How many gents was down there?" put in Harry Quinn.

"No one man could do it," said Dave Bates. "I told you *hombres* that it was no one-man job."

"Well," said Pop Dickerman, "tell us about the story, Reata. What you been doin' to put the yaller in your eyes?"

A huge tomcat jumped down off a window sill and started stalking Rags. The little dog sat down between the feet of his master and watched that approach without the slightest concern.

Reata said: "I had a ride on the railroad track, boys. Went faster than a horse could gallop."

"On what?" asked Salvio.

"On a hand car," said Reata. "But I couldn't keep on the way as long as I wanted to. I was just working up a good breeze, when the headlight of a train heaved around a corner and looked me in the eye, so I had to pry that old hand car off the tracks and roll it down the embankment, to let the train get by."

"Where was Sue?" asked Dickerman anxiously.

"She was following along."

"He's done something," said Harry Quinn suddenly. "Reata, what you been and done?"

"I picked up some loose horses," said Reata, "and brought 'em along. There's one for each of you fellows."

"You poor half-wit," groaned Salvio, "you ain't been stealin' hosses, have you?"

"I bought 'em," said Reata, "but I bought 'em so cheap that you wouldn't believe what a bargain I got." He pointed toward the door. "Go out and look at those horses. You'll like 'em. One apiece for you." He stood up and went to the stove where a number of pots and pans were simmering.

"What's in here worth eating, Pop?" he said.

"Look for yourself," growled Pop Dickerman. "Come on, boys. Let's see what kind of a fool Reata's been makin' of himself."

They trooped out through the rear door of the house, while Reata examined the pots and helped himself to some beans stewed in a hot Mexican sauce. He poured out a cup of coffee, cut off a large wedge of good bread, and sat down to his supper. From the outside he heard nothing, but presently all four men came in, loaded with burdens.

They piled small, much discolored chamois sacks on the table in front of Reata. He ate on, unheeding that pile of treasure. And the four men stood about the room silently, looking at the sacks, and then at one another. Their faces were a little drawn, and their eyes bright.

Pop Dickerman said: "Harry, you and Gene go out and get the saddles off of them hosses, and turn the mustangs out where they can roll in the south corral."

The two men hesitated. Harry Quinn said: "Can't that wait?"

Dickerman's lip curled till his yellow teeth showed. "Wait till some gents ride up and spot them hosses. Sure, they can wait, I guess."

Quinn and Salvio, cursing under their breath, left the kitchen. Pop Dickerman moved softly around the room with long strides. He was rubbing his hands. His furtive eyes kept traveling to the doors and the windows. He even glanced up to the ceiling, as though he felt that glances might be spying upon him from that direction.

"There's only twenty-one of these here sacks, Reata," he said softly, at length.

"One of 'em paid for the four horses. Cheap, weren't they?" asked Reata carelessly.

Dickerman extended his long arms above his head as though he were about to call down a curse, but he only groaned. Then he lowered his hands and stroked the discolored chamois. Strings and shreds of the marsh slime still clung to the leather.

That was Dickerman's occupation when Salvio and Quinn returned and came in with the breathless haste of men who fear that something very important may have happened during their absence.

Now the four men were standing around the room.

"We'd better split the stuff and break away with it," said Bates.

"All right, boys. All right, boys," said Dickerman soothingly. "I'll take my third. I'll take my seven sacks, and then you can split up the rest any way you wish." He began to pull some of the sacks to the end of the table.

Reata swallowed some coffee at the end of the meal and rolled another cigarette.

"You furnished the news about where the stuff could be found, Pop, is that it?" he said. "Well, you ought to get your share for that. But these three fellows saved my hide in a little saloon brawl up the line. The way I see it, we split the stuff into five equal lots."

Dickerman uttered a low, moaning sound. "Rob me of damned nigh half my rightful share that was agreed on?" cried Dickerman. "What you thinkin' about, son? It ain't like you, Reata. I ain't goin' to believe my ears!"

Reata lighted his cigarette and blew out some smoke. "Why do you argue, Pop?" he asked gently.

Dickerman stared about him. The other three with lowering brows met his glances. With another groan, Dickerman surrendered. "All right, Reata," he whined. "If you're goin' to do it that way, I suppose that there ain't anything that I can say. Into five parts, you said? That leaves an entire sack over, and. . . ."

"Take the extra sack, then," said Reata, careless always.

The clutches of Dickerman were instantly on a fifth of the sacks. "Get the stuff away . . . get it away quick. Up there in the attic in the corner. You know the place, Gene. Stow it all away up there. Here, I'll help you."

"Let them cart it away," said Reata. "What I want is a little more information about the gold, Pop. Sit down here and talk."

"Aye," said Pop. "But tell me first what happened?"

Quinn and the other two were instantly at work, burdening themselves with those ponderous little sacks, and their creaking footfalls went slowly up and down the stairs to the attic.

Reata simply answered: "They had fifty men working on the island all day. Tom Wayland was there. He got Colonel Lester to turn me off the place. At night they had a pair of

247

guards watching the island. I roped one of 'em, but the other touched off a signal rocket. I had to cart the stuff away from the hollow tree to the railroad track, and I loaded it on a hand car, got Sue to pull it up the grade, and with half the men of Jumping Creek out behind us, like the tail of a kite, we sailed down the far grade. A train came for us. I had to pry the hand car off the tracks, and roll the sacks down a hundred-foot cliff. I climbed down after 'em, got hold of a fellow who was willing to sell me four horses and saddles for forty pounds of gold, and loaded the stuff on the new nags and rode away. That's all. They nearly caught me at the finish, but I had fresh mustangs, and the Jumping Creek boys had been doing a lot of riding, by that time. So we pulled away."

Pop Dickerman, after he had heard this narrative, remained for some time, slowly opening and shutting his mouth as he framed more words, out of his imagination, to fill up the interstices of this tale.

The other three returned from their work, and Dickerman, slowly, always staring fixedly at Reata as though hypnotized, repeated the tale as he heard it.

At the conclusion, Harry Quinn was looking with a faint grin at Salvio, and Salvio made a sudden gesture of surrender. It was as though he had said suddenly: *Yes, he's the better man.*

"Now I want to find out from you," said Reata, "just where this gold hailed from."

"It's quite a yarn," said Dickerman. "Didn't you hear anything about it down there in Jumping Creek?"

"No. I was swinging a twelve-pound sledge on a drill head. I wasn't talking."

"The yarn goes back to a gent that found a rich strike up in the hills and worked it for pretty nigh fifteen years," lied Pop Dickerman. "And he ground his stuff out with a coffee mill, you might say, and then he loaded it away in sacks, but, when he come to his last sickness, he didn't know where he could hide the money where it would be safe. So he. . . ."

Here was a sudden and loud rap at the rear door. Dickerman, when he heard this authoritative summons, waved suddenly to Quinn and Salvio and Bates. "Out," he whispered.

They faded silently through the opposite door of the room. Then Dickerman opened the outer door upon the stalwart figure of Sheriff Lowell Mason.

The sheriff came in with a frown, that disappeared when he saw Reata. He gripped his hand heartily, saying: "I'm glad to see you, Reata. I'm glad to see you, no matter where you happen to be!"

"Thanks," said Reata. "I'm not back in jail, Sheriff."

"No," said Mason, darkening again. "And I hope that you never land there again. But bad company makes a lot of trouble in a man's life, Reata. A lot of trouble. I thought you were up north, taking up some land and building a cabin and getting ready to marry, but, of course, that's your own business." He turned suddenly on Pop Dickerman. "Dickerman," he said, "the time's come for you to move out of Rusty Gulch."

"Well," said Dickerman calmly, "that's kind of bad news. Who's goin' to move me?"

"*I'm* going to move you."

"You'll need a lot of drays, brother," said Dickerman.

"I'll need a warrant and a gun," said the sheriff. "I think there's enough stuff out to put you behind the bars, Dickerman, and I'm goin' to try to put you there. You've pulled the wool over the eyes of a lot of people, Pop, but I reckon you're more of a fence than you are a junk dealer."

That accusation made not the slightest change in the expression of Dickerman. "A high board fence is what I gotta have around my junk piles," he declared.

"You ain't as simple as you make out," said Lowell Mason. "Let me tell you this. You're a crook yourself, and you're a breeder of crooks. I've seen three of your men, from time to time . . . Quinn is the name of one of 'em . . . and they fit right into the descriptions of the three thugs who robbed the Decker and Dillon Bank in Jumping Creek and got away with eight hundred pounds of gold. I can't hang the thing on them just yet, but I know in my own mind that they were in it. I suppose they're over the border, by this time, but they'll come back, one day, and then I'll get 'em! As for you, I'd rather not handle the dirty job of collecting you for jail. I'm telling you to move on, and you'd better take my advice."

"Thanks," said Dickerman. "I always like to hear a gent talk even when he's wrong, if he talks pretty well. You been talkin' well enough to get yourself a pile of votes by election time, Sheriff."

The sheriff turned his back on the furry face of Dickerman and confronted Reata.

"Old son," he said, "I hate to see you in this place. Come and see me before you leave town. If you ever want a bunk for the night, you can have one with me. But if you stay around Dickerman, you'd going to get yourself into trouble. So long, Reata. It's great to see you, lad."

With this, and no further word to Dickerman, the sheriff walked out of the room and disappeared. The hoofbeats of his horse presently were trailing diminishingly toward the center of the town.

Reata and the junk dealer, in the meantime, faced one another silently.

"The old fellow that worked away at his rich strike, and ground out the stuff for fifteen years," Reata sneered.

"It's this way, Reata," pleaded Dickerman. "What I wanta tell you is this. . . ."

"It doesn't much matter what you tell me," said Reata. "Call the boys back in here, I want to talk to them."

When the three came in, in answer to Dickerman's call, Reata was standing near the door, with his Stetson on the back of his head, and little Rags on his shoulder.

He said: "Boys, the sheriff says that the three of you robbed the Decker and Dillon Bank at Jumping Creek. You got eight hundred pounds of gold out of the safe. Well, I want to know if that's the gold I've just fetched out of a hollow stump in the Jumping Creek marsh."

"Why, no, Reata," began Dave.

"Shut up, Dave," said Salvio. "There ain't any use trying to pull the wool over his eyes now. He knows."

"It's true, then?" said Reata.

None of the three made answer. It was old Pop Dickerman who said: "Listen, Reata. The folks in Jumping Creek knew the three of 'em. They couldn't go back for the stuff. There was nobody else to trust except you."

Harry Quinn looked at the grim, pale face of Reata and exclaimed: "Don't take it hard, Reata! Look it. What else could we do?"

Reata closed his eyes. "I thought I was pulling clear," he said slowly. "I thought that I'd washed my hands of the crooked work, but I see that I'm back in the dirt again."

"Go easy, Reata," urged Dickerman. "Don't say nothin' rash now."

"I'm not saying anything rash," said Reata. "I'm only seeing the truth."

"The truth is," broke out Gene Salvio, "that you're a better man than the rest of us, Reata! I'm not one to throw around the praise, and you know it. But you're a better man

251

and a straighter man than the rest of us. We may've done you wrong in this deal. We thought it was smart for us, and a way of putting a whole lot of money into your hands, too."

"Look here," said Harry Quinn, "you got enough money now to set yourself up right. If you think you wanta be a ranchman, you can do it now, and do it right."

"That's correct," declared Dave Bates, with ardor.

"Set myself up with stolen money, eh?" said Reata. "Thanks a lot. I'm not doing that."

"Hold on!" cried Dickerman. "You mean that you're pulling out and leaving your share behind?"

"What can I do? I'd take the loot back to the Decker and Dillon Bank, if I could," said Reata. "But there are four of you to one of me. All I can do is get as many miles between me and the rest of you as possible. And I'm going to put them between." He took a half step toward them with rage and with hate in his face. "I thought I was going clean, and you've made a swine of me again." That outburst of anger left him on tiptoe, but his rage vanished suddenly. He added sadly: "There's been life and death between us. You've saved my hide, and I've saved yours. And now this is the wind-up. I'm getting out of the country, and I'm staying out. It's like tearing the heart out of my body, but I know what the thing will be like, if I stay around here. One way or another, you'll get your hands on me again and drag me into some rotten business. I haven't the brains to handle crooks like you. Good bye."

He turned and went suddenly out into the darkness.

When the door closed, Salvio slumped into a chair, his head in his hands.

Dickerman said: "Well, we had to lose him some day, boys. But he's left a nice little farewell present for the lot of us."

Salvio jerked up his head suddenly. "You fool," he said. "You poor, rat-faced fool, don't you see that he was worth more than money to us?"

"Aye," put in Dave Bates slowly. "He was worth our blood!"

# MAX BRAND

# SAFETY McTEE

Here, in paperback for the first time, restored from his own typescripts, are three prime examples of Max Brand at his rousing best. In "Little Sammy Green," a son has a difficult time living up to the reputation of his gunfighter father, until fate forces him to prove himself. "Black Sheep" is the extraordinary story of a nine-year-old tomboy who comes up with a scheme to win an outlaw his freedom, even though it puts her own life in jeopardy. And "Safety McTee" tells of a gunfighter who earned his nickname by merely wounding, not killing, his opponents. But when he's forced to shoot an old man in self-defense, he finds himself hunted by a lynch mob that doesn't appreciate his past mercies.

___4528-1 $4.50 US/$5.50 CAN

# MEN BEYOND THE LAW

These three short novels showcase Max Brand doing what he does best: exploring the wild, often dangerous life beyond the constraints of cities, beyond the reach of civilization . . . beyond the law. Whether he's a desperate man fleeing the tragic results of a gunfight, an innocent young man who stumbles onto the loot from a bank robbery, or the gentle giant named Bull Hunter—one of Brand's most famous characters—each protagonist is out on his own, facing two unknown frontiers: the Wild West . .. and his own future.

___4873-6                                   $4.50 US/$5.50 CAN